BY ALAN DEAN FOSTER

BODY, INC.

BODY,

INC.

VOLUME II OF THE TIPPING POINT TRILOGY

ALAN DEAN FOSTER

BALLANTINE BOOKS NEW YORK

Copyright © 2012 by Thranx, Inc.
Frontispiece: © Eric Isselée

Published in the United States by Del Rey, an imprint of The Random House Publishing Group, a division of Random House, Inc., New York.

DEL REY is a registered trademark and the Del Rey colophon is a trademark of Random House, Inc.

LIBRARY OF CONGRESS CATALOGING-IN-PUBLICATION DATA
Foster, Alan Dean.
Body, Inc. / Alan Dean Foster.
p. cm. — (Tipping point trilogy; v.2)
ISBN 978-0-345-51199-7 (pbk.) — ISBN 978-0-345-53253-4 (ebook)
1. Genetic engineering—Fiction. I. Title.
PS3556.O756B64 2012
813'.54—dc23
2011040809

Printed in the United States of America on acid-free paper

www.delreybooks.com

2 4 6 8 9 7 5 3 1

First Edition

Book design by Liz Cosgrove

BODY, INC.

1

Whispr knew for certain that he was in Africa when the pair of black leopards shot past him in the airport corridor. His companion, cautious business partner, overbearing scientific advisor, and (dare he think it?) sometime personal physician, Dr. Ingrid Seastrom, let out a gasp and dropped to her knees as one of the big cats forcefully brushed her right leg in passing. Unlike their now panicky intended quarry the leopards tore through the terminal in complete silence. An equivalent airport Immigration and Security team back home in Namerica would have used dogs, an admiring Whispr thought as he watched the two carnivores take down their target. Amid screams and shouts, other equally startled arriving passengers were quick to scatter and give the cats room.

Pinning him to the ground beneath weight, fang, and claw they did not begin to devour the man they had trapped. In its excitement the larger of the two felines urinated on the frightened captive's legs. The smell of buttered popcorn filled the terminal. As Whispr had quickly assumed, both melanistic predators had been thoroughly maniped. Snapping against their muscular chests and flanks, loose-fitting lightweight vests flashing the SAEC's bright colors identified them as members of the Helen Zillie International Airport's security team. Strips of gleaming metal set atop their skulls between their ears testified to the skills of the biosurges who had installed the controlling implants.

Like the vests, the complex neuroplants were also probably South African Economic Combine products, Whispr mused. With impossibly slender and deceptively strong arms he helped the stunned Ingrid to her feet. The secrets of one peculiar kind of advanced SAEC technology—SICK technology—was what they had come all the way from Georgia and Florida to try to unlock. Less dramatic and more subtle, their purpose unknown, the quantum entangled nanoscale implants that had first intrigued and subsequently inveigled Ingrid Seastrom were infinitely more sophisticated than straightforward animal manips.

"Startled me." Ingrid continued to mumble to herself as she straightened her pantsuit.

She wasn't worried about her temporary dishabille or the fact that she had been knocked down. Overriding any and all other concerns was the need to keep safe the tiny silvery storage thread of metastable metallic hydrogen that lay hidden in a sealed security compartment within one cup of her brassiere. She worried about the shard's security because it represented a whole series of scientific breakthroughs and unknown social possibilities, some of them sinister. Whispr worried about it because if it were to be damaged or destroyed it surely wouldn't bring as high a price as it would if they could keep it intact.

Knowing her to be a consummate worrier, he wondered if Seastrom ever worried about *him*. Ever since he had obsessively but foolishly planted that scent-sucking zoe on her in Florida she had held herself even more distant than ever. Despite this her continuing disinterest in him in no way lessened his feverish desire for her. But he had vowed to act the gentleman, much as that remained an abstract concept to a street survivor like himself. Not because he didn't feel the urge every day, every hour, to pull her close to him and press his mouth against hers, but because at this point in their relationship it would be a bad move from a business standpoint.

He looked at her, drank in the sight of her, with great pleasure every chance he got. Even in her current disguise mode with her blond hair blackened, her cheeks puffed with temp collagen, the additional weight she had put on, and the contacts that changed her eye color every couple of hours, he still found her irresistibly enticing. He loved the way she looked, the way she walked, even the slightly stilted professorial way she talked. His attraction had nothing to do with the fact that he was a Meld and she was a Natural. Knowing full well that she would find any such expressions of admiration on his part unutterably annoying, he kept them to himself. Besides, they had work to do and surveillance to avoid.

Unlike the terrified young man who had been taken down by the leopards and was now being rescued and arrested by the big cats' handlers, they had made it quietly through Immigration and Customs without any difficulty. Traveling with only hand baggage, they headed for the nearest Transportation kiosk. Some of the other disembarking passengers had stopped to watch as a trio of cops placed the unfortunate lawbreaker in securestrips. None of them were citizens of the SAEC, for whom such sights were old news.

"I wonder what they're holding him for?" As Ingrid looked back at the scene she saw that the young man still wore a look of utter terror. She didn't blame him. Not with two full-grown maniped male black leopards hoping to make hors d'oeuvres of his toes and barely restrained by their handlers.

Whispr was more interested in finding immediate transportation into the city proper. He had been witness to far too many arrests to find this one worthy of his time, the exoticism of the circumstances notwithstanding.

"Probably trying to sneak into the country illegally," he opined. In the old days, he knew, the frenetic apprehension and subsequent arrest would likely have involved drugs. Imagine locking someone up for possessing recreational pharmaceuticals! What little he knew of history never failed to amuse him.

"As I understand it there's three Africas: North, Central, and South. North is philosophically and spiritually confused, Central is like downtown Old Atlanta at two in the morning—only with a quarter billion people, and the South is where everyone in the Central and much of the North wants to be. Mostly because the SAEC and the South is where the subsist is." Turning, he nodded back in the direction of the now stripped and secured illegal visitor.

"Gotta give the crazy Natural credit. Instead of sneaking across the border through a tunnel up north he bought a ticket and tried flying in like an ordinary traveler."

In her mind's eye Ingrid could still see the black slash of the police leopard streaking past her. "What do you think they'll do to him?"

Whispr shrugged. Among the many welcoming flads trying to cozy up to them was one for a vehicle rental company. Sticking a finger into the glowing sphere had instantly activated its functions. It trailed hopefully behind them as they continued on through the Arrivals area.

"Deport him if he's lucky. Slap him in detention if he's not. Feed him to cats if the cops are in the mood."

Her eyes widened. Where medicine and science were concerned Ingrid Seastrom was utterly up-to-date, but concerning Real Life she could be woefully ignorant.

"I'm kidding." A smile cut his angular visage and she favored him with a look of disgust.

Actually he didn't have a clue what the local cops did with illegal immigrants. With a lineage that included sjambok-wielding Afrikaans security, bomb-making ANC revolutionaries, fearless Zulu warriors, and modern police melds, it wouldn't have surprised him a bit to learn that the cost of securing borders that were under constant pressure from desperate would-be immigrants was occasionally offset by offering up pieces of said intruders in lieu of expensive leopard food. Did illegals from Mauritania taste different from, say, renegade Somalis? The thought would never have occurred to a Natural like Ingrid. To an ultra-slenderized Meld like Whispr it was perfectly—natural.

Hovering close to his left arm, the basketball-sized floating advertisement fended off competing flads with barely audible bursts of static electricity. As it urged them forward it declaimed with soft mechanical enthusiasm on the advantages of renting a roadster from the company it represented. Whispr ignored the sales pitch. They had engaged with the flad merely to help them locate the Arrivals Transportation desk. Whispr had no intention of renting a vehicle immediately upon entering the country. SICK had managed to track them down and send someone after the thread while they were in Florida. Though Whispr was pretty confident they had managed to subsequently elude the company's inimical attentions, he had not survived this long on the street by taking chances or moving too fast.

Once they reached the government-sponsored Transportation kiosk he dismissed the flad. It evinced no disappointment as it drifted off in search of other customers. Modern mobile advertisements preyed effectively on emotions but did not have any of their own.

Ingrid was already playing her hands over one of the several available holos. In response to her gestures all manner of public transportation lit up beneath her fingertips: taxis, buses, rail, aircraft, even maniped animals-for-hire. The latter were strictly for the tourist trade, an interested but realistic Whispr knew.

She eventually lowered her hands. "I've figured out how to get there, but how should we go? Where should we stay tonight?"

"Same routine as Florida," he told her. "Small hotel. Not too fancy, not too cheap. Same for the part of town. A suburb always draws less attention than the center of a city." He altered his voice to mimic that of an ancient Namerican actor whose work he had always enjoyed. "Ah'm a stranger here m'self."

As usual, she didn't get the joke.

With a nod she turned and put the request to the Transportation vorec. Connected to every other component of the greater Cape Town box it quickly provided half a dozen suggestions. One was quickly chosen, two rooms (Whispr let out a sigh but said nothing) reserved, and a deposit put down via her aliased credcard.

As they boarded the transport capsule at the airport's station they did not notice the two figures who stepped quietly away from the far wall and set off in their wake.

A small community of historic importance on the western shore of False Bay, Simon's Town was sufficiently developed to provide the facilities they needed while offering exactly the sort of quaint surroundings a pair of Namerican tourists would be expected to enjoy. Anyone looking for them in this part of Southern Africa would have a natural tendency to first seek them in central Cape Town. Simon's Town actually lay farther from the downtown area, with its famous harbor and grand tourist hotels, than did the international airport itself.

The main transport lines ran west from the airport to Downtown or eastward to Stellenbosch, the center of the wine and marijuana growing region. Every one of the automated cars departing the airport station was crowded with tired arriving passengers—except the one marked Muizenberg-Fish Hoek-Simon's Town.

Of the half-dozen other passengers taking the MFS service from the airport the one standing nearest to Ingrid boasted a full restaurant service meld. It took her a moment to realize that the impossibly short man was wearing nothing above the waist and that his bow tie, long-sleeved white shirt, pearlescent buttons, and neatly pressed pockets were nothing more than an artful spark tat. Such full body dimensional tats could be easily removed or customized should the owner change professions. They were particularly prevalent in hot, humid climates. A tat didn't cling, didn't show sweat stains, and never needed to be sent to the laundry.

Now that she saw that the little man had undergone skin stitching she found herself comparing the local work to its equivalent from Savannah. In addition to the uniform tat each of his hands featured two extra fingers apiece, the better to juggle trays, plates, glasses, and other dining paraphernalia.

Reflecting his country of origin his face was a neat checkerboard of black and white. It was the favored local melanistic meld. First at the airport and now on the transport she had seen alternating black and white stripes, spots, ovals, crescents, and in the case of one especially large woman, a direct vertical separation right down the middle of her face and exposed arms—half black and half white. Other Melds featured a smattering of brighter, less nationalistic skin colors. Turquoise seemed particularly in vogue this year, most notably among a group of loud, visiting Italians.

Seen firsthand it was clear that the old Rainbow Nation wasn't black or white. It was black *and* white.

Whispr could have fit his attenuated frame into any vehicle no matter how crowded, but he was glad of the space for his carryon pack. "Wonder why the cars on this transport line are so empty?" he mused out loud. An answer was soon forthcoming.

"Most folks are heading downtown or to the other main parts of the city. You're on a west bay express." The man boasting the restaurant service Meld and tat grinned at them. Every other one of his teeth, Ingrid noted with interest, had been stained a gleaming porcelain-black. "If this car was a local that stopped on the Wets it would be full by now also."

" 'Wets'?" Ingrid inquired.

"The Cape Wets. Used to be called the Cape Flats, which were just what it sounds like, but since the worldwater came up—well, you'll see."

As the transport line curved smoothly to the southwest the higher country around the airport gradually descended until they were traveling atop a guide strip mounted on pylons. The million poor people who had made their ramshackle homes on the flat-lands of the Cape Wets before the Greenland ice cap had melted had not moved when the sea level had risen. They could not move. They had no money, and no place to go if they had. So they stayed, and were joined by another couple of million of the Central African Diaspora who had migrated to the SAEC seeking work and a fresh start.

"It's like Greater Savannah," Ingrid insisted as she gazed out the transport car's window. But it was not.

"They say the Bangkok boatland has more people," the restaurant worker declared, "but there are more here than in any other stilted community, I think. Except of course for the Ganges Float."

Whispr's face contorted. "Never heard of it."

"It's where a country called Bangladesh used to be," Ingrid informed him.

Her companion grunted as he peered out the wide transparency of the transport car's wall. "Can't be any worse than this. I've seen a mess of buildings in my time, but this is just a mess."

"Careful what you say, visitor," the worker warned him. "People here are proud of their community, tumbledown as it may be."

The sleek air-conditioned car continued speeding on its way through a townscape unlike any Ingrid had ever seen. She had watched travelogue vits of South Africa, but those she could recall that featured Cape Town had made no mention of the Cape Wets. Passing through them, she could understand why. It was as if someone had engaged Escher's ghost to construct a vast urban landscape out of tin cans and toothpicks.

Like the transport track on which their comfortable climate-controlled vehicle rode, every one of the tens of thousands of individual structures they passed, whether domestic, commercial, or industrial, rose above the surrounding shallow waters on pylons or pillars or stilts that had been driven deep into the ground. Once a vast spread of flat dry land, the Cape Wets had been swallowed by the encroaching waters of False Bay. Now several million people lived just above the waterline in buildings that rose four, five, or more stories above the sea.

"I know what you are thinking," the restaurant worker guessed. "Those who live here thank God that the rising bay is one that is well protected from the elements and that the tide is sufficiently strong to flush it clean every day. Otherwise living here would be even more difficult than it is already."

"You don't live here?" Whispr asked him.

A foot shorter than the slender Namerican and hailing originally from central Gabon, the Baka immigrant drew himself up. "No, Meld-brother! I live in the town of Boulders, where I work. If you have time, come and see the penguins! Their beach has risen, but they still come to the same place regular as they have for hundreds of years."

"We don't have time to . . . ," Ingrid began.

Whispr cut her off quickly. "That sounds like a swell idea. We'll be touring around for a couple of weeks before we head up the coast to Durban and we sure wouldn't want to miss any of the local sights." He stared meaningfully at Ingrid. "Right, darlin'?"

"Oh, right," she quickly agreed, chastened at her forgetfulness. *Tourist*, she reminded herself. You are not on here a quest to solve scientific mysteries. You are a *tourist*. She held up her right hand and thrust out her forefinger. "I should have gotten that camera meld before we left."

"Don't worry about it," Whispr declared cheerfully. "I like you all Natural, just as you are."

The diminutive worker chuckled. "You like your women plain and simple, oo-ee? As Nature made them? Every man to his taste, I suppose. Myself, I like how science can improve on reality."

Ingrid bridled but said nothing. Over the decades national boundaries and much else had changed in Africa, but evidently not certain long-held cultural attitudes toward women.

The endless parade of makeshift structures flashing past the transport reflected the entrepreneurial skills of the locals and their ability to improvise construction despite a paucity of financing. Unable to expand horizontally because of the lack of available land, grown children built atop the homes of their parents, and parents atop those of their parents. Gazing in wonderment at the crooked, precariously leaning structures, it seemed to Ingrid that a brisk wind could bring down the entire district. But somehow, millions of impoverished citizens found ways to stabilize their clapboard and sheet metal and fiber dwellings, their half prefab businesses, and their salvaged shops.

The Wets might be poor and unstable, but it was not dull. Solar and wind and biomass powered the millions of lights that came to life as the sun began to descend over Table Mountain. Thousands of improvised walkways linked an equal number of buildings. Sometimes these informal paths floated on the water itself, else-where they hung like thick plastic vines connecting second- and third- and even fourth-floor levels. The transport raced past several ground-floor structures larger than most of the others. These blazed with cold fury, brazenly announcing the delights to be found within in a dozen languages or more: Xhosa, San, Afrikaans, Zulu, Baka, Himba, Shona and Ndebele, every imaginable derivative of the Bantu languages, every worldwide variant of English, Hindi and Tamil and Bengali, French. . . .

"French?" Ingrid mused in surprise. The pygmy restaurateur explained.

"Some of the shebeen owners think it lends a touch of class to their joint."

"What's a shebeen?"

"Whorehouse." Whispr was less fascinated by the lights of the Wets than the glow that seemed to perpetually emanate from the doctor. He would much rather look at her than their surroundings. To someone like himself who hailed from a poor neighborhood one slum was much the same as another. Even one lying halfway around the world that was as well lit as the Cape Wets.

"Sometimes can be." Their helpful acquaintance sounded slightly miffed by the sinewy Namerican's explanation. "More often it is just a drinking place, like an informal club, where one can meet friends, play games, and . . ."

"Whore around." Whispr's attention reluctantly shifted from his view of the doctor to the dark bulk of the flat-topped mountain whose eastern flank the transport track was curving south to avoid.

Anxious to compensate for her companion's lack of tact, Ingrid tried indirection. "Do you work in a shebeen?"

Her attempt failed disastrously, as evidenced by the small man's reply.

"Madame, I am the sous chef at Chez Sebeli in Fish Hoek." Turning away from her, he moved toward the door. "And this is my stop. Yours is the one after the next. Do not worry about the fading light. Simon's Town is a tourist place. It is well patrolled and safe after dark. The beach is lovely in the moonlight, but stay out of the water."

Ingrid blinked. Not that she had a nocturnal swim in mind. Not after their long flight from Florida. But she was curious. "Why?"

"Government white pointers," the affable sous chef explained. "Or great whites as you call them. Fully maniped and on beach patrol. Looking for illegal immigrants, but they have been known to have trouble in the dark distinguishing honest residents from interlopers. Once bitten, it is impossible to retract a bite." With that he was out and gone through the softly hissing doors, an energetic small shape from Central Africa who had found his calling and made good in the SAEC.

"White sharks." Ingrid mulled over the intimidating image. "Somehow I don't think the government has much trouble with illegals trying to swim ashore here."

Whispr shrugged. The near vertical mass of Table Mountain had consumed the entire western horizon and the cold dark sheet of False Bay the other, leaving only a few lights directly ahead of them to mark the last of the shrinking peninsula that pointed ultimately toward Antarctica.

"How would they know how many tried and failed?" he told her. "Truly desperate people will try anything, no matter the risk."

She had to smile. "Even to searching out a doctor to remove police traktacs?"

"Even to enduring such a doctor's sarcasm," he snapped back irritably. He lusted after Seastrom, he desired her with every iota of his being, but he would have liked her a lot more if only she wasn't so damned smart.

Turning away from him she leaned close to the transparent wall of the transport car to catch the last twinkling lights of the outrageous physical and human morass that was the Cape Wets as it receded behind the transport. The night was incapable of consuming the millions. She had been wrong in her assumptions, and wrong early.

This place was nothing like Savannah.

Horizontal strips of light cutting the backside of Table Mountain revealed the locations of holiday apartments while off to the north and northeast the frozen nova of the Wets drowned out the light of the moon. But to the south the stars of the southern sky were becoming visible. Out in the salt-stung vastness of False Bay seals snugged down for the night, safe until morning on their barren rocky islands from the depredations of Natural great whites. Meanwhile a handful of the great predators who had been extensively maniped maintained their nocturnal patrol for illegal immigrants, unlicensed fishermen, and hard-bitten smugglers.

When the sea level had started to come up, old Simon's Town had simply been moved lock, stock, commuter transport line and historical buildings a little farther up the steep mountainside. Continuing to occupy the original town site, more recent additions had been constructed over the water. These were not the rickety, tumbledown structures that grew like stalagmites of sheet metal and fiber and resin in the Cape Wets. Well founded on sturdy supports; hotels, restaurants, gift shops, commercial buildings, and expensive residences reflected architectural influences that ranged from old Boer farmhouses to ultramodern windsail powerfices.

Standing on one of the walkways that connected their pleasantly modest hotel to the main street on the sloping mainland, Ingrid contemplated the moonlight on the bay. She was chilly. The season was the reverse of what she had left behind in Savannah. Tomorrow she would have to buy some warmer clothes. Turning away from the enchantments of the bay, which were as much olfactory as visual, she nodded to the northwest.

"This is charming, but we can't spend much time here. We need to get into the city proper so you can start making inquiries."

"Yeah, about that," he began, "just how exactly did you have in mind for us to proceed?"

She stared up at him. "You're the one with the street smarts. That's why you're here." When he didn't reply she sighed and continued. "SICK has two corporate headquarters: one in Joburg and one here. I was able to confirm that much while using the box on the plane. But I couldn't find anything that shows the locations of their research facilities."

He nodded thoughtfully. "Stands to reason. Big companies boast about the discoveries they make, but not *where* they're made."

"Then," she continued with becoming if naïve cheerfulness, "we'll have to infiltrate their headquarters to find the location of their principal research facility."

Turning to face her, his slim form nearly disappeared in the overhead lights that dimly illuminated the walkway. As always, he looked as if a strong wind could pick him up off the faux wood planks and blow him out to sea. His tone was somber.

"Listen to me, doc. I've lived most of my life on the streets. I can riffle and flan with the best of them. I can zift a pocket or purl a purse and disappear before the mark knows what's happened." Reaching into a pocket he withdrew the flattened, flexible, form-fitting bottle from which he periodically sucked the fortified liquid that helped to keep his manip-thinned body properly fueled. As he pressed it to his nearly nonexistent lips he sensed that the curving container was almost empty. Tomorrow they would have to find a store that sold specialty foods for customized Melds like himself. Lowering the bottle he wiped his mouth with the back of an atten-uated hand.

"But I'm not an industrial spy. I don't have the right physical tools to break into a box node, much less the headquarters of a company like SICK. And you"—he looked her up and down, ad-miring her in the rising moonlight—"you don't have the mental ones."

She stiffened. "I might surprise you."

"Yah. You've surprised me already, or we wouldn't be standing here at the ass-end of Africa having this conversation. I just don't want to be surprised when some security lod snaps your arms behind your back and securestrips your wrists before hauling you off to the company query cage for a private interrogation session with Mr. Volt and Mr. Watt." A sudden thought made him grin. "Of course, you could buy yourself something slink and low and distract the security while I slip inside."

She bridled. "You never give up, do you?"

He affected innocence. "What? You want to get inside SICK's offices, I'm just suggesting one possible avenue of approach."

"Let's take that car down a different street." She hesitated. "For now, anyway. I'll consider your suggestion only if we can't think of something better."

I can't think of anything better, he mused to himself as he envisioned her in the kind of seductive outfit he was proposing. Out-wardly he gave no indication of where his imagination was straying. Leastwise, he hoped he wasn't.

"Okay. You're paying the bills."

"We'll go into the city," she reiterated firmly, "and you can start asking questions. You know how to ask. I know the address of SICK's administrative center: that's in the public box for anyone to see. What we need to find is the location of its main research facil-ity: whether it's also here in Cape Town, or in Joburg, or some-where else."

"Not the kind of information your average drift entrepreneur is likely to have readily at hand. But I suppose we might find some-body who knows somebody who knows somebody who knows how to get *at* that information." He didn't mince words. "Especially if you're willing to pay for it."

She sighed heavily. "That's becoming a familiar mantra of yours. How much is it likely to cost us? Me," she corrected herself.

He shrugged. "No telling. I don't know the local rates for that kind of inforeveal. Anyway, what price knowledge, right?"

Reaching out, she gave him a shove. "Easy for you to say. It's not your life savings we're spending here."

Turning away from her he headed up the walkway toward the town's single main street. His arm tingled where she had pushed him.

Then another hand was pushing him—far more forcefully. One of two very large black-and-white men slammed him up against the side wall of the two-story hotel while the other con-fronted a stunned Ingrid. Even in the fading light of early night Whispr thought he recognized them.

They had been on the transport car from the airport.

2

Given half a chance Whispr might have been able to defend himself. At six feet and barely a hundred pounds he was never going to overwhelm an assailant, but his melded body possessed a wiry strength than had been increased due to recent manip work. He tried to kick out with his recently enhanced legs. But his attacker had one huge hand pressed against the thinner man's throat, reducing the flow of air to Whispr's lungs and weakening him. Too shocked by the suddenness of the assault to run, Ingrid stood frozen in place.

The hand that was not clutching Whispr's throat held a heavy, thick-bladed knife while the other assailant brandished a neuralizer. The electronic weapon looked old, battered, and ill-maintained. That did not mean it was incapable of delivering a debilitating shock. Gasping for air Whispr still retained enough sense to wonder at the choice of weapons. They made no sense. For one thing, both appeared to be of local manufacture. For another, their primal nature and poor condition conflicted with everything he had learned about the professional assassin who had nearly slaughtered him and Seastrom back in south Florida.

Retreating from the black-and-white skin-swirled man before her, Ingrid looked longingly at the water below. She was an excellent swimmer. If she could get over the railing before he grabbed her she felt sure she could elude him in the dark dankness below.

But there was the small matter of the patrolling and not always scrupulous white sharks. . . .

"I'm not giving up the thread," she stammered as she took another step backward. "Not after all this. Not after all we've been through on its behalf. You'll have to kill me to get it!"

Bug-eyed now, Whispr gasped in her direction, "Don't—give them—any—ideas!"

The thug wielding the neuralizer blinked. *"Yerhali*—thread? What 'thread'? What you talk about, Natural? Give us you cards and jewelry and we let you go."

Realization now offered competition for the bright lights that had begun to flash before Whispr's eyes. His and Ingrid's initial assumption had been wrong. These were not minions of the hired assassin Napun Molé. Nor were they associates of the three melded women who had beat up Dr. Seastrom's elderly friend and mentor Dr. Sverdlosk. Having barely just arrived in this new corner of the world it appeared that he and his companion were being assaulted by common street crims. This wasn't a contract ambush: it was an ordinary riffle. Which did not in any way diminish the threat posed by the knife glinting in front of his face or the neuralizer aimed at the doctor.

"Doc—Ingrid," he sputtered, "they just want our valuables. That's all. They're not interested in threa—in anything else."

"Maybe." The heavyset thug blocking access to the street was not as slow on the uptake as he looked. "Now you got me curious, visitor. What is this 'thread' you talk? It is something valuable?"

Though she continued to contemplate the potential safety of the water below, Ingrid held her ground on the raised pathway. "N-no, he's just talking about—some thread I bought. Some gold thread. To fix a dress of mine. It's not all that valuable." She eased a little closer to the railing. It, and the water below, were close now. She was coming to the conclusion that she was more afraid of this moonlit mugger than any sharks that might be lurking in the shallows.

Further reinforcing her rising opinion of their attackers' mental acuity the man threatening her took a corresponding step forward, waving the aged neuralizer as he did so.

"If you try to jump in the water I will shoot you. With your limbs paralyzed, you will drown." He eyed her closely. "You do not look like a dress-type lady-person to me. Pretty, yes, but also practical, I think. I also think you must tell us more about this 'thread.'"

She had no doubt that his threat to use the neuralizer on her if she jumped was real. But if she managed to get over the railing first he would have trouble aiming at a moving target in the dark. One thing she knew for certain: she could not spend long minutes debating which course to take. Her leg muscles clenched in expectation and she had half turned toward the railing when a cry rang out.

"Biza amapolisa!"

Both muggers whirled. The shout was repeated, this time from multiple throats. They cried out in perfect unison, as though the call had risen from a single throat. The thug holding Whispr muttered something to his companion. They growled at each other for a moment. Then he sheathed his knife while his colleague pocketed the neuralizer. Both men started toward the street. As they hugged the wall of the hotel they and the threat they posed receded into the darkness. It was not so dark that Whispr failed to note the looks on their faces as they fled. It was an expression he knew well, and the same on this continent as on the one he had just left behind.

Something had frightened them.

After pausing another moment to make sure the two rifflers were really gone, Ingrid came over to Whispr's side. She stood close to him but was careful not to make contact. The cry of *"Biza amapolisa"* continued to resound in the darkness.

"What is it—what's going on? Why did those guys run away?"

"Wish I knew." He struggled to see deeper into the night. "That second word that's being shouted sounds kinda like 'police.' Maybe somebody saw what was happening and is yelling for the cops." He went silent again, listening. "Lots of somebodies, actually. I'll be damned if it doesn't sound like a bunch of kids." His expression squinched as he tried to focus on the unseeable. "Almost sounds like they're singing."

"Who cares? All that matters is that they've scared off our assailants."

"I suppose," he mumbled. "Except I don't like singing, and I don't like kids."

"Once again I get to reflect on what a jolly traveling companion I've been saddled with." She offered him a twisted smile.

He took no offense. "Jolly won't get you inside SICK's research facilities."

The singing-shouting finally stopped. She inhaled deeply of the bracing salt air. "Well whatever it was, at least now we're safe." She stepped briskly past him. "We can still go into the city and you can get started with your questions."

Whispr followed reluctantly. "We nearly got riffled, we only just got off the plane, and you want to go wandering around a foreign city at night?"

Her smile penetrated the darkness. "Isn't that when someone like you is most likely to run into the kind of people we need to pump for information?"

"Yeah, but..." He waved at the looming shadow of Table Mountain. "Those two may still be out there."

She shook her head. "Gone, they're gone. I can sense it."

"Oh, so now you can sense the presence of others? Was that part of your medical training?" His gaze rose past her. "If that's the case then how come you didn't sense *them*."

A cluster of figures stood on the near side of the street, blocking the way to the transport kiosk. Whispr tensed, then relaxed when he saw that the pack confronting them consisted entirely of children. A rapid survey suggested that with one exception all were between the ages of eight and thirteen. The one exception approached Ingrid. Whispr started to step between them, stopped himself when he saw that the man wasn't wielding a weapon. Only a smile.

Whispr didn't trust that, either. But he made no move to intervene.

Both the smooth-faced young man's words and expression were full of concern. "Are you two all right? Am I correct in assuming you are visitors?"

"We are and you are." A cool breeze off the bay nipped at Ingrid's cheeks. She really was going to need some warmer clothing here, she told herself.

The young man was shorter than her or Whispr; slim of build, well dressed, his appearance neat and well groomed. Like the twenty-five or so children gathered behind him, he was a Natural. All of the youngsters would naturally be Natural, she knew, since the legal age for receiving one's first meld was fifteen. At least, it was in Namerica. From the looks of the troupe staring back at her out of curious eyes it was no different in the SAEC.

"Were you the ones who scared those rifflers away?" she asked him.

"Yeah. I've heard of calling for the police, but this is the first time I've known anyone to sing for them." Whispr tried not to twitch. He always was uncomfortable in the presence of many unknowns, even if they were a bunch of schoolkids.

"So we did." The youthful leader of the group (he couldn't be more than nineteen, Ingrid felt) flashed a confident smile. "Such men are cowards in the face of the Lord."

Whispr blinked. "'The Lord'?"

"We are a Capella squad," the man explained. "We consider it our solemn duty to help keep the city free from such scourges as those who just threatened you. All Capellas are volunteers. Each of us has chosen a district in which to offer our assistance."

"That's wonderful of you!" Ingrid exclaimed.

"Yah, wonderful." Whispr wasn't buying it. He nodded up the street, past the glow from those Simon's Town business establishments that were still open at this hour. "You expect me to believe that those two thundering lods took off just because they heard a bunch of kids yelling for the cops?"

"Ah, not just any kids." The man beamed. "A *Capella* kids." Turning to face his young charges, he raised both arms high in front of him.

A mass clearing of throats was accompanied by the straightening of small bodies. Ingrid inhaled sharply and Whispr stepped back as twenty-five weapons made their sudden and unexpected appearance, flashing in the moonlight. Brandished by boys and girls alike was an uneven but unmistakably lethal hodgepodge of weapons built to fit a child's hand; everything from homemade shivs to single-shot pistols to highly unauthorized variations on neuralizers. Whispr even thought he recognized an injector or two; small pensized devices that held and fired a single poison dart. Accuracy might not be a hallmark of the small army, but if fired in unison the eclectic assortment of weapons would constitute a formidable threat.

The teenage leader of the group brought his hands down. Whispr flinched, but none of the myriad killing devices let loose. Instead, the children began to sing. Their small bodies quivered with emotion, their expressions were intense, and their harmony was angelic. All twenty-five weapons remained in clear view.

"He teaches my hands to war, so that a bow of steel is broken by my arms!" they intoned mellifluously there on the side of the dark Simon's Town street.

More than a little freaked by the Boschian combination of sight and sound, Whispr would have taken the opportunity to make a break for it. But Ingrid, perhaps unsurprisingly, remained where she was, clearly enraptured by the a capella street concert. Notwithstanding all they had been through, Whispr reflected, and despite everything they had survived, it was plain that she still had a lot to learn.

As the children sang the rest of the psalm he looked past them. It was noteworthy that despite the presence of open establishments and the comparatively early hour not a soul was to be seen. Except for the singing, the street had gone dead quiet. Evidently knowledgeable tourists and residents alike had chosen to give the impromptu concert a pass—or to take shelter until it had concluded. No doubt the visible presence of so many weapons, even in childish hands, perhaps especially in childish hands, was something of a deterrence to musical appreciation.

As the final verse faded into the night the leader (Choir director? Drill sergeant? Whispr wondered) paused briefly before resuming. For a second time the prepubescent voices of the neatly dressed and heavily armed seraphim trilled in perfect synchronization.

"Blessed be the Lord my strength which teaches my hands to war and my fingers to fight!"

Whispr stood and made himself drink it all in. He couldn't very well abandon Ingrid to whatever coda was to come. Well, he could, but he had come too far with her to flee now. Besides, without her he wouldn't have a rand to his name.

When the second psalm had concluded the leader turned back to her. Though he spared a glance for Whispr his attention was concentrated on Ingrid. His smile was as ingratiating as ever.

"That is how we sent packing those who would have robbed you. They cannot stand before the power of the Lord."

"Or the muzzles of a couple dozen weapons," Whispr muttered, but under his breath. He didn't want any encores or anything else directed his way.

"We don't know how to thank you," Ingrid gushed. "And the children's singing was beautiful!"

"Thank you. Psalm 18:30 and 144:1. Favorites of the children—especially if they know they might have to cut somebody. As to thanks, it pains me to say that our congregation is a poor one. Any contribution would be most welcome and would go to support and further the efforts of the squad."

Whether out of wariness or honest charity Ingrid hesitated only a moment. "I'd be happy to make a contribution. But I have no cash. Only the usual credcard."

"Of course you do." Reaching into a pocket, the choirmaster produced a compact wireless credcard processing unit. "If you will just quote me an amount...."

She recovered quickly and named a figure. The leader frowned.

"We just saved you from probable physical harm as well as from being robbed. *And* we gave you the gift of song. Can you not see it in your heart to augment your contribution somewhat?" There was a shuffling behind him. Still gripping their assortment of weapons, the children were edging closer. And spreading out along the street.

Ingrid stared at the teen, then looked to Whispr. He had no suggestions to offer and was beginning to wish he had made a run for it when he'd had the opportunity, the doctor's inane indifference notwithstanding.

She allowed a considerably larger figure to be entered into the choirmaster's processing unit. Apparently it was sufficient. Or else he chose not to push the matter further, perhaps because someone had called the real police. A conspicuously marked scoot sporting bright red and yellow lights was approaching from the north. Quickly he verified the exchange, slipped the unit back into his pocket, and turned to gesture to his flock. Pocketing their miniaturized armory they swiftly dispersed, vanishing into the darkness between and among the buildings that lined the street.

The scoot slowed to a stop before the pair of benumbed visitors. Both of the cops who got off were straightforward police Melds, black and white with weaponized hands and communications gear integrated directly into the sides of their shaved skulls.

"We heard there was some trouble here." His face a permanently melded swirling pattern of white, coffee-brown, and ebony-black skin, the officer addressed himself to Ingrid.

"We're—okay now," she murmured. "Some men tried to hold us up, but we were saved by an—by a 'Capella' squad. Or maybe I should say 'rescued.'"

Muttering a curse in Zulu the second cop turned sharply to survey their surroundings. Filing out of flanking buildings, pedestrians were returning to the street. The buzz of casual evening conversation had resumed in nearby shops and cafés. The first cop remained focused on Ingrid.

"I hope your 'rescue' didn't end up costing you too much."

"The request for a donation was—unexpected," she admitted, "but not unbearable."

"Maybe not for you." Turning away from her the cop headed back to the waiting, light-flashing scoot. His partner joined him. "These religious vigilantes usurp the function of the Cape police. They should be wiped out. But it's hard to wipe out well-meaning children, even if they are being used to extort money. I hope the rest of the night is better for you visitors. Watch where you walk. Stay on the main street. And beware of massed singing." The scoot revved to a whine, spun on its axis, and shot off back the way it had come.

Whispr came up alongside her. "Still want to go into the city?"

Ingrid was chewing thoughtfully on her lower lip. "Maybe—maybe it *would* be better to wait until tomorrow. Until daylight." She turned back toward their hotel.

He nodded sagely. "Good idea. Easier to see clearly in the daytime, less likely to get mugged by God."

3

Cape Town was lucky. Unlike so many port cities that had suffered from the great Greenland slide and the commensurate melting of the Antarctic fringe; cities like New York with its Great Wall and Hudson tidal barrier, or London-become-like-Venice, or long-lost Venice itself (now a scuba diver's paradise), the high green mountains that cupped the South Africa metropolis were sufficiently steep to have allowed its harbor to retain its original functions. Port facilities, docks, warehouses, hotels, and individual dwellings had simply worked their way up the surrounding hillsides. Much as had been done on a far smaller scale at Simon's Town, Ingrid reflected as she and Whispr disembarked from the cliff-hugging public transport.

As they strolled the elevated Victoria and Albert waterfront while doing their best imitation of a typical tourist couple she could see that Whispr was unhappy. Or rather, unhappier than usual. Her companion wore melancholy like a black headscarf. He ought to be feeling good, she thought. Hadn't they just escaped a potentially violent mugging, even if she had been "persuaded" to make a rather substantial donation to a local church group?

"What's wrong now?"

Long tapering fingers gestured at the lights shining around them, at the contentedly strolling couples and clusters of nattering tourists, at the placid cold waters of the harbor and the cargo ships docked across the way, their great computer-controlled carbon-fiber sails furled against the night like pupae in their cocoons.

"I guess—I thought it would be different. I thought it would be—I don't know. *African.*" He shook his head. "It looks like Greater Savannah. Or Charleston, or Baltimore."

She turned to indicate the immense cloud-shrouded monolith that loomed immediately behind them: Table Mountain. "Does *that* remind you of Savannah?"

"No," he groused. "It reminds me of a migraine I once had."

She sighed resignedly. "Nothing pleases you, does it?"

Bright eyes set in a narrow skull peered down at her. "I want it to be African. I want it to be exotic. I want to see wildlife."

"We will." Her tone was soothing. "I promised we would. Just like you said, going on a game drive will cement our identities as genuine tourists." She turned back toward the broad expanse of the harbor. Reflected lights glimmered on the dark water like flattened sprites suspended between reality and faery. "But first we need to lock down our goal. We need information so that we can blend touring with our real reason for being here." Shivering slightly, she wrapped her arms around her upper body and hugged herself.

"I'm sorry," he muttered. "I forgot that you need warmer clothing. I could do with some myself."

The shop they entered in the waterfront tourist complex was expensive compared to what they could have found in the city proper, but buying touristy jackets and caps was in keeping with their adopted sightseeing personas. Ingrid didn't care. The jacket she picked out was warm, thermosensitive, hydrophobic, and the rampant lions on the back that appeared to be chasing leaping impala depending on how light struck the material comprised an attractive scene. Whispr opted for less flamboyant accoutrements in the form of a sweater woven from pulse wool and standard mudenim safari pants. With shoes swapped for boots they felt ready to take on either city or veldt.

Their new clothes did not prepare them for the rhino that blocked their way up the street outside the shop. They did not panic. The outrageousness of its presence instinctively obviated any likely threat. This assumption was quickly proved correct. As the rhino addressed them a sampling of animated brochures slipped from its mouth like so many cards from an automated poker dealer.

"Hang-glide off Table Mountain!" one handout beseeched breathlessly. The others were equally strident in their description of things to do, from trekking to the tip of the Cape of Good Hope to taking a guided walk through the local fynbos forest.

"No thanks." Stepping to one side, Ingrid strode past the robot. Thankfully, the accuracy with which it had been constructed did not extend to emitting an appropriate scent. In passing Whispr looked for something useful to swipe: an instinctive reaction he had been forced to suppress ever since they had left Florida. Stuffed full of brochures and other advertisements the rhino's flank offered no obvious ingress. Instead of lions and leopards it was armored to fend off opportunistic rifflers like himself.

Sampling brews from Kenya to Tanzania, Ingrid downed a lot of coffee that night as she watched Whispr sidle up to every passing character and inviting cozy who looked like they might have info to sell.

"Just want to know where the SAEC mushes its hush-hush," he would ask. Sometimes the eager would feed him fresh-cut baloney, which he was adept at smelling. Sometimes the honest climbers and clamberers along the waterfront would tell him they knew nothing of what he wanted. And sometimes the mere mention of such a request would send Naturals and Melds alike scurrying away in fear as if he was asking directions to the vampire crypt of horror or some equally terrifying milieu instead of a division of a major commercial-industrial complex.

For a small consideration more than one of his interrogatories offered to provide the location of SICK's corporate headquarters. Whispr could only shake his head at the shamelessness of such responses. Just because he and his lady friend were from out of country didn't mean they had failed to bring their brains in their baggage. SICK's great hexagonal central office complex, its two-kilometer-high spires alternately lit red, blue, green, yellow, black, and white in homage to the colors of the combine's flag, dominated not only the city but the entire peninsula. Whispr didn't see any reason to hand over subsist in return for the self-evident location of the most prominent architectural feature in this part of Africa.

What he wanted to know and what the street informants could not tell him was whether the sextuple towers also contained within their radiant depths the SAEC's primary scientific research facilities.

Ingrid was leaning against a transparent railing gazing out at the water. Protected Cape Fur seals frolicked nearby, barking and playing tag beneath the lights of overhanging structures. Despite the danger posed by passing ship traffic the marine mammals were safer here than in False Bay, with its equally protected population of wild great whites. She turned from the calming view of the harbor as he approached.

"Any luck?"

He joined her at the railing. "Take me for a stupe the tide washed in, the locals do-do. Try to sell me mind goo, or think they can flash my pan, or perceive my perception as no broader than my beam." He looked over at her. Yet again she was struck by the mix of determination and anxiety in his expression. "I got nothing," he finished dourly.

She let it glide. "We just got here. It's our first night and it's been a busy one. Riffle, shopping, interrogating. We'll get a good night's sleep and try again tomorrow."

"Animals," he told her. "Wildlife. You promised."

"We need to pick a direction first." She was adamant as ever. Her nostrils were filled with the rich, dense odor of salt and kelp and scuttling crustaceans. "We need to at least learn where we have to go. Settle on a destination and we'll find a way to work your childish obsession into the going."

He made a rude sound. "Childish? You're the one who bought a jacket with lions running across the back."

"It was warm and it fit properly." She eyed his newly wrapped leanness. "At least I don't look like a pig in a blanket."

"I don't care what I look like," he shot back. "I'm a practical man. There's not enough room in me for vanity."

She laughed lightly at his comeback but it did not take away the sting of her words. He wanted her to like him, to admire him, to find him tolerable if not actually handsome to look upon. Instead she treated him as a tool, a means to an end, a human prybar with which to help unlock the secret of the thread. The misguided episode with the zoe hadn't helped his cause. That had not only been intrusive—it was juvenile. Pursuing the doctor was a hopeless quest, a cause lost before it could be fully formulated. He made himself turn his thoughts elsewhere. If she was unattainable the promise of the money the thread might bring would have to suffice. *If* what was on it was valuable. Or if it proved empty, if the storage device was valuable in and of itself.

All dependent, he knew, on whether they could survive long enough to learn the answers to those and other nagging questions. He rubbed at his eyes and his forehead.

"I'm exhausted. How come you're still awake?"

"Caffeine and practice. Doctors are used to working late hours. At least, I am." She stepped back from the railing. It moaned softly, trying to get her to stay and peruse the advertisements that ran along and through it. "But you're right. Tomorrow's another day."

4

Tomorrow's another day, Het Kruger mused, and hopefully he wouldn't have to okay the execution of any more fools like the trio who had set up operations not far to the east of the Nerens facility. Hidden inside a cave in the five-hundred-meter-high massif of the Boegoeberg they had probably believed their camp was safe from the installation's aerial patrols. Wearing lightweight thermoline suits that caused their heat signatures to blend with that of their chilly surroundings and working only at night, they had done their sifting solely by the light of the moon and stars. Thus rendered invisible to any patrolling seekers utilizing infrared or visible light they had plied their trade in self-assured secrecy.

They hadn't counted on the sniffers.

Kruger almost wished that the melded hyenas had torn the intruders to bits instead of just putting them down and holding them for pickup. It would have simplified his paperwork. But no, the loping patrol had complied fully with their training, merely incapacitating the poachers and broadcasting their location. A lifter had gone out and picked up the trio. There was no hurry. It was not as if the intruders were going to make a break for it, even if they had been so inclined following their takedown.

Demonstrating the meticulousness of their training the hyenas had neatly bitten through all six of the poachers' Achilles' tendons. The intruders weren't going to run anywhere.

And now they weren't going to do anything else. Their bodies had been cremated and poured into the recycler with the rest of the facility's combustible trash. Anyone foolish enough to come looking for them would meet the same fate. Anyone making inquiries would find themselves up against a bureaucratic void as vast and unforgiving as the Namib itself.

Kruger shook his head at the appalling stupidity of the intruders and their predecessors as he stepped into the lift and thumbed one of several illuminated squares. Not being a button, it did not depress. Instead, the internal electronics read both his fingerprint and individual heat signature. Thus appeased, the lift's computer permitted more prosaic mechanics to engage and the elevator commenced its nearly silent ascent.

He had not been present for the execution so he did not know if the three men, one Natural and two desert Melds, had begged for leniency. Having infiltrated the Restricted zone they presumably knew better. Illegal entry to the non-park section of the Sperrgebeit had been punishable by death ever since the world's best gemquality diamonds had been discovered there long ago. Thanks to marketing as clever as it was zealous, natural diamonds continued to hold their value even in a day and time when good synthetics were virtually indistinguishable from the real thing. So most of the Sperrgebeit Diamond Area I was still as much of a no-man's-land as it had been in the nineteenth century.

For SAEC's purposes this was very useful.

Diamonds continued to be mined in the vast southern portion of the Namib desert. Massive dredges worked around the clock in huge rectangular pits that had been scooped out below sea level, shoveling the diamondiferous earth into clunky sauropodian loaders. The gem-bearing soil was sorted and re-sorted at multiple locations before the final product was flown out on armed, escorted aircraft. The miserable excuse for a road that led more than a hundred kilometers south to Orangemund was suitable only for properly equipped tracked or multidrive vehicles and authorized tourist vehicles. The diamonds could have been sent by floater, but such small craft were too easy to shoot down or even capture intact. Armed aircraft were more expensive but safer.

In addition to more than paying for itself the ancient diamond mining operation and its enforced isolation provided excellent cover for one of SAEC's most important research facilities. The fact that as Chief of Security Kruger hadn't the slightest idea what the facility he was charged with protecting was researching troubled him not one whit. He knew a number of the scientists and engineers and their subordinates by name and could recognize a great many more on sight. Despite their wildly different specialties he chatted easily with them on many subjects, from food to football. But when they started talking about their business, to the limited degree that such general conversation was allowed, as far as he was concerned they might as well be from Mars.

No, that description was not quite apt, he told himself. He could understand the lilting patois favored by the Martian colonists quite well. The Titanites, of course, were quite another matter. Anyone who thought a bug-eyed top-heavy Martian was an extreme example of human melding had never set eyes on a Titanite. That included Kruger, who felt no need of such contact. He knew all about extreme melds because he had undergone the most radical of all.

The willing subject of one meld after another since the age of sixteen, he had been melded and remelded until he looked like — a Natural.

Gone were the forearm guns of which he had been so proud. Gone too the integrated vision and listening devices that had for years made his skull look more robotic than human. Gone the all-terrain lower limbs. To all intents and purposes he now looked like any other Natural, albeit one taller and more muscular than the average. As the quiet-voiced company interrogator who had conducted the final interview that had led to him being promoted to his present position had told him, "The SAEC prefers to cow those who might threaten it with integers that are at least outwardly unthreatening."

Though to all appearances now wholly Natural, he walked with a stiffness of gait that was the unavoidable consequence of so many surgeries. Of all his former manips he had retained only a single meld, pleading with his new employers that it was undetectable to all but the most expert onlookers. Some discussion had ensued, the upshot of which was that the concession of his right eye had been granted.

Immensely intricate and quite expensive, a unique system of flexible organic lenses combined with highly miniaturized internal optics to allow him to see well into the infrared. At maximum focal length he had the long-range spatial acuity of an eagle. Muscle-driven compression allowed him close-up vision that verged on the microscopic. Not only could Het Kruger see to the heart of a matter, given a portable flexscope he could see well into the heart itself.

Soon after the last operation he found he did not miss the more

macho melds, the guns and their accessories. He had matured beyond such tawdry displays of firepower. "Testostermelds" they were
referred to as in some quarters—often with derision. Now in his
midforties, after more than a quarter of a century in the security
business, Kruger did not need to flaunt instruments of destruction
to do his job or persuade the wayward. Looking into their eyes was
sufficient.

That had been the case with the three diamond poachers, whose
resolve had been broken and who had confessed quickly. Their ab-
ject pleas for sympathy did not save them. In the non-park portion
of the Sperrgebeit the SAEC was judge, jury, and executioner.
SICK justice, some would have called it. But such on-site jurispru-
dence and sentencing had been perfectly legal for a very long time
indeed; first under the Germans, then the South Africans, the
Namibians, and finally the SAEC. To Kruger's knowledge it was
the only part of the world where such summary justice could be
handed down. Legally, anyway.

The lift halted two levels below the surface. As a security measure, none of the lifts in the research complex extended all the way
from top to bottom. A vertical traveler always had to transfer
between at least two to get back to the surface. As Kruger headed
down the well-lit, comfortably air-conditioned corridor he exchanged brief glances or nods with those he knew. He never smiled.
He would have blanched at the artificiality of it and those on whom
such an expression might have been bestowed would have recognized it for the falsehood it represented. Within the facility he had
many acquaintances and no friends. None of them objected to the
seriousness of his mien. His task was to provide them with security
and privacy, not amusement.

Coming toward him was a researcher he knew only as Changl.
The scientist was conversing with a strange Meld. This in itself was

not unusual. The SAEC facility played host to the strangest Melds Kruger, who knew something about strange Melds, had ever seen. He had often suspected that the purpose of the installation was to conduct research into new, ever more extreme, and therefore freshly profitable melds. A cosmetic or medical meld that hit it big could generate tremendous profits for any multinational, the SAEC among them. Given the level of sophistication that had been achieved by contemporary industrial espionage it was no wonder that the SAEC would choose to situate such an important research facility in an isolated, inaccessible, and heavily defended place like the Sperrgebeit, whose diamond-mining operations provided excellent cover for the comings and goings of scientific personnel and equipment.

Changl's companion was a bloated, fat-faced creature who walked with a rolling side-to-side gait, as if struggling to negotiate the deck of a ship in a heavy storm. The individual's eyes were so dark as to render the pupils indistinct and wide enough to admit just enough light to satisfy a troglodyte. Though tempted to look around and examine the visitor's backside Kruger maintained his stolid forward gaze. He was religiously indifferent to that which did not directly concern him—another trait of which his employers approved. But he could not help but wonder at the existence of such excess avoirdupois. In a world where the most complex variations on cosmetic melds were readily available, what kind of person deliberately sought obesity?

The majority of technicians, scientists, machinists, craftsmen, programmers, and other employees at the desert facility worked two months on and one off. Given his senior position Kruger could have done the same. He chose not to. His idea of a vacation was examining personnel files and researching the latest in sophisticated security gear. His employers were very happy with their choice of security chief.

But he did occasionally feel the need to get away from the installation's subterranean confines. To stretch his legs on real ground and feel the sun flush on his face. He was not a termite, destined to spend all his waking hours underground. This time of year, when temperatures in the Namib were less than hellish, was his favorite. Stepping into a surface-access lift he acknowledged the four-armed Meld guard on duty, allowed the internal security system to read his biometrics, and waited patiently as it ascended the last two levels.

Emerging into the crowded surface warehouse, which had been carefully bedecked from the outside to look like an old metal storage building, he made his way among the stacks of crates and shipping cylinders and smaller packages to a side pedestrian exit. A visitor standing outside would see only an ordinary, weather-beaten door. To get to the ordinary door from the inside Kruger had to pass through a transparent domed tunnel sealed at either end and guarded by a large lod shouldering a massive automatic weapon.

As he walked the length of the short transparent passageway he drew a pair of automatically adjusting photosensitive shades from a pocket and slipped them over his eyes. Reaching the end he waited for clearance to sound. A moment later he was allowed to push open the door. With nothing left to impede his progress he stepped outside and into the Namib.

Sand. Sand and rock and sun. Not a tree, not a bush, not a blade of grass disturbed the sere serenity that assaulted his gaze. Leaving the warehouse and the rest of the deceptively ordinary-looking aboveground portion of the installation behind, he strode deliberately toward the nearest dune. Glistening like a lump of polished obsidian, a fat tok-tok beetle scurried to get out of his way. As he started up the dune he startled a burrowing lizard. It promptly vanished into the sand, surviving by sucking the air trapped between the grains.

Once at the top he turned and sat down. The panorama that greeted him would have appalled most people. As always, Kruger found it restful.

At his feet the visible portion of the research facility appeared to consist of nothing more than a cluster of dilapidated mining buildings, squarish structures of utilitarian gray metal zebra-striped with rust. Like so many other denizens of the Namib the ultramodern hospital-clean bulk of the complex lay hidden beneath the sand. Beyond the deceptively primitive upper layer of the facility, sand and dunes reached in all directions, the yellow-and-ochre surface of the earth broken only by folds of tormented rock or upthrusts of rust-red stone.

Against the edge of this isolated African coast smashed frigid white-crested waves tossed up by the Benguela Current, its dark green waters stretching to the western horizon and beyond; a sheet of uninterrupted ocean that ran flat and uninhabited all the way to the coast of South America. To the north and south the view was equally desolate. Save for the SAEC facility there was no sign of human habitation in all that silent, treeless wilderness. At once tortured and serene, it was a landscape only a geologist could love.

Sitting on the high dune, Kruger was content. Solitude was his friend, newcomers a potential problem. Propelled by the incoming breeze off the sea and utilizing the first thermals for lift, a seabird came soaring past on wings of dirty ivory. Perhaps it knew from experience that where humans resided, edible garbage was usually not far behind.

Mildly disconcerted at having his meditation disturbed, Kruger shot it in the middle of its querulous cry. Not for the research facility's chief of security a weapon as irresolute as a neuralizer. The small but powerful explosive shell his sidearm fired atomized all but a few feathers of the luckless visitor. Spiraling slowly downward they made little white sketches in the atmosphere where the unknowing avian intruder had only a second earlier gracefully displaced the air.

As he holstered his sleek, compact weapon Kruger tracked their forlorn descent to the sand. They barely had time enough to touch the earth before the wind swept them over the crest of the dune and out of sight. He was almost disappointed that it had been a real bird and not an espionage simulacrum or some other clever variation on an intruding spy meld. Putting the incident out of his mind he returned his full attention to contemplation of the vast expanse of empty sea. Oblivious to the brief, loud *crack* of his gun, the dark green rollers continued their remorseless, patient assault on the ancient shore.

He felt no remorse. Having shot people for unauthorized intrusion he saw no reason why a bird should be exempt. In today's world one could never be sure whether a nonhuman intruder was real, synthetic, or manip-compromised. One of the guiding tenets of his profession was never to take chances. As a consequence he trusted nothing that smacked of the living. Even a tok-tok beetle might conceal a clever tick-tock mechanism. He took great care and considerable pride in seeing to the security of he knew not what.

That was the greatest irony of his job: he had no idea what he was guarding. He knew no more about the purpose of the facility or the nature of the research that was carried out on its gleaming multiple subterranean levels than did those company workers who provided food for the scientists and engineers, kept the toilets clean, polished the floors, or serviced the air-conditioning. He was simply another employee, one rather more heavily armed than most. His staff consisted of armed Naturals and Melds as well as technical experts who monitored and maintained the elaborate layers of electronics that guarded the facility's interior and kept watch on its perimeter. The latter included maniped animals like the spotted hyena patrols as well as people.

Having been in the security business for some time now he occasionally found it difficult to tell the latter from the former. On the whole, he found that he preferred the company of quadrupedal hyenas to the two-legged kind.

It was not that he was uncurious about what went on at the facility. Surely an installation so expensive to staff and sustain, set in such an isolated location, must generate some kind of income for the company. But no product that he could discern ever left on the company helicopters. No direct mining that he could perceive occurred in its vicinity, the substantial diamond mining operation being entirely and completely a separate facility. As near as he could tell, those who worked at the research facility had zero contact with those at the nearby mining complex.

He never expressed such interest to the very few men and women who ranked as his superiors. Intellectual curiosity in a security chief was not a quality that was welcomed. Though cordial to fellow employees, he and his underlings stood slightly apart from them. This separation was not by choice but out of necessity. It was hard to become close to those on whom one was consistently spying. Sometimes it could be painful. For his part Kruger remained affable but reserved. It was a characteristic he strove to inculcate in all of his subordinates.

And now this alert. He didn't like surprises.

It had arrived a week ago in the form of a morning memo.

Nothing overly excited, nothing suggesting that someone corporate in Cape Town or Joburg was suffering from a panic attack. Merely a suggestion that for a little while security should be tightened, that the usual level of watchfulness should be raised a degree or two. There was no explanation for the request. Perhaps it was nothing more than a test, Kruger thought—though he took quiet umbrage at the notion that the security put in place and maintained by his team was ever anything less than optimal. Still, he went through the motions of complying. Called a meeting of his assistants and advised them of the contents of the memo. Laid on a few extra outlying patrols. Had all equipment checked for updates and reliability. Made sure all of the electronics were in working order.

Nothing happened. No armed assault took place on the facility. No maniped creatures attempted an intrusion. The usual comings and goings of unusual melded visitors and their Natural guides continued as they always had. Nothing in the nature of a threatening or even atypical activity manifested itself.

He had almost forgotten all about it when the call came in.

That in itself was not normal. Usually all incoming calls intended for or directed to specific personnel were routed through the facility's central communications center. There they were screened for content, traced to origin, and decrypted before being passed along to their intended recipient. This one rang his personal phone and when he acknowledged it, provided an image to accompany the audio.

He frowned as he studied the caller's portrait. It evinced no sign of encryption, almost as if the individual on the other end had been able to contact him directly. That was impossible, of course. Such a person-to-person exchange of information, however harmless, would constitute a grave breach of installation security.

That is, it would unless someone very, very high up in the

SAEC hierarchy had given permission for the direct contact to take place, and had supplied the caller with Kruger's direct number. That kind of exchange was virtually without precedent. Yet as he peered down at his phone the security chief could hardly deny the reality of the face that was looking back at him via the communicator's own pickup. He was at once intrigued and bemused, but not concerned. After all, his caller's aspect was hardly threatening.

The old man's voice, however, belied his appearance. It did not shake and more than once hinted at a confidence Kruger recognized immediately.

The old man sounded very much like one of his own kind.

"Am I speaking with Het Kruger, chief of security for the Nerens station?"

"Who wants to know?" Kruger's response was clipped but polite.

"I am Napun Molé. While I am an independent contractor, I also work for the company. My area of expertise somewhat parallels your own."

"Prove it."

A tiny hint of a smile tweaked one corner of the respondent's mouth. "I would think the fact that I am able to speak to you directly would be adequate proof of my status. However as an analog of sorts I appreciate your position and your concern. Please take a moment to review the following information."

The projection bubble on Kruger's phone fizzed to lux. A series of numbers and names appeared in the air before him. He scanned them rapidly. He had to, because they did not linger. When he had seen enough he looked down at the phone and nodded.

"You tote a weighty résumé, Mr. Molé. And such a sequence of recommendations and references as I have rarely seen. So, you also work in company security?"

"In a manner of speaking," the oldster replied. "My area of responsibility is broader than yours but my staff considerably smaller."

"What can I do for you, colleague?" As Kruger studied the small
image his practiced eye picked out enough hints to indicate that
the old man had undergone extensive melding. He wondered at
their provenance and purpose but knew better than to pry.

"I am in pursuit of a pair of thieves who have stolen company
property. Very valuable property that has connections to the facility
whose security is your responsibility. Though my pursuit was
briefly diverted I now have reason to believe that they may be here
in Southern Africa. And while there is no particular reason to
believe they will ever make an appearance in your vicinity, where
company business is concerned I am a firm believer in guarding
against the unlikely as well as the expected."

Kruger found himself nodding in agreement. "We would get
along, I think, Mr. Molé."

"Experienced professionals invariably do. I will now download
to your communicator the details of their backgrounds and, insofar
as it is current, their physical appearance."

Kruger hardly had time to inhale before the information transfer was completed. Making use of the communicator's projector he
studied the images and information that appeared in the clear
desert air before him.

"The woman is attractive. A practicing family physician of some
repute, it says here. Of considerably less standing, her companion's
profile makes more sense to me. Neither appears to be the usual
sort to trigger a company-wide security alert. Especially the
woman."

"I find her participation in this matter a continuing puzzle-
ment," Molé responded. "However it is no less real for its incom-

prehensibility. But having been in this business for as long as you have I am sure that you know how the promise of wealth and power can alter the behavior and personality of even the most stable-seeming of citizens. That is apparently the case where this Dr. Seastrom is concerned. Having barely eluded me in Namerica I can testify both to her intelligence and her exterior attractiveness, though her recent actions call her purported intelligence into question."

Kruger closed down the projection. He could study the fine details later at leisure. "For the company to put an experienced (he did not say 'old,' which was what he was thinking) investigator like yourself onto them they must have stolen something substantial. If it had happened here I'd think a large diamond, probably a colored stone."

"Nothing so inconsequential," explained Molé. "The object in question is a small storage thread. The material it is made from represents a proprietary manufacturing development of recent vintage of which the company is extremely protective."

"And its contents?"

"Even more proprietary." The old man's tone was courteous but unyielding. Knowing that further probing would garner distrust in lieu of explanation Kruger did not inquire further.

"Among the data that has been provided to you," Molé continued, "is my own private number. Though it is my hope there will be no need for us to talk again, should you encounter any information that might lead to the apprehension of these two miscreants you should feel free to contact me directly."

Kruger's lips tightened. "In other words, should I encounter them you don't wish me to have them arrested."

"In other words," the old man replied in a voice as cold as the depths of the offshore waters, "the company would prefer that I resolve the entirety of the situation quickly and efficiently. By myself if possible. By other hands if it should prove expedient."

"I understand." The atmosphere around the security chief seemed to have chilled slightly.

"I knew that you would."

"One thing before you go," Kruger prompted his caller. "Am I correct in assuming that I am not the only member of company security that you've contacted personally about this matter?"

"That is so. You are number thirty-two. I have forty more to call. I desire that everyone be suitably advised and prepared. One never knows from where a useful bit of information may be forthcoming. I wish you a pleasant day, Mr. Kruger."

The conversation was at an end. Replacing his unit in its self-sealing protective pocket Kruger once more returned to gazing out to sea. Ten minutes later he let out a long sigh, rose to his feet, brushed sand from his pants, and started back down the dune face. The information he had just received needed to be entered into the research facility's security database and his subordinates would have to be informed. Then, in all likelihood, they could all forget about it. As the site's maniped hyenas had recently proven, unauthorized travelers could not get within twenty kilometers of the facility even if they were aware of its exact existence and location.

Besides, having spoken at some length with the formidable old man who called himself Napun Molé, Het Kruger felt very strongly that the two Namericans for whom he was searching would soon no longer have the freedom to wander about Southern Africa or anywhere else.

HER NAME WAS THEMBEKILE. "But you can call me Thembe," the big woman told Ingrid and Whispr as she led them deeper into the complex of spider houses. "The name is Zulu and means 'trustworthy.' For a poor farmer my father was prescient. Or optimistic. Depends on which of my clientele you talk to." She favored them with a huge smile. "If you better like, you may call me the Electric Sangoma. That is my *professional* title."

She didn't so much walk as waddle Whispr decided as he followed in her wake. Ingrid's take on the woman who had been recommended to them was more nuanced. As a doctor she knew that their hostess could stand to lose some weight. On the other hand, it was entirely possible that within her profession physical size went along with spiritual heft.

In the old days Thembe would have been a traditional healer among the Nguni peoples of Southern Africa, dispensing herbal remedies and sage advice in equal measure. Possibly she continued to do so, Ingrid mused as they started up yet another flight of flexible steps. But even a sangoma had to change with the times. Repeated inquiries by Whispr had led them to this place and to this woman.

The synthetic ivory and hand-blown glass beads that were braided into her long black hair flickered with a rainbow of internal lights. Its internal dazzle-play notwithstanding, the multilayered electrophoretic gown that whipped around her hid considerably less of her than Whispr would have preferred. He was far too diplomatic to comment on the overpowering interaction of light and flesh. And sufficiently cautious. The sangoma must have weighed well over a hundred and fifty kilos and could have squashed his meld-slenderized self like a bug. As they ascended the mountainside her gown continued to dazzle-up hundreds of different colors, though because of the nature of the material the display was less intense than the one flaring from her hair.

Bringing up the rear, Ingrid noticed the presence in the complex coiffure of an object that was unambiguously organic, and in-

quired about it. Their hostess and guide offered an explanation that
was as unexpected as it was prosaic.

"That is the gallbladder of the goat that was sacrificed at my
graduation ceremony."

"I didn't know people in your chosen specialty had graduation
ceremonies." Now puffing hard, Whispr had long since stopped
counting stairs. How the massive woman in front of him managed
the climb without gasping prodigiously, much less having a heart
attack, was beyond him. There had to be some kind of advanced internal respiratory meld that kept her going. Certainly there was
enough room within the thickset rotund body to accommodate an
extra lung or two, be it transplant or mechanical.

"Indeed we do," she told him. "I value our traditions, skinny
man. They mean as much and are as important to me and my work
as is my degree in Communications from Witwaterstrand University." Looking back and down at him she smiled afresh, her gleaming cheeks bunching up like dark plums. "From the goat I got
gallbladder, from the university I got gall."

"I don't care if you shift sheep guts and read palms," a wheezing
Ingrid told her, "if you can help us."

The sangoma's expression tightened. "Palm reading is for char-
latans and swindlers and sheep organs are for the pot, my dear.
Surely you expect better from me than that! What a good sangoma
relies on is the throwing of the bones."

Uncertain whether the other woman was pulling her leg, Ingrid
replied with her usual honesty. "We don't know what to expect. We
were just told to seek you out because we were told you were someone who might be able to provide the answers we need."

"I know what to expect," Whispr grumbled as the house they
were approaching, in its perpetual quest for hillside stability, took
another step sideways and further widened the distance between

them. "I can read the future, too." He waved a hand melodramati-
cally over his head. "I predict the materialization of a large bill."

"You are insufficiently deferential." Their hostess pursed her
lips disapprovingly. "But Thembekile forgive you." She halted
before the house, which had finally stopped moving and adjusting
its position. "Here is my *ndumba.* In old times the place of healing
would be little more than a simple hut. I heal here, but nowadays I
only have to use one room out of many."

Halting before the front door she extended a hand palm out and
facing forward. The seamlessly integrated lock scanned the electronic key embedded beneath the skin of her hand and clicked,
opening to admit them.

A short entry hallway led to a room of modest size. Every corner, every square centimeter, was filled with part of what in total
comprised a fantastic panoply of the ancient and modern, the
organic and the synthesized. Animal skins hanging from the flat
ceiling flapped like primordial heraldic banners in the breeze generated by the building's climate control. Beyond and below the
steep drop outside, the entire Cape Town harbor and coastal metropolis could be seen, still spectacular despite the rise in sea level.
The soft whirrs and clicks of automatic machinery rose from beneath the marula-paneled floor as the house once again changed
position.

Outside, the entire hillside was peppered with similar mobile
structures. The community was in constant motion as each structure and its owner sought a more stable vantage point with a better
view. Each time a home or business settled in for a few days or
weeks or months it would spit forth a coil of animated seeker con-
duits. Searching on their own, homing in on the appropriate
community terminals, each building's sentient intestines would lo-

cate and link up connections for power, water, and sewerage. Seen from a distance the steep flank of the mountain appeared to be under assault by a swarm of boxy tentacular cockroaches.

Such mobility wasn't all, or even primarily, about the view. A house or business that was always on the move was one that was hard to tax. It also provided a complex but proven method of preserving one's anonymity. This feature was highly valued by, for example, certain individuals who might be operating a barely legal commercial enterprise.

Their hostess had alluded to a throwing of bones. Ingrid decided that the ones that ornamented the *ndumba* were much too big to toss around. Like Alice, she found herself drawn inexorably deeper and deeper into the improbable surroundings. One freestanding bone had to be the tibia of an elephant. From atop a cabinet overflowing with curiosities the bleached skull of a lion snarled silently down at her. Whether the skull was real or a reproduction even Ingrid, with her medical training, could not tell. Strings of beads hung like frozen rain, each strand irregular with bits of stone, seeds, bone, fish and animal vertebrae, shards of shining metal, chunks of colorful glass.

The room certainly might have put the easily alarmed in mind of a spider's web. Batik hangings illustrated scenes of death and destruction; semi-abstract portraits of a particularly African purgatory. Bowls and jars held an assortment of pickled and preserved parts of what seemed to be every phyla in the plant and animal kingdom.

In complete contrast a large flexible box screen stood on its own pivoting mount. Behind it, neatly tucked in between a petrified monkey and a crate overflowing with dried skates and stingrays, stood several powerful cloud couplers. Their lights gleamed as bright and steady as the beads in Thembekile's tightly braided hair.

Once more the house lurched beneath them as it shifted position. Whispr cursed and their hostess apologized as she settled herself into the big overstuffed chair that fronted the box screen.

"Sorry for that it be a moving day. Mountainside, she is getting crowded. Nowadaisys one person moves house, everybody has to move house." Her wonderfully reassuring smile appeared afresh. "Drives the municipal authorities crazy. Which of course is the idea." She folded her hands on her lap. "What can I do for you visitors? I know already it must be something unusual or you would not have sought me out. I specialize in satisfaction of the unusual. People do not come to me for restaurant recommendations." Her attention focused on Whispr and her gaze narrowed ever so slightly. "By finding me you have already gone to some trouble and risked your visitors' status. So I will try not to disappoint you. But I make no promises. Payment is in advance and nonrefundable."

Whispr grunted derisively. "Another prediction I could have made, and without the need for a goat's gallbladder in my hair."

"Be polite, Whispr." Ingrid fumbled inside her jacket, the unique signature from her right thumb and forefinger unsealing the special pocket that had been woven into the inside of the left cup of her brassiere. From the compartment she withdrew a small transparent capsule. It contained a single storage thread.

"What is this?" Demonstrating surprising dexterity Thembekile took the capsule between two fingers and rotated it as she held it up to the light.

"A storage thread," Ingrid explained. "We don't know what's on it, if anything, because we can't read it. Reading has been tried using an assortment of advanced and sometimes very expensive instruments. The thread itself is made of metastable metallic hydrogen, a material that according to physics and metallurgy ought to be unstable at normal temperature and pressure. In fact, it should be impossible. But the composition has been confirmed. We were told by our contacts in . . . ," she hesitated a moment, then resumed after careful thought, "we were told by our contacts that there is maybe one company in the world that is actually working on making such a substance viable. The SAEC."

Thembekile nodded thoughtfully as she handed the capsule back to the doctor. "You seem to know much already of what it is that you want to learn. What do you want of me?"

Ingrid wrenched her gaze away from the lion skull, whose hollow eyes seemed to be tracking her. "If SICK is working on MSMH it will be at their most advanced and secure research facility. We're hoping if we can find out where they're manufacturing the metal that it will lead us to whatever is on it. There are congruent social implications that relate intimately to my own profession. So . . . we need to know where that facility is located."

Their hostess looked from the doctor to Whispr and back again. "Sometimes SICK people are not very nice people. But in my experience people reply more courteously if you just ask them what you want to know. Why not simply go to one of their public offices and ask them about your little thread? They can always refuse to answer, or even claim they know nothing about such a material."

"That's just it. Nobody knows about it." Whispr was staring out the window, oblivious to the long drop below. "Nobody's even supposed to know about it. SICK is working real hard to make *sure* nobody knows about it." Turning away from the view and back to their hostess he smiled humorlessly. "It's a secret."

"A secret that leads to other secrets—we think." Ingrid did not elaborate.

"Oh, ho!" As the sangoma chuckled her entire body rippled and shook like a finely turned-out mousse. "You seek answers to questions you are not supposed to know. Is there more *I* should know?"

Ingrid glanced at Whispr, who threw her a warning look. They had come so far, she thought. They had come *this* far. She plunged onward. "This impractical material, this impossible substance of which the thread is made, has also been found in the heads of children. Children of many different backgrounds, from all over the world. Teenagers, mostly, who are suffering from depression and related problems."

Thembekile frowned. "The storage thread some way affects children? How?"

"Not the thread. Nanoscale devices made of the same substance that have been implanted in their heads. When you try to examine one of them closely they just—vanish. The tiny devices must do *something*, but we don't know what because they won't allow themselves to be studied. Likewise, the thread itself doesn't appear to do much of anything. Also, it's infinitely larger and it doesn't disentangle when you examine it. Why the minuscule devices do and the thread doesn't is just one of the mysteries we're hoping to unravel. We think the key might be among the information that's stored on the thread itself. Except we can't see the information, not with any known reading device." She jerked her head in Whispr's direction.

"My friend just wants to find out what it's worth. I want to learn its purpose and what it contains—if anything." She shrugged and sat back. "If we finally manage to find a way to read it and it turns out to be blank you're liable to hear two cries of disappointment all the way back here in Cape Town."

The sangoma sat and thought for a long minute. "I can see you have many questions. About this thread and about many very small things you cannot show me because you say that to look upon them is to make them disappear. But you only ask one thing of me. To play tour guide. To give you directions to a place that I am sure you have already determined is not listed in the government-sponsored visitor brochures."

Spinning alarmingly in her chair she faced the darkened, semi-transparent box screen. As soon as her eyes made contact with the unit its security mode sprang to life. Her back to her guests, she named a fee. Whispr blanched at the figure. Ingrid unhesitatingly agreed.

"*Ngiyabonga*—thanks. We have an agreement." Still fronting the box she turned her head to smile back at her clients. Ingrid was expectant. A characteristically wary Whispr rose.

"How do we know you aren't just contacting friends of yours to come and rob us?" The unnaturally lean Namerican had edged toward the hallway. "How do we know any information you give us will be valid and not just some address or location you make up on the spot?"

"How do I know that your credit is good?" their hostess responded good-naturedly. "How do I know you haven't come here on behalf of the authorities to arrest me simply for practicing my art?"

"Come on, woman," Whispr sneered. "Do I strike you as a cop?"

"Of course you don't." Her smile widened. "If you had, you would be dead by now and on your way down-mountain to feed the sharks." She turned back to her setup. As she did so the thick middle fingers of each hand began to elongate. The tip of each finger flipped up to reveal bare connector terminals. With ease born of long practice she slid them smoothly into waiting slots beneath the screen. Her voice was a knowing singsong.

"It is traditional for a sangoma to see through their hands."

Whereupon her eyes popped out of her head and retracted smoothly upward on flexible metal stalks.

5

Normally collapsed within the sangoma's eye sockets behind her real eyes, specialized lenses now unfolded to focus exclusively on the activated box screen. While using them Thembekile was effectively otherwise blind, the eyes now resting on her forehead still attached to the inside of her skull by extensible composite muscles, moisturizer tubing, and maniped elongated optic nerves. The extraordinary melds that had been performed on her hands and eyes were as complex as they were unsubtle. Neither Whispr, attuned to such extensive modifications from experience, or Ingrid, familiar with them from her medical work, had detected the manips until they had been activated.

Through them the sangoma essentially became as one with her mass of high-tech equipment and with the Cape Town box. This melding of human and machine did not restrict awareness of her guests nor prevent her from keeping in contact with them. She continued to speak to her customers in the same easy, relaxed fashion as she had prior to the revelation of her complex meld and the unexpected elevation of her eyeballs to their present position on the top of her forehead.

"Does my temporary transition to contemporary sangoma unsettle you?"

"No—no." Ingrid found herself fascinated by the continuing immobility of the eyeballs that had been retracted against the woman's hairline and the two long flexible fingers that were now embedded in the box console. "I'm a doctor. I've seen a good deal more extreme manips than the average person."

Not to be outdone Whispr added, "And I've seen some straight out of nightmares. Freely chosen nightmares."

"I am pleased you are not uncomfortable. Now I will go to work for you."

Behind the screen a constellation of glowing telltales sprang to life, their light reducing the screen itself to near invisibility. It was impossible to tell how far back into the wall the complex of electronics extended. Insistent and primal, the rhythmic pounding of drums echoed throughout the reception area.

An uneasy Whispr found himself searching the crowded corners of the increasingly dark room. "Why the drums?"

"Very important part of sangoma ritual," the temporarily eyeless woman explained. "Necessary to the summoning of the relevant ancestral spirits."

Ingrid looked uncertain. "You're not telling us that you're trying to use the box to summon ancestral spirits?"

"Of course not," came the pleasant reply. "What do you think I am—some kind of primitive fakir?"

"Then why the drums?" Whispr wondered edgily.

Her explanation was as simple as it was straightforward. "I like drums. They put me in the mood."

While she worked he studied the technical aspects of her setup.

It was impressive but not overawing. He'd seen elaborate conjoined boxworks before. Most recently in the Alligator Man's workshop and on the houseboat of the late and not especially lamented Yabby Wizwang.

"I get what you're after with the drums. Atmosphere, to intimidate your less sophisticated clients. But what's up with intimate box connection? I thought you relied on the throwing of bones." He sniffed. A strong loamy fragrance had begun to seep into the room. Ingrid smelled it, too. Its unannounced intrusion did not worry Whispr. If their host had intended to knock them out or otherwise subdue them with some kind of gas it most likely would have been odorless. "And what's that stink?"

"Burning *imphepho*—another sangoma tradition. As for throwing the bones, that is what I am doing." Thembekile kept them informed without looking away from her work. Indeed, with her eyes resting comfortably almost on top of her head she could not do so even had she been so inclined. Light flared from the box screen and the interwoven mass of instrumentation behind it. "I am casting forth your request together with what relevant information I can summon from the box. To enhance the chance of success we should also sacrifice a chicken or goat, but I feel it is not something you would understand. Or appreciate."

"I told you: I'm a physician." Ingrid was staring closely at the now explosively alive box screen. "I've probably worked around more blood than you have."

Whispr was equally unfazed. "Wouldn't bother me, either, woman. I'd like to see how you carry out the procedure. When it comes to sacrificing meat I personally favor grilling or frying."

"Ah, sociocultural convergence." Thembekile spoke softly and without turning away from the closely contained lambent cosmology she had called up. "Traditional African societies sacrifice animals to gain wisdom. European-derived societies do it to gain weight."

Out of the forest of lights multiple shapes and reader platforms started to appear. They began not only to fill but to surround the screen as its integrated minijectors coughed up three-dimensional responses to the sangoma's stream of queries. Leaning forward Ingrid was able to make out a rapidly shifting succession of maps, reports, news articles, pictures, brief video clips, and a vast assortment of tangential information. To an unintegrated onlooker it all appeared very much unrelated. Drawing conclusions from the mass of material was impossible unless one was virtually a part of it. Meanwhile synthesized hide and wood drums continued to fill the room with their portentous beat. Twice she found herself tapping her feet in time to the rhythm and had to make herself stop. The throbbing might inspire their host but she found it distracting.

The pounding didn't seem to bother Whispr. Equally intent on the glowing river of information he evinced no visible reaction to the drumming.

Eventually the data stream began to slow down. Far-reaching and all-inclusive as the box was, its supply of relevant info was not infinite. Surely their host, who no doubt had been probing locked and supposedly private corners of the box as well as public resources, had by now acquired more than enough data to parse. The refulgence from the box faded and the telltales behind it that served to identify active electronics winked out in rapid succession. As her two extensible fingers disengaged from the depths of the console her gel-protected eyes slid neatly down off her forehead and retracted back into their sockets. The sangoma blinked a couple of times, took a damp medicated tissue from a nearby box, wiped at first her right eye and then the left, and swiveled in her chair to face her customers. As she tossed the used tissue aside a small hard copy was printing out from a slot in the console beneath the box screen.

"Good news?" Ingrid did not try to hide her eagerness. Whispr considered this one of her greatest faults. In the brief time she had spent in his company she had learned much, but not yet how to dampen her zeal.

"I have some *Muti* for you, if that is what you mean." Pulling the hard copy from its receptacle with one hand she touched one arm of her chair with the other. Hidden motor humming, it rolled toward her clients.

Though thoroughly fed up with this latest manifestation of African obfuscation Whispr kept his feelings to himself. This was not Greater Savannah. He was nothing if not adaptable. He could even, when the occasion demanded it, show patience.

"What," he asked slowly, "is '*Muti*'?"

"It is that whatever which you want." The sangoma grinned. "Traditionally *Muti* can be swallowed, snorted, smoked, smeared, or even given as an enema."

Grinding his teeth in frustration Whispr turned away so that she wouldn't see his expression. "Oh, yeah, that's what we came half-way around the planet for."

Thembekile ignored him and her chair motored a little closer to Ingrid. "You say you a doctor. A sangoma is also a doctor. Even today many people without much education come to us for treatment. But times change and even sangomas must change with them. So in addition to doctoring people, some of us have learned how to doctor information. That is the kind of *Muti* I have for you." With great ceremony she handed over the single sheet of hard copy.

Ingrid took it impatiently. "This is the location of SICK's main research facility?"

"Ah, but there are three." One thick finger tapped the waterproof, fireproof printout. "I have rank them in order of perceived company importance. I make of this *Muti* a hard copy because it is safer than electronic." Pivoting her chair she rolled over to a wall of shelving and scanned the contents briefly before selecting a small jar. Holding it she returned to her fellow physician.

"I have some other *Muti* for you." Popping the lid on the vacuum-sealed container she shoved one index finger inside, twirled it briefly among the contents, and then extended the newly coated digit toward Ingrid. It glistened. "If you will allow me to continue one older tradition . . . ?"

Eyeing the pointing finger, a dubious Ingrid drew back slightly. From the greasy substance that now coated the sangoma's fingertip came an unholy reek.

"What is . . . is it harmless?"

"To you, yes. To those with whom you may have to deal if you continue your search, hopefully not." Extending her finger Thembekile drew a long streak across Ingrid's forehead. As she suffered the attention the wincing doctor tried not to inhale. The sangoma turned to Whispr. "Now your turn, skinny man. Or are you afraid?"

"Of a little grease?" Rising from his chair Whispr came toward the sangoma. "There were times when all I had to eat for days was a little grease." He bent toward her. She smeared a streak above his eyes, then resealed the jar.

The snarky odor lingered. Ingrid wanted to wash it off, but desiring not to offend decided she would wait until they were back at their hotel. Folding the hard copy carefully she slipped it into a side compartment in her purse. Their hostess had been as helpful as word on the street had promised and the doctor did not want to do anything that might upset her, such as violating an ancient tradition. Reaching up to gingerly touch her forehead her finger came away glossy with a bit of the slick, viscous, smelly substance.

"What is it?"

"Lion fat," Thembekile told her brightly. "To stimulate bravery and ward off attackers."

Doctor or not, Ingrid almost gagged. Whispr only smiled. "How do we know it's not just pork or chicken fat from your last meal?" He wanted to say "from your last meld" but did not.

His skepticism did not offend the sangoma. "You will find out the next time courage is required of you, stick-man. If you are confronted by danger and run away with your dick between your legs, then you will know I was untruthful with you." She turned back to Ingrid. "And now makes itself known the disagreeable business of authorizing final payment."

"I have a feeling dealing with *that* will take some courage," Whispr muttered as Ingrid fumbled in her purse.

The grease that had been applied to their foreheads by Thembekile could just as easily be cow fat, or guinea fowl fat, or any other kind of lard, Ingrid knew. Not that it was important. All that mattered was the information on the hard copy that was now resting safely in her purse. At last they had a physical destination, a goal. It might prove unreachable, but at least it was no longer theoretical.

Actually Thembekile had provide them with three destinations. A glance at the hard copy had shown that they had indeed been ranked in order of likely importance.

Ingrid could hardly wait to head for the one at the top of the list.

"THIS WOULD BE SO much easier," she told Whispr over dinner later that night at their small hotel in Simon's Town, "if we knew even a little of what was on the thread and why SICK is so desperate to get it back. Maybe all they're trying to do is just protect an unprecedented discovery in metallurgy." She shook her head in frustration. "But that wouldn't explain the MSMH link between the thread and the nanodevices that are turning up in unsettled young adults' heads."

Whispr stared across the table at her. "You think maybe the devices are what's unsettling the teens?"

"No. From what we've been able to learn the affected individuals are disgruntled before they get the unrecorded implants. They're put in as part of one kind of cosmetic meld or another."

He considered. "Someone has to insert them at some time during the cosmetic procedure. Why aren't we questioning the melders?"

Her mouth tightened. "I'm not sure they're even aware of what they're implanting. The devices are so small it would be easy to conceal them as part of standard, mass-produced cosmetic melds. That has to be what's going on. If a hundred melders or so around the world knew about the nanodevices, more information on them would be available. And you and I wouldn't be the only ones looking for their source or trying to find out what it is exactly that they *do*."

Whispr gazed down at his food. "The funny thing is, from what you've told me, doc, they don't seem to do *anything*. The subjects — the kids — don't seem to suffer any harm or aftereffects from the implants. So what's the point of 'em?"

She paused with her glass of tea halfway to her mouth. "That's one of the things I'm hoping to find out. Nobody goes to the trouble of developing a quantum entangled nanodevice made out of an impossible material and having it surreptitiously inserted into the heads of numerous young adults all over the world without some sort of plan in mind."

He grunted. "You make it sound diabolical."

She didn't smile. "I'm hoping, Whispr, I'm really hoping, that it's not."

Their table was built out over a shallow shelf of False Bay. In the distance a swath of clouds like brushstrokes lifted from a Turner glowed a dying crimson over Seal Island. Unwilling to stray too far from their slips this late in the evening, private watercraft cruised back and forth while hugging close to several small boat harbors. Powered by sail, by electric engines, or by a combination of the two they resembled fistfuls of paper crumpled into fanciful shapes and cast out on the darkening water.

"The longer we chase after this the more convinced I am that there's something important and valuable on the thread." Whispr dipped a spoon into his perlemoen bisque. It resembled a number of seafood soups he'd enjoyed in Savannah (on those rare occasions when he'd had the money to buy such luxuries) but with a richer, deeper flavor. In addition to cream, spices, and chunks of the meticulously aqua-cultured shellfish the bisque included a healthy dose of the supplements necessary to support his melded digestive system. "Forget about the implanted nanodevices for a minute. If it's just the nature of this special metal the company is trying to keep secret, why go to the trouble of using some of it to make an ordinary storage thread?"

"It's not ordinary," she corrected him. "For one thing there's that very low-level signal it's putting out."

"Real low-level," he agreed. "Or we would've been surrounded by company agents by now."

She shoveled something round and fried between her lips and chewed reflectively. "Maybe it has to be in direct physical contact with its intended receiver in order to carry out its function." Sitting across the table from him with her left side facing the water she allowed her attention to be drawn to the evening's entertainment. "Do you know *Sleeping Beauty*?"

"Personally?" He blinked at his companion.

She hid her smile. "The ballet."

He stared down at his bowl, embarrassed. "I don't know any-thing about ballet. And the only sleeping beauties I know are Melds too broke to afford a place of their own or those who are rent-ing themselves out instead of renting a codo. They're all sleeping beauties to me. They're my friends." He looked up, his gaze sud-denly startlingly intense. "Just like you're my friend."

"Business partner," she shot back. Seeing the downcast look on his face she added reluctantly. "And friend, I suppose."

He brightened at the concession, however forced it sounded. Meanwhile the maniped seals in the bay outside the restaurant continued their performance, executing aqueous flips and pirou-ettes that no human, not even one who had been specifically mani-ped, could have duplicated. The preprogrammed dance was as charming as its company of performers, though there were un-avoidable lapses in the choreography. It's hard to execute a grand jeté in the absence of legs.

"I think before we go any farther we should get some minor vi-sual manips."

"What, again?" She stopped chewing. "Maybe melding is noth-ing to you, but getting the makeover before we went to Florida was the first time I ever had to go through all that. And now you're sug-gesting we do it *again*?"

"Florida's exactly the reason why. The pronasty who scattered junior Wizwang all over the inside of his residence got a good look at both of us in our present traveling mode. He may have had access to what we looked like before we underwent melding, too, but seeing us subsequently and in person would've made a much stronger impression. We need to make some new changes."

"Maybe we could change back to our original appearances?" she asked hopefully.

Every time her companion's narrow head shook briskly from side to side atop its attenuated neck, Ingrid worried it was going to fall off.

"No." He was insistent. "We need third, brand-new façades. Hair do-overs first—it's warm here so I think for myself I'll just undergo a temporary depilation. Then body shape. I'll have to add some mass. Hate the flesh, but preserving anonymity's more important than adhering to an aesthetic." He looked her up and down. "You could lose some of the facial collagen and osseoputty."

"Well, that's a relief. If that's the kind of meld you're talking about it's one I can get behind."

"You ought to get taller, too, but that's bonegrow and we don't have time for it to heal properly." His gaze dropped. "I'd recommend breast enhancement."

"To preserve my anonymity, no doubt?" she replied icily.

"I'm serious. You have to change your body shape quickly. Keep the fat pads—you already paid for them—but use them to change proportions."

She took a swallow from the self-chilling glass of a fruit juice whose name she couldn't pronounce. "All in the interests of safety, of course."

"Look, I'm just making a suggestion." Surprisingly, his exasperation seemed genuine. "If you prefer you can opt for a chest concavity. Anything to accomplish a quick shape-change. I'd also suggest going with long red hair." He sniffed. "Or if you think long hair is some kind of personal fetish of mine you can join me for a depilation."

Ingrid envisioned herself bald. It was a common-enough look, and not only for patients being prepped for surgery. "Long red hair it is, then." That image was far more appealing. "Maybe I'll add some twinkle. I've seen it on a couple of the nurses at the hospital in my tower. I didn't think it appropriate for someone in my position."

Off to her companion's left a seal was cruising along the harbor front soliciting donations on behalf of the evening's performance. Half the money would go for maintenance of the ballet program, the other half for herring. Whispr edged his chair a little farther inland and tried to make himself even more inconspicuous than usual.

"Well, doc—your 'position' has changed. I'll make the necessary inquiries about a good, discreet melder tomorrow." He scrutinized the several couples who were sharing the above-water dining platform with them. All appeared utterly engrossed in the pinniped ballet. But then, a company agent engaged in surveillance would naturally be skilled at diverting attention from his or her actual task by blending in with a crowd. "And I think it's time to change hotels," he finished.

Upset was prominent in her reply. "Change hotels?" She indicated their surroundings. "But we just got here, and I like this hotel."

"So do I." He pushed back from the table. "First rule for avoiding the attention of lods and nasties: never stay more than two or three nights in the same place."

AVOIDING THE FANCIER MELD parlors in the upscale areas of Cape Town, with their spalike recovery rooms and expensive post-op customizers, Whispr settled on one in the commercial section of the harbor whose owner-practitioner came well recommended locally. Having checked out of their hotel earlier that morning, her spine-conforming luggage pack slung against her back, Ingrid eyed the shop front less enthusiastically.

"I don't know about this, Whispr. It doesn't look any too— clean."

"Unlike the hospitals you work in, it doesn't have to look clean: it just has be minimally hygienic." He considered the security door set in the center of the battered faux-wood entrance. "I cross-checked this biosurge both via the box and with people on the street. Her local rep is stellar."

A touch on the door activated an automated synthvoice response. Information was exchanged. As soon as it was determined to the door's satisfaction that the two visitors represented neither the police nor local medical surveillance they were admitted.

Patience Nonyameko was short as the gold miner her father had been and delicate as a rare shore bird. Almost fragile, Ingrid thought. But there was nothing flimsy about the female biosurge's hermetic operating chamber. As near as Ingrid could tell the instrumentation on view was completely sterile and surprisingly up-to-date. The presence of a large amount of heavy equipment prompted her to question its purpose.

"Most of my customers are sailors, my dear. Those of them who choose to be melded tend to request fairly extreme manips, to make their work easier." Her smile revealed a rainbow. Entrancingly, the tooth tinting was different each time she opened her mouth. The panoply of colors was activated by melded salivary glands that had been chromocharged.

"Then there is the diversity and intensity of the sexual manips. They are sailors, after all, and little in seamen's tastes have changed over the centuries." When she beckoned to a large metal-bound book the mobile tome slid across the desk toward her. "If you would like to see some examples of..."

"That's okay," Ingrid replied hastily. She was no prude, and the human body kept no secrets from her. No secrets—but since the advent of melding there were always surprises. There was always something, usually customized, that you'd never seen before.

When it came to individual tastes in sexual melds, some surprises were best kept hidden.

"We don't need any major work done." Having chosen not to take a seat, Whispr continued to stand nearby. Sitting with a door at his back, even in a biosurge's secure inner office, made him twitchy. "Just a few cosmetic touches here and there. We're—on vacation, and we'd like to take the opportunity to experiment." He winked conspiratorially. "You know: spice things up a bit. But nothing radical."

"Ah. Very well then." Directing the sample book to crawl back to its resting place the diminutive Nonyameko activated the desk's projector. It scanned first Ingrid, then Whispr. A moment later a pair of body images materialized in the space between the biosurge and her customers. "Which of you would like to go first?"

"I will." Ingrid didn't hesitate. The sooner this was over with the better. Also, going first would allow her a little more healing time than her companion and, more importantly, a little more time to get used to her third appearance in barely a month. "I want long red hair—shoulder length, anyway. My eyes are fine with that color but you'll need to do an all-over match."

"Of course." Nonyameko did not have to take notes. The conversation and description were being recorded.

Putting her hands to her face Ingrid pinched her cheeks. "I want any recently maniped collagen and osseoputty removed." Sitting straight in the chair she mentally resculpted herself. "A longer neck, if you can manage it without a bone push. Same for longer fingers." Certain that she could feel Whispr's eyes burning into her back, she lowered her voice as she continued describing the changes she wanted made to her face and body. "Breast enhancement."

As she continued checking her notes the biosurge never looked up. "What size, my dear?"

"Um, let's go for an even ninety-four centimeters, same cup size."

As the biosurge's client enumerated her requests they were automatically entered into the appropriate hovering image so that Ingrid could see how the requested finished manips would appear on her body.

"How many?" Nonyamenko continued politely. "I can do a half dozen in a perfect circle or . . ."

"Just the usual pair," Ingrid added hastily. This was a sailor's establishment for sure. For emphasis she added, "Horizontal."

Nonyamenko still wasn't finished. "Color? Technological enhancements?"

"Color body match." Ingrid shook her head uncertainly. "I'm not certain what you mean by technological enhancements."

Whispr spoke up helpfully. "She's been a Natural most of her life. This is only her second meld ever."

"I understand." The biosurge's tone was sympathetic. "We can add a variety of sound effects that respond according to the degree of contact, rise in body temperature, or extent of digital manipulation. Then there's chemophoric color flow, music responsiveness, adjustable tactility . . ."

Ingrid had heard enough. "How about feeding a baby? Can you manip for that, too?"

"You are being cynical, my dear." Nonyameko pushed back slightly from the desk. "Perhaps I am not the right person to perform your melding."

"No, no!" Whispr stepped forward quickly and offered the biosurge a reassuring smile. "Like I said, she's new to all this." He glared down at the seated Ingrid. "Though I would have thought she'd be more knowledgeable."

"I'm pretty familiar with *standard* melds," the doctor shot back frostily. "But you're right: some of these kinds of manips are indeed new to me." She returned her attention to the patient biosurge. "Don't mind me, Ms. Nonyamenko. I'm just a little nervous, that's all."

"This being only your second meld, I can understand." The petite biosurge rose. "Come with me and we will start prep. I don't want to rush either of you, but my time is reserved to do half a dozen stevedores late this afternoon. You would be surprised that in this day and age how many essential occupations still require the application of manual strength and labor." Her eyes twinkled. "I like working on big, strong men."

Ingrid wanted to say to Whispr, "That lets you out," but though her propensity to sarcasm seemed to be increasing day by day, this time she kept her feelings to herself.

Soothing music supplemented the sedative chosen by the biosurge. Having administered a vast variety of medication herself and only recently undergone her first manip, Ingrid knew what to expect as her prone form was lifted from the gurney to be held suspended in the medical magnetic field. Despite her foreknowledge she was surprised at how little time the procedure took. As she sat up on the white carbon metal platform she expressed grudging admiration for the biosurge's skill.

"Thank you, my dear." Nonyamenko gently helped her toward the recovery chamber. "I'll do your friend now and then we'll finalize arrangements. I won't be long."

"I know. You're fast. Very fast." *I only hope you didn't sacrifice skill for speed*, she thought to herself.

More soft music was playing in the recovery room. As Ingrid took a seat on the soft padded circular bench in the center she could feel the tautness in places where fresh synthskin had been applied. Almost afraid to look down at herself, she called up the reflectors. Even through the fine therapeutic, healing mist that filled the chamber she could still see her likeness clearly. She was shocked by what she saw. Doubtless someone who had been a Meld all their life would not have reacted so strongly to what were after all little more than a few comparatively minor cosmetic manips. Still new to the process, Ingrid responded to changes with wide eyes.

Her new proportions were not only stunning, they were downright daunting. Long red hair cascaded down her back almost to her waist. Her eyes had been enlarged slightly, fostering a boldness wholly in contrast to her age and experience. Her ears had been trimmed and her lips returned to their former thickness. Rajeev would have been pleased to see that her nose had finally been fixed. He would have been pleased by other alterations as well.

She had always been attractive. Now she was, if only by older and somewhat historical standards, beautiful. Having always valued the small imperfections that constituted a visible reminder of her individuality it appeared that at least for the foreseeable future she was going to have to live without them.

Studying what she now had to work with she knew she could spice up her appearance even further, could modernize it, by adding some of the latest gengineered cosmetic accoutrements, whether sparkling eyes or flame-firing ear cartilage or spark-emitting fingertips. Changing her height or skin color or adding limbs (or any other body parts) would alter her appearance more completely, but she wasn't ready for that. Not mentally, not emotionally, and they didn't really have the time. But she could not deny that she found intriguing the notions such images conjured.

She needed to be careful. Meld addiction was a widespread and well-documented psychological condition against which education and knowledge offered only limited defense. As she knew from experience as well as from keeping up with the relevant literature it posed a particular danger to always body- and appearance-conscious teenage girls. The trouble was the same as it had been since the beginning of time: cosmetic fads came and went with demoralizing regularity. In a matter of months today's concept of beauty could be yesterday's idea of gruesomeness. This was not a problem when one was speaking of trends in fashion or styles in jewelry. It posed considerably more of a dilemma if the changes that were incurred on behalf of trendiness involved manipulation of muscles and fat, tendons and ligaments, skin and keratin. Being, say, sixteen only magnified every change and option, only made every decision taken that much more significant and potentially permanently damaging.

She was a long way from sixteen, she told herself. She should not be having such thoughts. She was a *physician*, for heaven's sake! But now that she'd undergone melding twice, albeit for what any biosurge would regard as minor manipulations, she was coming to a greater understanding of the temptation in ways that no reading of the literature or listening to distraught patients could convey.

Suffer one meld and you were tempted to try another. Try another and you became convinced that a third would make everything just right. Undergo the third and ... It was all too easy, if one possessed the time and the inclination, to be melded and remelded out of all recognition by the time one reached thirty. And that was speaking only of cosmetic melds. Industrial melds, sports melds, commercial melds—some of these made simple cosmetic manipulation look positively juvenile. Professional melding was where the really radical alterations were made to the now easily manipulated human body. Beyond the professional lay scientific melding of the kind necessary to transform a terrestrial into *Homo maritianus* or *titanus*.

Seen in such lights a little hair lengthening, eye widening, nose shaping, and boob enhancement seemed positively unworthy of comment. One more time she reminded herself that the manips had been required not to satisfy personal vanity but to maintain her anonymity. To veil her from the view of possible pursuing assassins. In that context traditional female beauty, no matter how perfect, was less likely to draw attention than more radical or avant-garde melds.

She found herself discussing her thoughts with Whispr as soon as he had recovered sufficiently from his own operation to engage in coherent conversation. The irony of a doctor seeking advice from a patient did not escape her. Anticipating being on the receiving end of some of his characteristic sarcasm, she was surprised when he was immediately empathetic. Understanding, even.

"I've seen too many friends die from bad manips." He sat nearby in the recovery room, inhaling the lightly aromatic mist that enveloped them. "I know just what you're talking about. A lot of people start with the small stuff because that's all they can afford. If they're lucky enough to glom onto some really significant subsist, that's when they go crazy. They want bigger muscles, they want more classic proportions. They want smaller ears, they want better hearing. Bright eyes, subdued eyes. Back and forth, in and out, around and down. There are some bad biosurges out there, doc. Take your money and treat your body like putty. Twist and pull and tug and then one day you can't manip it anymore. There's just not enough foundation left on which to build recovery." He stared across at her. "You've probably seen examples in hospital."

Ingrid had: broken and twisted bodies that had been roughly and faultily maniped until the addict could no longer walk properly, or walk at all. Other poor, overmelded souls who had been left blind, or deaf, or impotent, or worse by the kind of inept or outright

inadequately trained biosurges who plied their efforts in unregis-
tered and unmonitored facilities. Human grotesqueries who would
have been right at home in a Bosch landscape. No matter one's
chosen specialty, every student had to study such failures in medical school. Even a GP like herself.

You rarely saw such failures on the street or elsewhere in public.
They kept to themselves, to the poorer and least visited corners of
dark cities, fumbling in the shadows for subsistence and assistance,
wondering if it was worthwhile to fight to stay alive.

And always, always, dreaming of that one grand final meld that
would ultimately make everything right again.

Something brushed at her bare shoulder. Irritated, she slapped
at it, only to discover that it was strands of her freshly lengthened,
newly tinted hair. In light of recent musings she started to see them
not as a flattering flow of red but as slender components of a deceptively soft, unbreakable tentacle just waiting for the right moment to strangle her in her sleep.

She forced the disconcerting image out of her mind. Her newly
maniped hair was nothing more than part of a disguise, like dark
glasses or a heavy coat. She could dispense with it as soon as all this
was over, as soon as she returned home to Savannah.

Or she could try to fine-tune it. All it would take was one simple and quick meld. One more brief meld that . . .

What's happening to me? she thought a little wildly. She made
a conscious effort to slow her breathing.

Nothing. Nothing was happening to her. She was the same quiet,
responsible, cultured physician she had always been. To be sure,
one who was presently engaged on a mildly obsessive quest in the
name of science and satisfying a personal curiosity, but not one
whose personality and self had undergone any kind of elemental
shift.

Whispr was staring at her; doubtless because she had not responded to his last comment.

"Yes, I've seen examples." Her voice, she was pleased to note, was perfectly normal. "Enough to understand the addiction." She indicated her just-melded appearance. "As soon as we're finished with this and I'm back home I'm getting maniped right back to the way I was before. I'll revert to my Natural self as soon as I can. There's no reason to maintain any of this . . . this . . . falsehood."

"Of course there isn't. I'd argue with you, of course. And not just because I'm a Meld." He rose. "We need to find a place for the night. Starting tomorrow I'm holding you to our agreement to see some animals. It'll be relaxing as well as constructive to play tourist for a while. Anybody *is* watching us, they'll see that we're not going anywhere near any of SICK's facilities. Therefore we can't possibly be anyone they'd be interested in." With one long, slender finger he traced a sweeping arc through the air. "Instead of heading straight for the first spot on that sangoma's list we'll make a real journey out of it. Work our way around and come at the location from a different direction."

She rose to join him. "You're rationalizing a roundabout approach so we'll have more time to look at wildlife, aren't you?"

His small mouth pursed in a smile. "Both reasons are valid, doc. I want to see wildlife, yes, but I also want to confuse and deter anyone who might be suspicious of us. By the way, and this is a completely impartial opinion, if I haven't said so already you look fantastic." He pivoted on a bare heel and headed for the exit.

From the standpoint of her just-established resolve to change her appearance back to what it was as soon as she returned home, it was the worst thing he could have said.

6

The two tardy lods were locals. As supplementary staff they had been forced upon the organization representative who had rushed down from Joburg as soon as the two Namericans had been positively identified. Unfortunately for everyone both the rep and the local hirelings were, as had been their counterparts in Savannah, a day late. Furthermore, the Namericans had checked out of their Simon's Town hotel without leaving a forwarding address or contact information of any kind. Frustrated and fuming, the restless overseers of the organization could no longer even be certain that their quarry was still on the same continent. There was talk that they might have gone to Tokyo. There were rumors they had returned to Namerica but not to Greater Savannah. There was, as is common in such organizations, a great deal of yelling and disproportionate expenditure of cuss words in a multitude of languages.

The result was that many fingers and related melded digits were crossed in the hope that the two surprisingly evasive targets were still in South Africa, perhaps even still in Cape Town. Despite lav-

ishing significant subsist on concentric rings of informants, only
one lead as to the fugitives' present whereabouts and activities had
come forth—but it was a good one.

The upshot was that Sela Chelowich found herself sitting on
the deck of a perambulating café sipping bad coffee imbued with
absinthe as the two local hirelings came rushing breathlessly up
to her.

While the other women settled themselves into the remaining
empty chairs at the circular table, fastened their seat belts, and ordered Rooibos tea from the pickup protruding from its center,
Chelowich regarded her newly acquired backup. Boo Terror didn't
need her wince-inducing moniker to intimidate. Big as a football
player, bulging with maniped muscles, the Meld still affected girly-
girl accessories like long dangling earrings, lipstick, and color-
shifting eye shadow. The hair that reached to the back of her broad
shoulders was tied in a thick black braid whose diameter approached that of some of the old-fashioned hawsers coiled on the
decks of cargo ships in the harbor.

Though no bigger than Chelowich the other lod had to coil her
upper limbs to keep them from sprawling on the floor. Lindiwe was
a partial tentacular Meld, one who had traded in her arms for far
more flexible grasping appendages. The flex meld was a common
one that involved removing the entire arm including the bone all
the way up to the shoulder and replacing it with gengineered
sucker-lined cephalopod limbs. The resultant manip had proven
its worth in numerous businesses where strength and flexibility
were prized above precision control, from shelf stocking to long-
distance driving to the sex industry. The skin of Lindiwe's upper
limbs shone a striking glossy black that alternated with wide bands
of equally brilliant carmine. Among other things, tentacles were

very useful for holding on to anxious individuals in a hurry to be elsewhere.

"We found someone who has saw them for sure." Though a deep rumble that originated somewhere in the lower registers of the human voice, Terror's words still had a surprisingly feminine lilt.

Seated next to her Lindiwe gestured with the tip of one tentacle while the other dexterously accepted a large tea mug from a Natural waitress. A complimentary plate of cookies and petits fours was placed between the three women, its underside adhering to the occasionally shifting tabletop to prevent it from sliding off and down the steep slope on Chelowich's right. Each cookie and cake, be it chocolate or vanilla, emitted an individual ringtone that identified its contents. Picking one up, the hunter munched on the music.

"Well then why are we sitting here babbling over the bubbling?" Swallowing the last of the melody, Chelowich started to rise. Lindiwe put up a restraining hand and the bald blond hunter paused.

"Boo said 'saw' them. The same person also saw them leave the place where they were seen. Saw them go back toward the city."

Chelowich's gaze automatically turned toward the metropolis spread out below. Cape Town was not a small place. It would not be easy to find the Namerican pair—especially if they'd had enough sense to change their appearance again as well as their local address. At least she could report back to her superiors that as of this morning the two visitors were still in South Africa. She knew full well that by this evening they could be pretty much anywhere else on the planet. If that was the case no one in the organization would blame her. As had been proven in Savannah these two

Namericans knew enough to keep on the move and not to linger too long in any one place. But neither would their flight bring any credit her way.

"We're wasting time with tea and cookies. Where is this place where they were seen?"

The local Melds exchanged a glance. "Very close to here," Lindiwe replied. "They were visiting a local business."

At last something promising, Chelowich thought. "They might have left word at this business of where they're staying. Or if they're not staying, some mention of where they're going next." She quickly downed the last of the sweet brew in her cup and, in petulant protest, let it drop over the side of the café railing instead of putting it back on the table. "Let's move."

For a second time Lindiwe raised a cautionary appendage. "Maybe we should not go so quick to this establishment. Maybe we should look for another way to learn where the two visitors have gone."

Compared to the two locals seated across from her the melds Chelowich had undergone were minor. Since one involved a complete and permanent depilation, she had no brows to draw together when she frowned.

"Are you screwing with me? When you smell shit you don't run away from it—you buckle down and clean it up. That's my job. As of today, it's also your job. Why should we look elsewhere?"

A plainly uncomfortable Lindiwe turned to her larger colleague for support. The hulking Terror looked away. Incredibly to the impatient Chelowich, the massive woman looked more than a little intimidated. The tentacle Meld was forced to continue by herself.

"This establishment, this business the Namericans visited: it is the shop of a sangoma."

"A very well-known sangoma," Terror added quickly.

Chelowich made no effort to conceal her frustration. "I'm from Brno and I've only been working for the organization's local branch for a few months. What's a sangoma?"

Lindiwe's tentacle tips curled in on themselves. "In the old days, a witch doctor."

"Nowadays," Terror muttered, "still a witch doctor."

Chelowich was flabbergasted. These two brutes, one capable of suffocating even a strong man by strangling him with her maniped upper limbs and the other able to do so simply by sitting on him, were frightened of some primitive childish institution from their ancient past! If she was not hearing it for herself she would have laughed at the scenario.

"You're *scared*. Both of you are scared." Her hard gaze flicked from one local woman to the other. "Of a 'witch doctor'? I can't believe what I'm hearing."

Lindiwe spoke up defensively. "As you say, Sela, you have only been in this country for a little while. Sangomas have great power here. Make no mistake—Boo and I are not afraid of old tales in which such people laid curses on and threw bat blood at those who offended them. Sangomas have come into the modern world with much of their mystique and many of their talents intact. That is why they are still respected by the general population. That is why they are still in business."

Chelowich rose and pushed back her seat. Raising her right leg and putting her foot on the chair she tapped her right thigh. The trendy balloon pants she wore were useful for concealing the multibarreled splat that was strapped against her skin.

"I've got something here that will blow apart any mystique. Besides, if this sangoma is all about business, then there'll be no need to get rough. I'm authorized to pay whatever is requested in order to acquire any necessary information associated with our hunt."

"That's right." Terror was clearly relieved. "We'll just be customers, like the two Namericans."

"This sangoma, though," a more cautious Lindiwe pointed out, "has a big reputation. She may not agree to give up information she considers confidential."

The spiderweb pattern hennaed on her bald pate gleaming in the sun, the hunter Chelowich cracked the knuckles of her right hand. "Then we will persuade her. As three women to another." She stepped away from the table. "Where is this house of archaic cultural tradition? You said it was not far."

Terror stood, looming over the sunbrella, and turned to point out a location partway up the mountainside. "Walking distance from this café. Of course the house may also be walking. But we will intercept it."

"Yes we will," declared Chelowich. "A destination in motion is better than none at all."

THE HUNTERS WERE FORTUNATE. No matter where it went as it ambled among the other oft-shifting hillside houses, the dwelling-shop of the electric sangoma was well known to all who passed by it—or to all it passed by. The shifting (and shifty) neighborhood was blessedly quiet as the trio of women worked their way upslope from the café. Most of the residents were off at work down in the city, over the hills in the Wets, or preoccupied with the press of everyday domestic concerns. The demanding echoes of squawling babies rose above the continual creak of buildings moving and grinding against one another. Moans, yelps, shouts, imprecations, and implorings resounded from overcranked vit connections as stay-at-home mothers and somnolent grandparents sought to distance themselves from their lives by numbing their neurosystems with the narcotic of popular entertainment.

Lindiwe led the way with Chelowich in the middle and Terror bringing up the rear. The one crinkle-haired old man they encountered as they approached the house of the sangoma Thembekile nodded at Lindiwe, smiled at Chelowich, and widened his eyes and increased the speed of his servo-assisted old legs as he gave Terror a wide berth.

Standing on the building's small porch among its simple rattan furniture, Chelowich studied the structure's entrance with professional detachment. When no one responded to her repeated caressing of the pressure-sensitive material or to her shouts of inquiry, she tried to force the door manually. Despite her best efforts the old-fashioned, almost ancient handle did not respond to pushing or pulling that would have overcome most such barriers.

Off to the left of the trio's leader Lindiwe was trying to see inside through a window that was almost completely blocked by a cascade of colorful streamers and cloths. "I can't see anything moving inside. It's dark."

Chelowich replied while conducting a detailed examination of the doorway. "Afraid of the dark?"

Lindiwe straightened to look over at the European. "Boo and I do our best work in the dark. It is our friend, and we are not afraid of friends."

"Well said." Terror corroborated her colleague in her subdued but deep voice.

Chelowich had removed a small device from a pocket and was using it to slowly trace the door's outer limits. Each time it passed over a contact point it beeped softly and words appeared on the integrated readout. '

"What's that?" An interested Terror looked over the smaller woman's shoulder.

The blonde continued her work. "Think of it as a sedative for alarm systems. There are a couple built right into this door. The device also silences as it unlocks." Having completed a complete circuit of the barrier she pocketed the device, reached out to grab the handle once more, smiled thinly at her cohorts, and pushed. There was a click as the door swung inward.

Once inside, Chelowich's expression turned from satisfaction to disgust. The hand she waved back and forth in front of her face did little to dissipate the swirl of repellent odors that assailed her nostrils.

"What a dump!" Her pupils widened to adapt to the dim light. There was just enough interior illumination to let her eyes make sense of the disagreeable surroundings. More light would have been welcome but she didn't want to waste time checking the building's internal lighting system for another possible integrated alarm system. Also, the sudden flare of lights from inside the house might spark unwanted curiosity on the part of neighbors or passersby. Though weak, there was enough illumination to work by.

"Spread out, look for any kind of record-keeping gear. Vit or audio pickups, main drive, box links—anything that's likely to keep records of recent visitors."

"If we do find anything it's probably encrypted." As a muttering Terror shut the door behind them and took up a defensive stance next to it, Lindiwe roughly pushed a pile of small clay sculptures off a cabinet that was in her way. Several crashed to the floor and broke. She stepped over them without looking down.

Having already located the box console and its flanking accoutrements Chelowich was plowing through a pile of hard copies she'd found in a drawer. She was pleased to see that the majority of printouts were in English. If there was a recording showing that a pair of Namericans had paid a recent visit it would be easy to read. With any luck there would be at least a note. If nothing could be found then the three of them would have to settle down to wait for the sangoma's return and request the necessary information in person. She had no doubt that this would be forthcoming. Lindiwe and Terror were professional persuaders, an area of expertise in which Chelowich herself had ample experience.

Deeper back in the overcrowded dwelling, something snarled.

The portable recorder Lindiwe had just found slipped from her fingers. At the doorway Terror turned to face the room so that she could press her back against the wall. The snarl sounded again. It was too thick, too primal, to arise from a dog or a housecat. At least, not from a typical housecat.

Chelowich didn't bother to look up from where she was sorting through the materials that covered the top of the sangoma's console. "Sounds like a lion."

"Yes, lion." Seeing her boss's calm demeanor encouraged Lindiwe to relax. Positioned by the door, Terror straightened up out of the fighting stance she had assumed.

The snarl came a third time. It was much louder now. Toward the rear of the reception room a shape began to materialize out of the darkness. Though increasingly uneasy, both local contract workers held their ground. Observing Lindiwe gazing at her for guidance, an exasperated Chelowich finally looked up from her searching.

"It's a sound and vit projection. That's all. Typical traditional anti-intruder contrivance, same as you'd encounter anywhere in the world. In Brno it would be a big dog, or maybe a wolf." She nodded curtly in the direction of the growling shape. "Here you get a lion. Look."

Stepping away from the console she moved toward the back of the room. At the doorway Terror tensed. The outline of the lion was very coherent now. Dense, fully three-dimensional, and active, it looked real as real could be. Until Chelowich stuck a hand into its mouth—and out the back of its neck. The image of the big cat reacted with another snarl and a snap at the offending hand, causing Lindiwe to jump slightly. But the unperturbed Chelowich was unharmed. The lion was a superb simulacrum, even a responsive one, but nothing more.

"Get back to your work." Ignoring the image of the huge-maned male cat that was now pawing at her hips, she resumed going through the contents of the console. Chelowich's thoroughly debunking demonstration notwithstanding, Terror was still unaccountably relieved when the feline simulacrum vanished. Its presence was replaced with a sharp, warning voice.

"*Lumkela—qphela*—beware!" it barked in the three principal local languages. "Your presence here is unauthorized. Vacate the premises immediately or suffer the consequences! The wrath of the electric sangoma Madame Lulo Thembekile be upon you!"

How suitably biblical, Chelowich thought as she continued to plow through the console's contents. No doubt it would have the desired effect on the ignorant. Pulling out one drawer after another she dumped the contents onto the top of the console and sorted swiftly and efficiently through the growing pile of papers, devices, and witch doctor paraphernalia. Terror continued to guard the entrance and keep a watch through the small side window for visitors or busybodies while Lindiwe was plowing through the contents of the big cabinet that stood against the far wall.

Clipped to her belt, the European's monitor hummed softly for attention. Irritated at the interruption, Chelowich pulled it out and glanced at the readout. Pausing in her excavating, Lindiwe glanced over.

"What is it? Something wrong?" She looked around uncertainly. "Another projection coming?"

Chelowich shook her head and reattached the monitor to her belt. "It's picking up a very low-level, very short-range broadcast. Might activate another projection. Be advised and don't let the boogeyman unnerve you." Having found nothing informative she had settled herself into the chair in front of the box screen and was preparing to activate the unit. If there was any information in local storage regarding their quarry a quick and straightforward hack ought to produce it.

"Look on these clever vit apparitions as entertainment. Something to keep you from getting bored while we're searching." Her fingers began to move swiftly over the keyboard. She couldn't hack the aural input to activate the unit, of course. That would be coded to its owner's voice and unlikely to respond to the demands of an intruder. But she felt confident she could get in utilizing one or more of the specialized devices she had brought with her.

A crawling sensation tickled her left leg. Whenever she sat down her stylish balloon pants drew up slightly to expose a couple of centimeters of skin between boot and hem. The tickling might come from a microwave projection designed to unnerve and irritate. If it intensified to the point where it felt hot then it would bear monitoring, but given the state of the residence and the previous feeble attempt to frighten them off with a simple projection she didn't anticipate the presence of anything as sophisticated as a bloodboiler. One powerful enough to be small yet effective would demand more juice than a modest dwelling like the sangoma's could safely or anonymously draw from the municipal grid.

Sure enough, her skin did not grow hotter. There was no perceptible temperature rise at all.

In front of her the box screen sprang to life. Removing yet a different device from a pocket she clipped it onto the base of the screen. It would feed wirelessly into the box console itself, burrowing through defensive passwords and decoding any protective encryption. Once in, it would also allow verbal access. A couple of quick questions ought to bring up whatever useful information the witch doctor's private files contained. Chelowich's left leg itched again. Absently, she reached down to scratch it.

Something bit her. It was small, sharp, and decidedly more consequential than a projection. At the same time Terror yelped and stumbled sideways. As the big woman did so she grabbed for support at the cloths that were hanging from the nearby window. They ripped loose in her strong fingers. Gray afternoon light flooded the room, banishing the darkness.

Looking down at her leg Chelowich saw the spider. Two spiders. Then a third. All were small, fat, and an almost metallic glossy black. Lindiwe was screaming and slapping at herself, leaping about and contorting as if infected with the latest shebeen dance craze.

Rising, the increasingly wide-eyed European stared down at herself. Her lower body was covered with the scuttling arachnids. Having reached her hips they were continuing to migrate rapidly upward. As she frantically slapped and brushed them away she could feel the weight of their tiny but undeniably substantial bodies. Looking around she saw that the room had been flooded with hundreds of the ugly little black biters. The interruption was unexpected but not necessarily . . .

She was starting to have trouble getting her breath. Her heart began to beat faster. Another sharp twinge on her other leg indicated a third bite. Despite having eaten little that morning she felt as if she was going to throw up. Having been bitten many more than three times, Terror was now lying on the floor writhing and moaning. Her defensive slaps were growing more and more feeble, her huge melded muscles useless against the multipronged, multilegged attack.

A frantic figure was suddenly in Chelowich's face. Lindiwe's fingers clutched wildly at the European. "Button spiders, button spiders! Real ones!"

Chelowich shaped a ready reply only to discover that her tongue wouldn't work. Fire seemed to be infiltrating her entire body from her navel to her chest. Sweat began to run from her pores and her eyes started to water. Drool bubbled in her mouth and spilled from her lips as she fought to form words. Though unfamiliar with the cause she knew pretty well what was happening. Her body was reacting to multiple injections of a powerful neurotoxin.

Shoving the panicky Lindiwe aside she turned and stumbled toward the door. Whatever the toxin's exact chemical makeup she could tell that she needed a significant injection of the appropriate antivenin, and fast. Stepping over the recumbent and now barely audible bulk of Terror, she reached for the door handle. It seemed to dodge out of her reach. Given the other subtle and unpleasant surprises the house had already dished up Chelowich wouldn't have been startled to learn that the handle actually had moved and that her inability to grasp it was not an illusion. Still upright and unbitten, Lindiwe came up beside her. But the local had no better luck as the handle proceeded to migrate off the door and climb up the wall. It hung there out of their reach, gleaming down at them like a muscular brass bat.

" 'Nother door. Look for another door." Chelowich felt her lips going numb. Her heart was undergoing severe palpitations. "Get out. Need antidote, fast." She reached out toward Lindiwe, looking to her subordinate for support.

Something small, active, and fast-moving bit her in the left eye.

If not for the surprising amount of soundproofing contained within the walls of the dwelling her scream would have been heard throughout a sizable portion of the ambulatory suburb. It was sufficiently forceful and penetrating that a few nearby dwellers did hear it. Those who did put it out of their minds. Strange and sometimes disturbing noises were often heard from the house of the electric sangoma, and were best ignored.

A less tortured but equally shattering exclamation interrupted the relative calm of the neighborhood as a female figure threw herself through one of the dwelling's locked windows. Bleeding from numerous cuts but still unbitten, Lindiwe staggered to her feet. Brushing off shards of glass, she stumbled down the nearest stabilized walkway. Like the exceptionally unsettling sounds that had preceded her violent exit from the house, she was dutifully ignored by the neighborhood residents.

Within the slowly striding structure nothing moved that was bigger than a mouse. Sensing no living presence larger than the soldiers of the small black impi it had silently dispersed, the house's defense system altered the high-pitched and highly localized signal it had been emitting. Responding instantly and without thinking to the precisely tuned stimulus frequency, the several hundred electronically aggravated, marauding button spiders halted their continuing assault on the two already dead women and hurried to scurry back to their concealed holding pens. Hidden in small dark corners of the building these were exactly the kind of locales *Latrodectus indistinctus* preferred. A banquet of captive crickets was promptly disgorged by the house and an orgy of contented arachnidan consumption ensued. No triumphant roaring accompanied the feasting.

The intruders' odds of survival would have been far better had they merely been forced to deal with a threat as simple and prosaic as a lion.

7

The view was beyond stunning. From the top of Table Mountain they could see not only all of Cape Town but a great deal of the coast to the north and nearly all of it to south. This early in the morning the clouds that normally hugged the top of the massif like a gray fox stole around a matron's neck had not yet woken themselves sufficiently to obscure the crown. Dark green water edged with foam like white lace crept up the distant shore, the sound of breaking waves smothered by distance and height.

They were alone near the edge. The few tourists and couples who had ascended with them in the cab of the antique cable car had wandered off among the fynbos on their own. Declaring her desire to avoid their attention Ingrid had insisted on walking away from the protective railings and along the trail that paralleled the edge of the escarpment. Rimmed by bushes and exotic grass, Whispr felt that the fringe of the great mountain probably looked much as it had for thousands of years.

He trailed slightly behind and to one side, letting her take the lead. She was wearing the light jacket purchased in the city the night before. A gusty, intermittent wind puffed it out around her small form and made her look bigger than she was. Pausing beside a dark stone outcropping she turned back toward him and smiled. Women didn't often smile at him. When they did, no milk bath of Cleopatra's could have felt as enveloping and warming.

"What a sight! There's nothing like this on the East Coast." She gestured seaward, her arm taking in the vast sweep of shore, city, and sky with a shared flurry of arm and enthusiasm. "You can see halfway to Namibia!"

You couldn't, of course. That immense and empty desert country lay too far to the north to be visible even from the crest of Table Mountain. Drawing in his gaze he let it focus on her to the exclusion of the grand panorama spread out before them. She was too lost in the landscape to notice that he was staring.

He was struck again by how small she was. Small and Natural despite her recent cosmetic manips. While the mystifying thread was reasonably safe within the special compartment in her underwear he would have felt better with it sequestered in the secret hollow in the sole of his shoe. But she insisted on retaining possession. He had to admit that in its present location it really might be less likely to be discovered than it would be anywhere on his person.

Below the sheer drop the first brush-covered rockfalls beckoned. Unbidden, he found his thoughts turning naturally if alarmingly to ill-met options all too reminiscent of his life on the streets of Greater Savannah. Willowy lightweight that he was, he had no doubt that street life had toughened and strengthened him physically as well as mentally to a far greater degree than his view-distracted companion.

It wouldn't take much, he knew. Compared to encounters he had survived on the streets, it would take very little effort at all.

Though still wary, she was by now used to him being close to her. He could approach even closer while complimenting the view. A single brusque two-handed shove and over she'd go. He looked around. They had walked quite a way in the opposite direction from the other visitors. No one would hear her scream, and in any event her descending shrieks would be swiftly swallowed up by the wind and the speed of her descent.

He imagined the impact on the rocks below. It would all be over instantly, almost painlessly. As a doctor she would be aware of that. While she fell she would have a few seconds to appreciate the looming finality and the fatal consequences of her misplaced trust. He doubted he would be able to hear the final smash.

He would run screaming back the way they had come, his face contorted into a rictus of despair as he howled out his woe. Barely able to stand, he would collapse gasping into the arms of startled but compassionate strangers. The police would be called. The SAEC police had become exceptionally efficient ever since the massacre and mass purge of '23. They would ask plenty of questions. The spot where the two Namericans had been standing just prior to the tragedy would be combed by local forensics. Suspicion would immediately fall on him. But in the absence of any eyewitnesses other than himself there would be no proof of foul play.

Sobbing, overcome at the loss of his friend, he would be asked to identify the remains. Whispr had been in morgues before. Unless procedure varied radically here, the opportunity to recover the thread would present itself. He would be able to continue with the journey of discovery unencumbered by a smart but oftentimes gullible traveling companion. Most importantly any subsist, any proceeds that might be realized from the trip, would accrue to him and him alone. In one push, with one shove, he could instantly double any potential profits.

He edged nearer to her. Wholly absorbed in the splendid panorama she paid him no attention. She was now within easy reach of his long, spindly, but strong arms.

One shove, he told himself again. A quick thrust with both hands and it would all be over in seconds. No more disapproving sideways looks. No more clumsy efforts at concealment.

Several things gave him pause. For one, if she was dead it would be difficult for him to make use of her credcards. Her easy access to subsist was something he had relied upon ever since they had formed their partnership. For another, despite her frequent sarcasm her companionship was more often pleasant than not. And he had not given up hope of somehow, someday, hopefully bedding her. Most important of all . . .

She was smarter than he was, and he knew it. But he was smart enough to recognize when he was in the presence of someone smarter than him, and to make use of that. As he would continue to make use of her now—at least for the foreseeable future. He knew what kind of person he was. Knew all too well. The real question, he asked himself, was what kind of person could he *become.*

He took a step backward. The movement caught her eye and she turned to him. Curiosity replaced awe.

"You're looking strange, Whispr." She was teasing him. "Stranger than usual, even. Something wrong?"

A local crow went soaring past just below the edge of the cliff. An omen, he wondered—or just a hungry bird on the wing. He felt an instant kinship with the black and white scavenger.

"No, nothing wrong."

Her grin faded as she continued to stare at him. "Why are you looking at me like that?"

He turned away—from her as well as from deeper, darker

thoughts. "Not looking at you, doc. I just—I don't like heights, that's all."

She started past him, heading in the direction of the tramway. "It didn't seem to bother you when you were staying at my codo in Savannah."

He was glad of the opportunity to change the subject—and to divert his thoughts. "That was way different. It was enclosed, and there was lots of entertainment to take my mind off how high it was. And there was food. Which reminds me—I'm hungry."

"Must be the air."

"Yeah," he agreed quickly. "The air."

He said little during the descent from the top of the mountain. She was still too enraptured with their surroundings to notice the lack of conversation—or if she did, she found his uncharacteristic silence not worthy of comment.

Unaware of the fact that two-thirds of a criminal pursuit that had been less than a day from making contact with them had early that afternoon died deaths as primitive as they were painful, they posited a query to a floating info sphere outside the tram station gift shop. From a list it provided they settled on a local transport company. Local was cheaper. More importantly and unlike the case with an international vehicle rental company, its database would be far less likely to be sitting on alerts that could be triggered by their inquiry.

Riding on the small public transport that slowly worked its way toward downtown they had plenty of time to discuss what kind of vehicle they ought to rent for the remainder of the journey.

"Has to be something inconspicuous." Whispr's seriousness was never more in evidence. "Can't be something that draws attention. But at the same time it has to be tough enough to handle any conditions." He looked down at her. "Because where we're trying to go we'll be showing up unexpected and unannounced, and that means going off-road."

She readily agreed. Behind her a middle-aged gentleman in suit, tie, bowler sporting two backward-sweeping yellow bird feathers, and the battle paint of a well-known international conglomerate was concentrating intently on the projector that filled the left-hand lens of his designer glasses. While the right eye looked out onto the world of transport and passing pedestrians the other was deeply engaged in the small but still three-dimensional episode of a locally produced soap opera. Seeming to float in front of his left eye, their turgid but addictive dialogue communicated itself via the induction insert comfortably nestled in his left ear. The faint hiss of two women shrieking at one another was barely audible above the rattle of the public transport. Ingrid ignored the well-dressed viewer and his choice of semiprivate viewing just as she paid no attention to the commuter-dominated crush of Naturals and Melds packed in around her and Whispr.

"I always thought we'd have to go that way," she added. "We can hardly pull into the company parking lot, assuming the facility we're seeking has one, walk up to the front door, and ask to be shown around." Her expression turned grim. "My money will get us as far as that door. Getting us inside will be up to you and your street expertise."

Not to mention getting us out again, he thought glumly. "Assuming we can get in, what then? You can't dangle the thread in front of somebody's face and expect them to tell us anything about it."

The determination in her reply didn't surprise him. She could waver and equivocate—except where science was concerned.

Then she turned as tough as a football center. It must be wonderful, he mused, to be able to sacrifice all recognition of reality in the hope of acquiring a new fact or two.

"I'm planning on passing myself off as a researcher. I think I can do that, for a little while, anyway. And you can pass as my assistant."

He had to smile at that. "I'll be sure to remember to keep my mouth shut. But what makes you think anyone will accept you as a fellow researcher at this site?"

"Act like you know what you're doing and people will believe that you do," she told him assuredly. "Because most of the time they won't. I learned that in medical school. The three research facilities of the size and importance that the sangoma singled out for us won't be populated solely by scientists—suspicious or otherwise. There'll also be janitors, lab staff, drivers, stockroom people, clerks, administrators—none of whom are likely to question on sight anyone they don't deal with directly. They'll assume we belong among them because we'll *act* like we belong among them."

He debated. Never having been brave enough to brazen his way to any kind of success in life he found himself intrigued by the opportunity to do so now. Especially with someone like Ingrid Seastrom to show him the way.

"Assuming we can get inside, how long do you think we can get away with it?"

She was gazing out the window at the passing cityscape. "I guess it depends on how intense their internal security is. I've spent time in hospitals and medical facilities where the external security would prevent so much as an unauthorized mouse from getting inside. But once in, he'd have the run of the place for a while. That's because industrial security, or at least the kinds I've been exposed to, is designed to keep intruders out; not look for them once they're inside." She returned her attention to her companion. "The standard assumption that unauthorized visitors won't be able to get inside is the one thing working in our favor, Whispr."

"It'd be nice to be able to believe something is," he grumbled.

"If SICK's installations are anything like secure medical facilities, then the tighter perimeter security is, the greater the freedom of movement we're likely to have once we're inside. The more the SAEC thinks their research centers are impenetrable, the less likely they are to run daily security checks on personnel already inside."

"They probably have reason not to worry." As the public transport slowed he nodded toward the front exit. "If memory serves, this is where we should get off."

She let him lead the way through the tightly packed clutch of commuters. Once more out in the ocean-cooled air they walked past one row of modern building fronts, turned a corner, started to cut across a small park that was a green blister on the surrounding world of concrete and hardened construction foam—and found themselves in the middle of a war. Or so it seemed to a worried Ingrid. Having been witness to or a participant in a fair number of street confrontations, Whispr was considerably less taken aback by the local confrontation.

Several hundred potential combatants armed with everything from advanced pockshocks to antediluvian wooden clubs faced off against one another in the center of the park. A dozen or so cops stood off to one side looking bored. At the moment the two Namericans stumbled into it, the altercation consisted of little more than taunts, shouts, and the trading of insults. This was accompanied by much threatening waving of unused weapons. Whispr hastened to reassure his anxious companion.

"Calm down, doc. We'll just go around."

"Go around?" Her recently re-maniped face gazed up at him.

"Shouldn't we get out of the area as fast as we can? Go back the way we came?" She nodded in the direction of the loud but largely immobile mob. "Before things get ugly?"

"What makes you think they're going to get ugly?"

Her expression twisted. "What makes you think they're not?"

"My guess is that mobs are pretty much the same most places, whether made up of Melds or Naturals." He leaned toward her and pointed toward the lollygagging police. "See the cops? Don't look real anxious, do they? That's a sure sign they've got a handle on this. Otherwise there would be more of them, they'd be spread out with weapons drawn, and looking around for reinforcements. I don't know this part of the world—but I do know cops. When they're this relaxed you can bet they've got everything under control."

They waited for the confrontation to disintegrate or move on. Instead, the yelling from the two opposing groups continued to increase in intensity and viciousness. The atmosphere was not improved by several participants on both sides who had undergone serious throat melds. Their necks bulging like bullfrogs, they hurled amplified insults and challenges that rose above the general cacophony.

Confronted with the prospect of more violence Ingrid vacillated between running for cover and trusting in her companion. Where street smarts were concerned she had to admit that his advice had been accurate so far. But still, this wasn't Savannah.

As they looked on, one group launched into a rhythmic stamping and chanting that was as mesmerizing as it was intimidating. The opposition responded immediately with an entirely different series of steps and vocalizations. The effect, uniting outsized and often outré Melds with equally enthusiastic and unabashedly profane Naturals, was as if two armies were battling it out with dance and song instead of the weapons they carried. Which, in point of fact, was exactly what was taking place.

"It's called 'toyi-toying.'"

Ingrid hadn't heard the young man come up behind them. That was not unusual in normal surroundings, far less so when the ambient sound was being overwhelmed by a raucous demonstration like the one taking place right in front of them. What *was* exceptional was that Whispr had also failed to detect the new arrival. Staring at him (doctor or not, she couldn't help but stare) she guessed him to be around eighteen, though it was impossible to tell for certain. He might have been fifteen, or sixteen, or thirty. The thick brown fur that covered his distorted, maniped skull was as off-putting as it was distracting.

And then there was the not-so-small matter of his anything but small eyes.

Though she could not see them clearly through the enormous sunglasses that covered a good portion of his face, enough light was admitted by the lenses for her to determine that they had been enlarged by an ophthalmological biosurge who knew his business. Doubling the size of the eyeballs had required suitably enlarging their sockets as well. Despite this the skull was narrower than normal. Not as slenderized as Whispr's, but when measured against the size of those enormous glistening oculars the brain-case looked more than just unnaturally thin.

After first having been removed from their usual positions and grafted onto the top of the skull, the ears had been triangulated and aimed forward. The brown fur covered every visible square centimeter with the exception of a wide bald streak that dominated the face. Some of the teeth were pointed, and the left incisor (only the left) protruded outside and over the shrunken lip. Letting her gaze drop she saw that the young man's fingers had been elongated and thinned. The knuckle joints were far more pronounced than in normal human fingers.

While unsettled at having had someone come up on him from behind, Whispr was not in the least disturbed by the appearance of this fellow Meld. He was acquainted with far more radical manips back home in Savannah.

"Is that a veldt Meld?" he inquired. "I've read about them."

The adolescent shook his head while keeping his enormous eyes trained on the demonstration that was taking place a stone's throw distant. "It's based on a creature that lives on an onshore island. A lemur Meld. Ever since I was little I loved lemurs. Saved my subsist for years so that when I was old enough I could afford a good one. Got it all. See?" Proudly he pirouetted in front of them. Something like a brown rope just missed Ingrid's face. Melded muscles allowed the grafted tank-grown tail to be fully functional.

Its existence was no surprise to Ingrid. Ever since the advent of melding, tails had been among the most popular and easy to perform manips. On those rare occasions when she had contemplated surrendering her Naturalness it was among the first bioaccessories she had considered adding. A well-turned tail was an easy way of turning heads among members of the opposite sex. Psychologists said that it had something to do with atavistic longing and the natural rhythms of the moving body. Without a doubt this lemur Meld was proud of his altered appearance.

"Toyi-toying?" she asked him.

"Dance and chanting designed to register protest or disarm an adversary. Very old local tradition, though some say we stole it from the Zimbabweans. No one bothers about such things much anymore ever since all the local tribes joined together to form the

SAEC." The enormous sunshades turned toward Ingrid's companion. "This kind of demonstration is harmless to nonparticipants, like you said."

Whispr wasn't about to be disarmed by casual small talk. "How long have you been hiding and watching us, bug eyes?"

In protest the lemur Meld raised furry long-fingered hands. "Hey, I was just going on my way and overheard you in passing. I got curious because you didn't sound like local. You don't look like local, either. Where you from?"

"Somewhere else," Whispr replied tautly.

The teenager nodded understandingly. "Not mean to pry, I don't." He turned back to Ingrid. "I don't know your stick-friend, but *you* looked and were sounding afraid. So I tell myself; Phosa, just go and be civic and reassuring to the pretty lady. Even if fighting breaks out no one will come after you. Because you two are not affiliated with either group."

"What *are* the groups?" Ingrid continued to divide her attention between the furry commentator and the furious confrontation. "Is it some kind of political rally?"

Pointed ears twitched as he shook his head. Behind the shades the huge maniped eyes looked sad.

"You would think in this day and age would no more be tribal disputes. Like I say earlier because SICK running most things from Cape to Congo, you would think would be only fights between companies. Excuse me for cliché-making, but old ways die hard." He nodded toward the confrontation. "Here we have running free no charge before you interested visitors, anthropological movie called 'tribal dispute.'" His ears strained forward. "From what I can filter out I think has to do with allocation of government money for over-air communications services in certain section of Wets." Looking away from the increasingly tense standoff he stared sorrowfully at the ground. "Is very sad."

"I'll tell you something else that's sad." Whispr had moved closer to both of them. "Engaging us in polite conversation while trying to zift your grubby maniped self into my friend's purse." At which point he made a grab with both hands for the teen's melded tail.

Slender, lithe, and suitably prehensile, it had been trying to forge a way into her purse while its owner used his body to shield the effort from view. As a startled Ingrid clutched at the container with both hands, the teen threw a punch at Whispr so feeble it would have been laughable if not for the youth's desperation to free himself. Having fought off significantly larger and far more dangerous opponents Whispr had little hesitation in taking on the fur-covered teen.

"Let me go, let go me!" The youth struggled violently in Whispr's spiderish grasp. "I am sorry but hungry . . . will leave you in peace, I promise!" Behind the dark glasses, saucer-sized eyes pleaded.

As she followed the struggle Ingrid was moved to compassion. The young would-be pickpocket was hardly in the same criminal league as the pair of muscle-bound thugs who had tried to mug her and Whispr outside their Simon's Town hotel. He was just some poor street kid struggling to survive, with nothing to boast about or rely on except his expensive meld. She said as much to Whispr.

"Yeah, right—what d'you want me to do, just let him go?"

She eyed her companion steadily. "You could always call the police. They'll take him into custody and then they'll need some information from the offended. From us. They'll ask—the usual questions."

That gave him pause. In a threatening situation Whispr was

quick to react, but thinking ahead had never been one of his strongest virtues. Reluctantly he released the teen and stepped back, panting softly.

"You're damn lucky my friend has more compassion than common sense! Come anywhere near us again, meld-mistake, and I'll strangle you with your own freluking manip."

The lemur Meld was backing away carefully. "May you go down Cape, straw-man, where the wind blow you to the southern ice!" Vast eyes gazed liquidly at Ingrid. "Blessings upon you, lady of all that is Goodness. I apologetically am for try borrow from you. I'm hungry and need food for help saving others, but must press on regardless." He slapped at his own coiling, curling tail, knocking it sharply backward. "Stupid bad meld! Three times I pay to fix biosurge's bungling and still it not work right!"

Ingrid blinked at him. "Saving others? What others?"

His retreat accelerated. Not back the way he had come, as one might have expected. Nor toward Whispr to challenge him again. Instead, the furry adolescent was withdrawing in the direction of the clashing mobs.

"Must help to try and stop quarrel from advancing beyond angry words and defiant dance steps."

Whispr frowned. What the kid said didn't feel right, didn't match up with the theft he had just tried to pull off. "Why should you care? Are you a member of one of the tribes?"

"Neither tribe is mine, but would not matter," the Meld declared. "The old ways must go passing by. Tribal feuds *must* be stopped. Not only here but everywhere. Is for betterment of human species I go."

An alarmed Ingrid stepped toward him. "Are you crazy? You can't put yourself in the middle of that! You'll get yourself trampled—or worse."

"Must try. Not sure why." The youth smiled for the first time, revealing polished white teeth and more of that oddly elongated left canine. "It a feeling that run deep within me. Anyway, not alone — you'll see." He waved, turned, and rushed toward the rapidly shrinking open area that now barely separated the two howling parties.

"Wait, kid!" Whispr cupped his hands to his mouth. "I want to see animals! Where should we go that's close to see animals? And if you tell me a zoo, I'm coming after you!"

Halfway across the street the Meld turned to shout back at them. "Sanbona! Get yourself to Sanbona. Is a very special place, even for MMBA Africa!" Then he was across the street, and his voice as well as his body were swallowed up by the mob.

"He's going to get himself killed." Ingrid could not contain her disbelief. "And for what? For a noble but futile gesture?"

Whispr shrugged. "Seen kids get killed for less. But it doesn't compute, doc. First he tries to scam you, then he goes all rubber-legged righteous in the service of humankind?" He shook his head. "And he was lying to the last; he's all alone."

Ingrid's attention had been drawn to a rising commotion on the far side of the small park. "More people are coming."

Only marginally interested, Whispr made no real effort to see. "More cops? About time. Even back home they prefer to ignore political demonstrations, unless they've got no choice. 'Cause no matter what they do, one side is gonna end up hating them."

"No, I don't think it's more police." She strained to make out the advancing figures. "They're not uniformed and they're not carrying weapons. Leastwise, none that I can see. They look like they're toyi-toying, too."

Whispr truly couldn't have cared less. Delays were dangerous: they meant that anyone on your tail drew that much closer. They needed to rent transportation and he wanted to see animals. But the doctor stood transfixed, staring across the street at the ongoing altercation and showing no sign of wanting to be on her way.

What to do? He could grab her arm and pull, except that she would instinctively resist any such effort on his part. Not to mention that he had promised not to touch her except in an emergency. The only emergencies they faced here were boredom and impatience, to both of which she appeared immune.

The newly arrived third group was singing. Their high-spirited lilting voices soared in harmony above the ongoing salvos of multitribal imprecation. None of the newcomers appeared to be older than nineteen or so. Their dance steps were energetic as they advanced in pairs, swaying and shifting first to the left, then to the right, and back again. The sight put Ingrid in mind of the sinuous windings of a Chinatown paper dragon, only without the costume. The newcomers appeared oblivious to threats and attempts at intimidation from both sides.

Youthful hands were extended to the infuriated, the enraged, the incensed. Under assault by empathetic words, soothing touches, and imploring looks, even the most belligerent individuals found their fury beginning to subside. Like an angry wind that had blown itself out, the din gradually subsided. Weapons both modern and traditional were lowered. Expressions of uncertainty and even discomfiture began to replace those of rage and resentment as the group of newly arrived teens cajoled and persuaded the quieting adversaries.

"I'll be damned." Intrigued in spite of himself, Whispr joined Ingrid in looking on as the young newcomers quietly put an end to the incipient altercation—and without raising anything except their voices in song. "What was it he said? 'For betterment of human species'? I swear he wasn't the type. Right, doc? Doc?"

Ingrid continued to stare across the street. Her expression had changed to one of fascination.

"There was something else he said. Something else. About bungled biosurge work. Work that he'd had to have redone three times, and it still wasn't right."

"So?" Frowning, Whispr gazed over at her. "What's that got to do with anything?"

"Maybe nothing. Probably nothing. It's just that as you know I have an interest in individuals in his age group who've had to have bad cosmetic melds repaired." She nodded toward the park, where the near riot had been muzzled by the group of young interlopers as smoothly and efficiently as a simmering pot could be reduced to silence by the touch of a button or a single verbal command.

Whispr didn't understand. "There are a lot of dumb pre-adults in this world who have to deal with messed-up melds. What's so special about one furball who tried to riffle your purse?"

Her gaze lingered on the park a moment longer. Then she shrugged and turned away. "Probably nothing. It just struck me as kind of an odd coincidence. Like all the peacemakers being from the same age group. No older adults and no young children."

"Uh-huh. Next you're gonna tell me they've all got slipshod repair melds with brain-bugged nanodevices that disappear when you try to look at them."

"No." Turning, she started back the way they had come. She was not going to go through the park. They would find another way to their destination. "No, I'm not going to tell you that."

"That's good, doc. Because I can only handle so much weirdness at one time, and I don't need for you to go all weirdness on me, too. Not now. Not here. It would spoil my day. Last day in the big city, I'm not gonna take my leave from here without taking in a little entertainment."

Setting all preposterous hypotheses aside for the moment, she eyed him guardedly. "What kind of 'little entertainment'?"

"You don't wanna know, Ingrid."

"I am an experienced physician, Whispr. I doubt there is anything of any entertainment value whatsoever that you could engage in that would unsettle me."

"Okay." Leaning over and down, he whispered into her ear and then straightened. It was good that he did so.

She would have slapped him hard if she could have reached his face.

8

Even walking the long way around it didn't take much time to find
the rental service that had been recommended by the mobiad they
had spoken to at the Table Mountain lift station. Could the human
agent manning the front desk of such an outwardly modest enterprise satisfy their request for something small, efficient, inconspicuous, and tough? He could. After registering a deposit would it be
possible to defer final payment until the vehicle was returned? It
would. As they were traveling incognito in hopes of closing a highly
sensitive business deal might they complete the necessary forms
under a set of mutually agreeable aliases? A short pudgy Natural
dark of mien but bright of eye, the agent responded with an ac-
commodatingly conspiratorial nod. They should.

Promising to return at the hour of opening tomorrow morning
to pick up their chosen vehicle and declining to indicate where they
were staying, his highly satisfied customers then departed. The
agent watched them go.

An odd couple, he mused. A Meld slender to the point of

invisibility and a reticent but highly educated companion. He wondered what sort of secretive business such a patently mismatched couple were intent upon. For a brief moment he toyed with the idea of having them followed. Deciding that his curiosity had been overstimulated from spending far too much time watching locally made immersion vits, he put the notion aside. Merely because they were mismatched did not mean they were worthy of further interest or speculative expenditure on his part.

Stimulation of another kind was much on Whispr's mind when he and Ingrid returned to their new hotel after lazing their way through an early dinner. Centrally located, pleasantly modest, in fact not unlike the smaller one they had utilized in Simon's Town, the mobiad-filled entry admitted them in response to a flick of the doctor's room card and a qwikcheck of the guests' retinas.

Back in their eleventh-floor room he watched as she hung her jacket on a hallway coat hook and headed for the single bedroom. Though the convertible couch on which he had enjoyed a decent night's sleep the previous night beckoned, he made no move toward it. The single large window was becoming more transparent as the sun descended behind it.

His brain told him to stay where he was. Sometimes he listened to it, sometimes other organs raised their voices higher. He had repressed as long as he could. Fortified with a pocketful of the doctor's subsist, he felt he had done so as long as he could.

"I'm going out."

In the process of removing her shoes, she poked her head out of the bedroom. "Going out? But we just ate."

"Yeah. I told you earlier. I'm going for dessert."

As she emerged from the bedroom he noticed that she had one shoe on and one off. The humanizing asymmetry made her look almost approachable. Almost.

"Can I come with you? I wouldn't mind something with a little sugar in it."

"The kind of sweetness I'm going shopping for wouldn't appeal to you."

She cocked her head sideways as she looked back at him. "How do you know what kind of dessert I like? We haven't eaten together all *that* much."

"I'm not talking about eating. I alluded to this particular need earlier." His tone was flat. "I'm going to find the red-light district."

"Oh." She was clearly taken aback. "That. You're right. I don't think I do want to come." She hesitated. "We're leaving first thing in the morning and we're safe and undiscovered here. Is this— diversion—really necessary?"

"No," he snapped. What was she now—his mother? "It's not 'necessary.' What it is, is long overdue. I wouldn't expect you to understand."

Her expression froze. "Oh, wouldn't you, now?"

"No I wouldn't, now." He turned to go. "I'm not going to stay out all night. For one thing I know as well as you that we're leaving early in the morning. For another, the allowance you give me isn't nearly enough to buy a whole night of what I want."

She nodded curtly. The detached systematic physician was plainly warring with the inquisitive single woman. "If you don't mind my asking—what are you going to 'buy'?"

He allowed himself a smile of misplaced self-satisfaction. "Don't know. Don't know this city. Don't know what's available, don't know where, don't know for how much. Right now I'm in smorgasbord mode. Don't worry. I'll fill you in with all the juicy details when I get back. If you're still up."

Her tone turned as frosty as her look. "I was just mildly curious. I hardly require all the 'juicy details.'"

"That works for me." He smiled thinly. "This way I won't have to worry about remembering them." Pivoting, he headed for the doorway. "Don't wait up for me, doc. You need your beauty sleep."

A redness rose in her cheeks that threatened to match her newly maniped hair color. "What's that supposed to . . . ?"

But he was already out the door.

WHISPR, NÉ ARCHIBALD KOWALSKI, didn't know much about history, didn't know much about biology—but he did know at least one truism of supreme importance. Knew it because it had been imparted to him by the Mad Scholar of Iron Mountain Park. The Mad Scholar was reputed to be a Turkish-French ex-professor from the Atlanta branch of Kaust University who had undergone one too many delicate brain melds in eternal and ever-frustrated hopes of increasing the size of his integrated organic hard drive. The result was that his brain now cut in and out with the same unpredictability and irregularity as a small town's electrical supply. Having lost his position, his reputation, and his family, he eked out a half-crazed existence wandering the park and the streets that bordered it on four sides by dispensing sagacious bon mots wrapped in varying degrees of accuracy. Sometimes he requested a donation in return for portions of this uncontrolled erudite spew, sometimes not.

Having encountering the wild-eyed bearded old man on more than one sojourn of his own in that part of Greater Savannah, Whispr knew him for the harmless if loquacious crank that he was. On this particular occasion, however, the Mad Scholar of Twenty-third Street and Jackson had stepped sideways to block Whispr's path. Grabbing the wary but self-possessed pedestrian by his nearly nonexistent shoulders, the unhinged learned one had gazed glaze-eyed into Whispr's own.

"D'you know, skinny Meldman, the secret of humankind? D'you know what it's all about?"

"No." One of Whispr's hands was drifting surreptitiously in the direction of the pocket in which resided the expandable stiletto he often carried. "But I get the feeling I'm about to find out."

"It's simple, it's so simple and so obvious!" The hands digging into Whispr's clavicles were large but weak from lack of proper nutrition. "I'll tell you, no charge because it's so obvious, and you can do with it what you will." The bearded one looked around and licked his lips, clearly on the verge of imparting the answer to some great mystery.

"Sex and power. That's all there is to it. That's all there is to *us*. Those two and nothing more. Everything devolves from them. All else is meaningless—art, music, literature, science, history, mathematics, engineering—everything." The fingers dug deeper into Whispr's lean shoulders. "We've not advanced hardly at all from the chimps. The bonobos are better than us, if less literate. It's all about the location of the larynx and a few fortunately mutated brain genes; otherwise the differences are moot."

"Your moot's a hoot." Whispr had firmly removed the other man's hands and pushed him aside. "And your secret's no secret. Everybody on the street knows that. Even a few high-lifers know that. Politicos certainly know that."

So saying he had left the baffled, befuddled, and bemused Mad Scholar in his wake; a deranged elderly ex-academic who through madness and the passage of time had finally come to a truth known instinctively to anyone who had spent the majority of their life on the street.

Sex and power, Whispr mused as he strolled purposefully deeper into the inner intestines of Cape Town. As if that was some kind of great revelation. Like most of his friends he knew all about sex and power because like them he had never had more than a very little of either. From a lifetime of experienced observation he also knew that you could use the former to get the latter, and the latter to obtain the former. Of course everything else was incidental; nothing else was more than an accessory.

The red-light district was easy enough for an experienced urban explorer like himself to find. A few questions pressed on passing citizens of increasingly deprived social status led inevitably to encounters with other citizens of increasingly depraved social interests. Cape Town being an international port of far greater importance than Savannah, its late-night "entertainment" district was of correspondingly greater extent and complexity. As he crossed the invisible yet clearly defined boundary between the genteel and the genital, moving with the easy edgy grace of a nervous cricket in search of fresh offal, it would have been apparent to anyone tracking his progress that here was someone who was operating in familiarly dissolute surroundings.

Surroundings in which, he reflected, the good doctor Seastrom would have stood out like red licorice in a bowl of salted nuts.

The bowl of nuts flowing around him took the form of hawkers, barkers, sales folk, and a plethora of shockingly uncensored mobiads whose franchise was restricted to the district. In a metropolis as cosmopolitan as Cape Town there was little in the way of sexual variation that was not on offer. Most of it was accepted, or endured, or otherwise legalized, though no matter how broadly statutes were written or deviances from the social norm tolerated there was always a new perversion or a variation on an old one that was sufficiently shocking even to the contemporary mind's eye to get itself banned.

These too were, of course, also unashamedly on offer.

Though there was much for the lonely to avail themselves of via the box, science had not succeeded in finding an electronically generated substitute for actual physical human contact. Not yet, anyway. While the military was reputed to have made considerable strides in the development of what were known as tactiles, such expensive and difficult-to-manifest articulations of what were as yet little more than incredibly complex programs had yet to make their way to even the high-paying illicit marketplace. Short of genuine physicality, however, those who sought sexual surcease through the box did not lack for diversion. That was not what Whispr was looking for, however. In a world drowning in simulation, he sought a dose of reality.

He had managed to ward off the screeching beseeching of half a dozen persistent touts until a short, youthful Natural fell into step alongside. Well, he wasn't completely Natural, Whispr realized as he gave the local a quick once-over. A series of intense colors climbed from the base of each individual hair to flare off at the tips. Instead of being composed of keratin, the man's blossoming natural was a ball of gengineered fiberoptics. Nor were the colors entirely random. They formed patterns that changed with each couple of steps: images that were animate, expository, and occasionally obscene. The young man's skull had been transformed into a mobile animated ad.

Whispr mused that it was sensible to choose a short man for a walking advert. If he was of average height or taller, then the potential customer wouldn't be able to see the ads without straining. Doubtless when not on duty the walking advertisement could turn his head display off, perhaps merely by thinking about it. Being part of the peddler's body the advert's movements would not be electronically restricted to a limited area like those of the floating motile advertisements known as mobiads.

Despite the increasingly salacious nature of the displays Whispr kept his attention on the road ahead. It proved harder to ignore the tout's voice. In its own way its content was no less colorful than the man's artfully melded pate.

"Good evening, my friend."

"Not yet it isn't." Whispr did not turn in the direction of the bipedal remora.

"You are looking, I can tell, for something special. I can direct you. I am Vusiquos." An arm extended. When Whispr declined to take the proffered hand, it segued smoothly into a sweeping gesture. "I know everything and everyone in this part of the city, and I can tell you are hungry—looking for a late-night snack. I am proud to say that I consider myself a gourmet of late-night snacks." He chuckled. "Low in calories and low in fat. Unless you are looking for fat. Or something made with saturated oils."

"And you take no commission, of course," Whispr murmured as he strolled. "You're doing this because you want to be my friend."

The much shorter local drew back as if offended. "Do not speak crazy talk, my friend! I hope to make big commission off your as-yet-unknown perverted tastes. On a personal basis, already I don't like you."

Whispr slowed a step and a thin smile spread across his face. It didn't have far to go. "That's more like it. I can trust a man who admits to his own self-interest."

The remora looked pleased. "Your self-interest is my self-interest."

Whispr pushed out his lower lip slightly. "And I suppose my perversion is your perversion?"

"Probably not. Myself favors tall white women who are partial amputees. I like them to have *some* range of movement when I . . ."

"That's sick."

"Yes," the tout agreed readily, "and your tastes are for sure

Catholic-Kosher-Halal, which is why you are wandering alone through this dignified corner of the city at this respectable hour of the night. Judge not, my friend, lest you be found wanting in the tools department." His own reciprocal smile spread. "What can I unveil for you? What do you favor? What is your pleasure-obsession on this fine brisk evening?"

Whispr did not have to ponder. "I'm looking for a virgin."

"Aren't we all?" The remora chuckled at his own comeback; one that could be freely employed as punctuation for several dozen straight lines. "Not a problem, my friend." He studied his angular customer closely. "Male or female? Human or animal? New or re-conditioned?"

A fight was spilling out of a performance club across the street. Since it involved women, it drew its own crowd of spectators. Glad of the free entertainment, they cheered the battling pair on. No weapons being in evidence, Whispr turned away. It was not a serious fight, and he had seen all too many of the latter on the meaner streets of Savannah to be entertained by this one.

"Human. Female. As to the last, it doesn't matter," he told the remora.

The tout was making mental notes. "How many arms? Legs? I know an Indian-run place famous for its banging lore that has a couple of she-vas with enough melded arms to make a man think he's getting a three-for-one deal!"

Whispr shook his head. "The normal number. Same for eyes, ears, boobs, and all the other usual appurtenances. In proper and acceptable proportions."

The remora's eyes widened. "You want a—Natural?"

"Don't be silly. Do I look like I can afford a Natural virgin?"

"No you don't, but I never presume. Presumption is the way of bad business. A bad appearance often masks the existence of good money." He drew himself up. "Okay—one virgin. You positive-sure nothing else?" He eyed his new client intently. "No add-ons of any kind? No surprises? No 'specialty' manips at all?"

Whispr shook his head. Somewhere out beyond the insistent drifting mobiads and light-emanating shopfronts and squealing bars and retina-blinding lights lay the rest of the city. Beyond that lay vineyards and orchards, and beyond them, if one went far enough, were to be found the exposed bones of old Africa, with their ancient tales and energetic tribesfolk, mysterious legends and exotic wildlife. Beyond also lay the most prominent and secretive and well guarded of the SAEC's research facilities, which the quest to penetrate would probably result in his incarceration or death.

But not now, not here.

"Maybe just one," he added quietly.

"Ah!" The remora looked gratified. "I knew it! What is it you desire? Your perversions, my friend, are blowing in the wind. Tell me and I will pluck them for you."

"I want," he told the eager tout, "for her to be kind."

The considerably shorter man blinked at his foreign client. " 'Kind'? What kind of 'kind'?"

"Kind," Whispr repeated. "As in, nice to me."

Small shoulders shrugged. "They will all be nice to you. It is part of what you are paying for."

"No." Whispr leaned forward and down so sharply that the remora took an uneasy step back. "*Kind.* As in understanding. As in empathetic. As in compassionate."

"I don't know...." Genuinely at a loss, the remora was shaking his head doubtfully. "Holes and appendages I can supply in quantity, some of it Natural and some of it Branded. But kindness..." His voice trailed away, and then he brightened. "I have someone for you, I think. Come with me." Turning, he started off at a brisk pace up a sidestreet that was a river of neon-bright light and color. Whispr followed, hopeful but without any real enthusiasm. He did not expect much from the remora who had corralled him.

He should have been less pessimistic. The building they eventually entered was neat, clean, and well fitted out. Multiple drifting monitors ensured client safety while protecting an individual's privacy. The lod in the entrance foyer was there as much for show as for security.

A short walk brought them to an open garden walled off from the outside world by two floors of rooms and a high peaked tile roof. The absence of any overhead dome or other transparency allowed the unobstructed African moon to shine directly into the fynbos-filled courtyard. Fragrances emitted by flowers strange and unfamiliar filled the air and set the mood.

In the center of the small but elegantly appointed courtyard a large rotating holo image hovered above a projector camouflaged to look like a fountain. A succession of fully-realized miniature women paraded, contorted, or masturbated beneath the benign distant moon.

"I'll leave you here-now." The remora was already backing up. "To make your choice. I would suggest Imalo or Trinca. If they're not ready for what you want, a twenty-minute qwikmeld should do the trick. Then they'll do the trick, which is you."

"What about your commission?"

The remora pursed his lips. "I am touched, my friend—but fortunately not by you. My delivery, which again is you, has been duly noted and recorded." He gestured at the garden and its heavily soundproofed surroundings. "Depending on what you spend, my portion will be forthcoming. Enjoy your virgin." He turned and was gone.

Whispr was left to choose from among the redacted pixies who inhabited the rotating projection sphere. While he could have spent a contented hour simply watching, an actual woman was waiting for him in a hotel across town. Tomorrow they would want to get out on the road early, to avoid the queue that invariably backed up on auto-controlled routes. The name "Imalo" having slightly too exotic a ring to it, he voiced a request for Trinca.

She was a slightly built redhead complete to maniped freckles and permanently widened eyes. Not quite a Kewpie doll, with the aspect of someone aged fifteen or so, she was probably closer to her midthirties. As a Meld himself Whispr was not troubled by the skillful yet obvious manip work. A small shudder of delight went through him.

"Trinca?" She nodded. "You're a virgin?"

"That's what you ordered up, Hardly-There." The woman spoke with the maniped voicebox of a teenager. Her response neither confirmed nor denied his query. He chose not to pursue it.

"Where should we go?"

Trying not to appear bored she sighed as she turned to indicate the surrounding apartments. "We have pretty much every imaginable kind of environment to choose from. Conceive one and I'll let you know if it's here, and available."

He did, and it was. Beneath trees that swayed and caressed his bare back and a brook that babbled encouraging obscenities, he had his virgin. It was her first time, she moaned with practiced conviction, and would he be gentle? The illusion being nearly as effective as it was expensive, he was well pleased with the experience when he departed an hour later, having been much lightened in wallet and bodily fluids.

He was more than a little shocked to find that Dr. Ingrid Seastrom had waited up for him.

"Did you get what you went for?" The coldness in her voice was gone. Now it was more a mix of curiosity and disapproval.

"And then some!" He pushed past her into the central sitting area. The door to the bedroom was open and he could see that the linen had been mussed. Resolute as well as exhausted, he turned away, muttering, "I need a drink. I need replenishment." He lurched toward the small cooler that projected slightly from the far wall. "Why'd you stay up? Why aren't you asleep? You're the one who's desperate to get out of here first thing in the morning." The cooler yielded a self-icing Tusker that on command ejected its cap. He drank thirstily, noisily, and unapologetically.

She came toward him. "Which is why I'm still awake. I didn't trust you to get back in time and so I knew I wouldn't be able to sleep until I was sure you had returned."

He lowered the half-empty bottle and sneered, wondering why as he did so. "Afraid I'd take off on you?"

She shook her head. "Not while there's still a chance to make money at stake. I've learned that much about you."

"How well you have learned about me, Ms. Prof. Doc." He dragged the back of a bony hand across his lips, mowing foam that had dried to the consistency of flaking skin. "Want to know something else about me?"

Though calm, she remained well out of arm's reach. "Not if it relates to your evening's dissolute activities."

Thanks to its gengineered hops Tusker was a powerful brew. He was feeling the effects already. Contrary to some popular beliefs, being able to instantly metabolize beer actually saved money and reduced alcoholism. The ability to get a good buzz on while imbibing less alcohol got drinkers off the streets and home sooner Whispr, having never had a real home, usually had an easier time of it than most. Ignoring the advice fighting for prominence in his brain, he took a step toward her.

"C'mon, doc—you don't fool me. You want to know the details, don't you? All the ripe, plump, tickly-tickle, nasty little details." He smacked his lips theatrically as his voice dropped to a melodramatic murmur. "It was a class operation. Despite the extra expense I always go for the best available whenever I can afford it. Want to know why?" He leered at her. "Because no matter what you order up, a class outfit always lets you take your time. Always lets you savor—things. Isn't it the same with a class hospital—or a class doctor?"

Her attitude reflected growing distaste. "Actually, it's the exact opposite. Except for hypochondriacs, visitors to a hospital or a doctor can't wait to get away as fast as possible."

His expression twisted, visual confirmation of what was going on in his head. "Oh, yeah, I guess that'd be right, wouldn't it? See what happens when I try to impress you? See what happens when I struggle with metaphors?"

"I see what happens when you're quick-drunk," she told him coolly.

He tried to take another step toward her only to find himself moving laterally. "I'm not drunk. Just coming down from a physiological high. It's called orgasm. Maybe you've heard of it?" He stared down at her. "Or maybe not."

She would have punched him square in the mouth except that she was wary of getting too close to him. "When you came into my office in Savannah I thought you were just a common thief. Now I see that you're a common bastard. A spiteful, miserable, low-life son of a bitch. I should never have let you in. I should never have removed those traktacs."

He drew himself up, inflated with false pride. "Umbrage! I take umbrage, Ms. Doc. You wound me. I am at worst an *un*common bastard." He wavered a moment longer in front of her, a pathetic stick-figure of a Meld. Then he began to cry.

If it was a ploy to gain her sympathy it wasn't going to work. If it was sincere and not a ploy it still wasn't going to work. As he crumpled in upon himself, physically as well as emotionally, and dropped into a crouch with his hands covering his face, she turned toward the bedroom.

"Try to get some sleep. Your unenumerated debauchery notwithstanding we're still going to make an early start in the morning. You demand that we see some wildlife, remember? Also to convince any possible watchers that we're just ordinary tourists. So we'll go look at some animals. You should feel right at home. Try not to throw up on the floor. I don't want to have to pay a cleaning fee."

He wanted to say something as she marched out of the room, but his voice didn't seem to be working. In fact, a sizable number of frustrated organic functions were in the process of shutting down. When the last of them clocked out, he collapsed on the synthetic tile in a pool of his own spittle.

In the bedroom Ingrid Seastrom locked the door behind her, removed her clothes, laid them neatly across a chair, and slipped unclothed into the waiting bed. She paused a moment before closing her eyes. No sound came from the main room. The crying had ceased and not been replaced.

I should go check on him, she told herself. If not out of personal interest, then out of her responsibility as a physician.

Screw that. If he died she would go on as best she could without him. If he lived she would tolerate his presence and make use of him as necessary. The man was an accessory, an appurtenance, a tool she hoped could help her unravel the mystery of the thread.

Nothing more. He meant nothing to her. She would remain civil to him because that's who she was. When their search concluded, successfully or otherwise, she would discard him as indifferently as she would the rental vehicle.

Lying on her right side in the bed, her knees drawn upward, she thought of her beautiful eighty-first-floor codo, of its modern conveniences and reassuring familiarity. She missed her friends and colleagues, her patients, the fresh daily lunches in one of the tower's restaurants. Here she was, on the run in the SAEC, forlorn and pursued, her only companion an unpredictable degenerate malefactor who had crawled out of the sewers of Greater Savannah and presented himself in her office. She ought to have known better. She ought to have dismissed him out of hand.

But she couldn't dismiss the thread. It glowed in her mind, flush with the promise of impossible technologies and hidden secrets. Her determination to understand it was as powerful, as compelling, as ever.

It struck her with a start that in its own way her obsession was no less a compulsion than perverted sex or drugs or whatever else a creature like Whispr engaged in for entertainment. She had heard and read on more than one occasion that the unrelenting pursuit of scientific data could be considered an addiction as powerful as any narcotic. That was what she was: a knowledge junkie. She was mainlining the mystery of the thread. Otherwise how to explain the contradictions inherent in her present situation? This wasn't like her. For Ingrid Seastrom a weekend at the beach constituted a serious break in routine. Now here she was in Southern Africa, chasing technological phantoms.

She should pity Whispr, she realized. Not loathe him. Otherwise he might loathe her. Not that it mattered. Loathing or friendship; so long as they could continue to function together and help each other out. Drunk and attracted to her as he was, she reflected, he still had not laid a hand on her. Not since that evening in her condo. Lack of desire expressed did not necessarily mean lack of desire felt, she knew. Or maybe his depraved evening had simply left him too drained to try anything.

By morning he would either be dead or well rested, she told herself. Only then would she be able to know for certain how to proceed. She rolled over onto her back, unable to sleep and hating herself for it. Hating herself because she knew he was right.

She did want to know all the details of his evening, and in lieu of the realities that could have spilled from his teasing but now stilled lips, her imagination was working overtime and unbidden to fill in the lascivious, sweat-inducing blank spaces. As a conse-quence (or perhaps a punishment) she spent the next hours tossing and turning, unable to shut off the flow of lubricious images that as-saulted her mind's eye, unable to sleep, until mental as well as physical exhaustion finally combined to render her unconscious.

By far the worst of it was not the prurience itself, nor the fact that it revolved around her thoroughly dissipated companion, but the awareness that in more than one lewd and salacious scenario Whispr was not the central figure.

She was.

NATURAL AND MELD, WOMAN and man, doctor and riffler were both unusually subdued the following morning.

Screwed up, Whispr was thinking to himself as he silently packed his simple luggage for the journey ahead. *Lewd up leads to screwed up*. What could he have been thinking? The answer to that was simple enough: he hadn't been thinking. Ordinarily he would have had no trouble keeping a lid on his desires. That was easy enough for someone who was not exactly a magnet for women, melded or Natural. It was his constant proximity to Seastrom, he told himself. She was driving him crazy. The way she moved, the way she smelled, the way she looked, even her frequently patronizing speech; all combined to generate an erotic frisson he could no more ignore than he could the occasional pangs of hunger that rose from his meld-shrunken stomach.

The worst thing was that she seemed oblivious to it all. She gave no indication that she was in any way aware of the effect she was having on him. Furthermore, his yearnings were patently not reciprocated. The only attraction she felt toward him had to do with his ability to negotiate the less cerebral difficulties that threatened to derail their progress.

He could tell her how he felt, of course. Confess his attraction, beg for a crumb of attention, beseech her to look at him as something other than a two-legged utensil. But he had already tried that once, clumsily, in Savannah. A second botched attempt and despite the advantages his presence offered he had not the slightest doubt she would dump him like the skinny sack of street trash that he was. As if to confirm his worst fears and frustrations she was ignoring him even more than usual this morning.

He knows. As she gathered her travel gear, Ingrid would steal a glance in the direction of her silent, lean companion. Whispr wasn't saying anything because he suspected, she told herself. He was too wise in the ways of society's bottom rungs, too adept at reading expressions and emotions, not to know what she had gone through the previous night.

Naturally she had said nothing about it. By his continuing silence was he choosing to respect her privacy? She found herself analyzing every step she took, every gesture she made, for hidden meaning.

This won't do, she told herself. You're crediting him with far more perception than he possesses. He doesn't know anything. How could he? Maybe he was good at analyzing expressions, but he couldn't read dreams.

"You all right, doc?"

"What?" Startled by the sudden query after nearly an hour of mutual near silence, she looked up sharply.

His brows drew together. "I asked if you were all right."

"I'm fine. Why shouldn't I be fine? Why do you ask if I'm all right?"

He raised both hands defensively. "Hey, I was just expressing concern. Take it easy."

She turned away. *Yes, I'd better take it easy*, she thought angrily. Otherwise this was going to be a long road trip and she was more likely to break down before their rental vehicle did.

"Got everything?" At the door, clutching her travel pack in one fist, she took a last look back at the unprepossessing room.

He was standing very close. It still made her a little bit nervous to have him in such proximity, looming over her, but in the absence of a valid reason for complaint she felt obliged to keep her unease to herself. He was careful not to touch her or otherwise make contact. The lesson of Savannah had been well learned.

"Let's get moving." He smiled, not at her or at the room but at images he had carried with him since childhood. "Let's play tourist."

She was shaking her head unenthusiastically as she let the automatic door close behind them and they started down the hall. "We're just wasting time." When he looked about to protest she raised a hand. "I know, I know—I promised. Wildlife first, then the research center. But this is unnecessary. Other than a few local thugs with only their own interests in mind no one's come near us."

He nodded as he walked alongside her down the narrow corridor, deliberately shortening his stride so she would not have to move fast to keep pace with him.

"Some might consider that confirmation that we've been doing all the right things."

She favored him with a jaundiced eye. "How is throwing away a couple of days or so gawking at antelope and elephants a right thing?"

"It's right for me." He spoke a little more harshly than he intended. "If there's nothing on that stupid thread and its supposedly unique composition turns out to be some kind of false positive or fake, at least I'll get something out of this trip. Meanwhile, I'm glad you're feeling so confident. Go ahead and relax." He raised his gaze, scanning the last of the hallway ahead. "I'll stay paranoid for the both of us."

9

Molé studied the unpretentious hotel. It was typical of the places where his surprisingly elusive quarry chose to stay. Didn't they realize that by now he would have built up a profile on them? Repetition of choice was a hallmark of amateurs. The realization made him feel a little better and helped to mitigate some of his frustration. He was close now and looking forward more than ever to his inevitable reunion with the good doctor and the bad riffler.

He'd had plenty of opportunity to reflect on the seemingly interminable delays. It allowed time for contemplation of what he would do once he again made their acquaintance. Their expensive and time-consuming evasions demanded reciprocity. Consequently he would lavish more time on their demise than was his custom. The pathetic riffler he would educate piecemeal. With the doctor he would take longer. It would be more enjoyable. For one thing he was something of a student of the human body himself, and not only because he had undergone a succession of radical melds so extensive that it was difficult to tell how much of him remained human and how much now consisted of customized synthetic add-ons. The images such thoughts conjured cheered him. Yes, he and the doctor would have an extended conversation. The riffler could listen and watch, provided that Molé permitted him to retain the basic organic components necessary to do so.

As was typical of such middle-grade establishments there was a human clerk at the front desk. It being the middle of the afternoon, no one else was around. Tourists were off sightseeing and business travelers bemoaning their miserable individual fates. Smoke coiled upward from the tip of a stimstick stuck between his lips as the clerk intently manipulated the details of a projected war game grounded in ancient local lore. In addition to the rapidly changing statistics displayed on the portable box screen, miniaturized African warriors and British soldiers of an earlier time fought in the air around him. Though muted, their shouts and battle cries were clearly audible. The preoccupied clerk was literally in the game.

Stepping forward, Molé ignored the spears, knobkerries, and bayonets that briefly inclined in his direction. A soft but demanding cough failed to draw the attention of the clerk, who continued to ignore the elderly figure now standing next to the counter. Coughing a second time as he waved away a cloud of Zulus and smoke, Molé spoke loudly enough to ensure he would be heard over the martial din of the game.

"Excuse me. I beg your pardon?"

The clerk did not so much as glance up from his gaming.

Pulling his comm unit from a pocket, Molé flicked it to life. Accompanied by their respective portraits a pair of full-length three-dimensional images took shape in the air between him and the clerk. As the figures rotated the portraits morphed to reflect, as best Molé's intelligence sources had been able to discover, the most recent incarnations of the pair he sought. The hovering images did not interact with those projected by the game, but the large visuals did interfere.

"Please, it is important that I know: have you seen either of these two visiting Namericans?"

Making no effort to conceal his annoyance at the persistent interruption the clerk finally responded—with unconcealed reluctance and palpable disdain.

"Yebo, I seen them, old man." As he spoke, each word was accompanied by a dip and rise of the stimstick clamped in his mouth.

A small spark stirred within the hunter. "You are certain?" The casually dismissive remark about his age he filed for reference.

The clerk looked to be in his midtwenties. Cocksure and apathetic, it was plain that he had finally responded to the presence of his elderly visitor only in hopes of getting rid of him as quickly as possible. Around the attendant the faultless images of nineteenth-century African warriors, tough-as-leather Boers, and her majesty's dedicated soldiers drifted in cybernetic limbo as they awaited a resumption of their master's commands. Responding to programming, several of the soldiers lit cigarettes in cynical imitation of the games master who controlled their highly transitory existence. In advanced gaming, idle time and downtime were not the same thing at all.

"Of course I'm certain." The clerk's affirmation was accompanied by a scowl. "D'you think I'm half senile like you?"

Molé added this as a footnote to the previous comment about his age. "No, I certainly do not think that. Please, when did you last see them?"

The younger man shrugged indifferently. Interruptions like this he did not need. Gaming time was ever precious. One never knew when a serious interruption like the arrival of a guest, or even worse the manager, might take place.

"Why should I tell you anything, old man?" Looking his visitor up and down, he was plainly not impressed. "You don't look like police. You don't even look like a private investigator. You look too—old."

"Yes, I am old," Molé genially agreed. "But not too old."

The clerk's brow crinkled. He liked puzzles, even when they arose from unexpected sources. " 'Not too old' for what?"

Molé's expression and voice did not change. "You'll find out, if you don't tell me when last you saw these two visitors." A touch on the comm unit ghosted the aliases of Archibald Kowalski and Ingrid Seastrom.

"If I don't . . . ?" The clerk gaped at his caller. Not only was he old, the quietly brash interrogator was short. A threatening presence he was not. But the last thing the clerk wanted was a time-wasting argument. As the oldster had pointed out, the white couple he was interested in were not even Africans. So why should the clerk care if some petrified elder wished to get in touch with them?

"Oh, what the hell—yebo, I remember them pretty good. They struck me as a real mismatch, even for a mostly Natural traveling with a Meld."

"You cannot imagine," Molé murmured in agreement.

"They checked out yesterday morning." Puffing furiously on his stimstick, the clerk was already turning back to his game.

Yesterday morning. It would soon be over, Molé told himself. He was close enough to the end now that he felt he could relax. "I don't suppose they happened to mention where they were going?" he inquired casually. "A destination, perhaps, or even a direction?"

Having resumed the game where he had paused it, the clerk

replied without looking up. "Nawso. They just left. Didn't volunteer nothing about where they were headed and I didn't consider it my place to ask."

"No, you wouldn't." *You mindless box-dwelling nit. Life is passing you by and like so many of your ilk all you can do is sit and stare with vacant eyes into the bottomless hollow depths of a wholly artificial existence. The excitement you purport to feel, to experience, is as synthetic as your soul.* Napun Molé considered himself something of an expert on realities.

When the clerk's stimstick suddenly flicked out, his aged visitant saw an opportunity to introduce a touch of one reality into the younger man's life.

"*Isihogo* and damnation!" Yanking the half-finished narcotic twig from his mouth he began searching through the desk on which the portable box screen rested. Molé extended a hand.

"Allow me. In repayment for your kind and considerate assistance."

"Blow it out your arse, old man." Rising, the clerk leaned toward Molé's extended hand. "But thanks for the relight." He regarded the middle digit his elderly visitor had extended toward him. "Finger lighter meld, yes? Something like that seems appropriate for you." He smiled thinly. "Can't lose your lighter if it's part of your body."

"That is very true." Molé waited as the clerk put the stimstick back in his mouth and extended himself still farther in his visitor's direction, nodding at the proffered finger as he did so.

"It's a traditional meld, right? From the old days?"

"Not so old," Molé countered. "Not so traditional." As the tip of his finger popped back, it simultaneously came to life.

The hellish narrow jet of yellow-orange flame roared as it instantly carbonized the stimstick and flared past to slam into the clerk's face. Screaming at the top of his lungs, his voice reaching the very apex of agony, the younger man fell backward clawing at himself. His eyes had melted away like two scoops of vanilla gelatin and the rest of his face was on fire. So was his shirt. Flailing wildly at himself only served to spread the flames to the rest of his body and to the furniture around him. Their eternal battle interrupted, unfeeling Zulu impis and proper British battalions stood down as they flicked out around the sagging box screen.

Molé had long since turned and headed for the exit. In his profession one never knew what small and seemingly insignificant accessory might one day prove useful. That included the need to make fire. As he reached the door he glanced back in the direction of Reception. The clerk was moaning now, no longer screaming, a flaming near corpse lying like a burning Yule log in the center of the increasingly engulfed front desk. The hotel alarm was sounding and the building's integrated fire suppression system was spraying white foam everywhere. Molé was not put in mind of the holiday season.

"I never go anywhere without a little napalm," he murmured softly as he pulled the entry door shut behind him.

By the time the first fire floaters and ground units arrived, the hotel was fully engulfed. In addition to the clerk, whose body could be identified only through dental records, two panicked guests and one bystander died. More were taken to area hospitals while others were treated at the scene for burns and smoke inhalation.

Smoke inhalation. Ignored by fire and police personnel, the old man strode purposefully in the direction of the vehicle park where he had left his roadster. That was what the disrespectful clerk had perished from. Smoke inhalation. He recalled the semaphoring stimstick. It was, to Napun Molé's way of thinking, almost . . . funny. He nearly smiled.

Alien to the marching orders they had been given, his facial muscles were not quite up to the task.

THAT THE N1 HAD BEEN the main route between Cape Town and Joburg for a very long time was evidenced not only by the amount of traffic the wide roadway carried but also by the fact that the express lanes were completely automated. Guide strips running down the center of each lane could control and convey anything from a suitably equipped one-man scoot to a road train all the way from the SAEC's main port at the Cape to the massive industrial-commercial complex centered on Johannesburg and Pretoria. Once they hit the outskirts of Parow, Whispr programmed their turnout for distant Worcester and eased back in the driver's seat. Accelerating to a relaxed two hundred kph, the rented roadster settled into one of the middle lanes.

Hissing by at even higher speeds, electrically powered speed-sters rocketed past them in the fast lane. With their maximum ve-locity controlled by the guide strip embedded in the roadway they were no danger to themselves or their occupants. At the other ex-treme, individual trucks jockeyed for position with massive road trains consisting of a hauler attached to four or five engineless containers. Swiveling the driver's seat sideways, Whispr let his long legs extend to the far side of the passenger compartment. He had room to do so because Ingrid had already ratcheted her own seat backward on its servo and was engrossed in a manuscript on her reader.

Dividing his time between enjoying the rapidly changing scenery that was blurring past, monitoring the car's perfectly inde-pendent systems, and sneaking furtive sideways glances at her, he stood her indifference for half an hour before he could take the si-lence no longer.

"Are you going to read all the way to Sanbona?"

She glanced up at him. "Maybe. Why?"

"I just thought..." He hesitated, desperate to engage but not wanting to put her off. He waved a hand at the terrain speeding by outside the vehicle. "We're in *Africa*. Doesn't it interest you at all? Don't you care? We may never have the opportunity to do this again." His expression twisted. "What happened to your goddamn overriding sense of scientific curiosity?"

She indicated the reader. "I'm indulging in it right now. Reading the most recent update to *The Journal of Atlantean Medicine*. Just because my body is here doesn't mean my mind can't attend to business." She smiled sardonically. "You, of course, suffer from no need to keep current with an ongoing profession."

"Is that so? Might surprise you to know that people in *my* 'ongoing profession' have to—"

He broke off. What was he going to tell her? That information on the latest methods of breaking and entering or taking down a mark was shared among thieves? That discussions on the best way to remove subsist from the unwary took place every time he encountered another of his ilk? That devices for defeating or confusing police functions while the latter were carrying out their duties were updated as fast as law enforcement techs could invent new ones? She didn't give him any time to catch his mental breath.

"What exactly is it that you *do*, Whispr? Besides eke out an existence on the fringes of conventional society. I don't know that I've ever asked you."

Should have left her to her reading, he reproached himself angrily.

"Odd jobs." Leaving his long legs where they were he let his gaze drift back to the road ahead. "Pick up a little subsist where I can."

There—that was truthful enough.

She was staring at him. "Some of those jobs must be pretty odd, I imagine."

He turned back at her. "Look, you knew what kind of person I was when we decided to make this trip. I'm not a saint and I don't live on alms. You want the nasty particulars, you'd better wait until this is over. Otherwise you're liable to start having second thoughts, and this is no time for second thoughts." He looked away. "If you're gonna go all ethics on me we'd be better off calling it quits right now."

"Take it easy." Though she looked back at her reader, her attention was still focused on him. "I'm not judging you. I was just curious, that's all."

His tone turned sarcastic. "That's why we're here. Because Ingrid Seastrom is just curious."

She smiled kindly. "If it wasn't for you, Whispr, I'd probably be dead by now. If not at the hands of that assassin Molé then by others who want the thread. You speak of ethics. It would be unethical of me to presume to render judgment on someone who's saved my life."

"Nothing wrong with that logic." Shifting in the seat, he turned on his side. Between his attenuated body and slender lower limbs he stretched from one door of the roadster to the other, a fleshy pillar that in any serious accident would crumple like cream cheese.

She eyed him a moment longer, then gave a mental shrug and returned to her reading. While interesting, the landscape racing by outside their vehicle was nothing remarkable. Besides, diverting herself with the long list of recent medical articles allowed her for at least a little while to forget that she was embarked on the last stages of a journey as bizarre as it was dangerous. With a common street thief and maybe murderer as her sole companion, protector, and business partner. Without a doubt she had taken complete leave of her senses.

Then why, she wondered not for the first time, did she feel so exhilarated?

When automated road services transferred them to the Off lane and the roadster began to decelerate, she finally looked up from the reader. Whispr had left her alone since their last conversation and she had managed to lose herself in the medical journal. She had not really noticed how quickly they had left civilization behind. They were entering the Karoo, a region of deeply folded mountains and canyons far removed from the urban delights of Cape Town.

They were still several kilometers from the exit when their vehicle suddenly slowed to a stop. It was not alone. Though traffic had thinned quite a bit they could see that every roadster, family transport, truck, scoot, and other vehicle had similarly been stopped. While traffic heading south toward Cape Town continued to flow unhindered, all four northbound lanes had come to a standstill. Whispr could have disengaged their vehicle from the automated roadbed and gone off-road, but assuming that the situation in which they currently found themselves was akin to what they would experience in a similar set of circumstances back home, he did nothing. No one else was breaking from the stalled lines. Had any of the stopped vehicles attempted to do so their occupants would have been subject to an on-the-spot fine.

The reason for the disruption soon manifested itself in the form of a pair of police vehicles that came screaming up behind the travelers. Ignoring the in-road guide strips and utilizing their onboard anticollision hardware they were able to weave a relatively consistent path through the stopped traffic. Floaters, of course, could have traveled off-road and aboveground—but not at the speeds achieved by the law enforcement vehicles.

As soon as the police pursuit had blasted past, the roads re-engaged and traffic was allowed to move again.

Ingrid had turned off her reader and was slipping it back into her backpack. "Wonder what that was all about?"

"No idea." Whispr forced his muscles to unclench. Police sirens of any stripe unsettled his nerves. Had the two chasers slowed down and settled in behind them he had been prepared to break contact with the road and take off on his own. Though he had not voiced his concern to his blissfully unperturbed companion he was not prepared to be questioned by the local police. The last time police had tried to question him he had been forced to flee through night and swamp unaware that they had killed his partner. He did not want to go through anything like that again. He most especially did not want anything like that to happen to Dr. Ingrid Seastrom.

In all likelihood she would probably have disagreed with his line of reasoning, he knew. She'd probably welcome the police. Never give a thought to the possibility that some of them might be working with a delister like the assassin Molé. She was right about one thing, though. Just like she'd said, if not for him and his life-time of accumulated street wisdom she probably already would be dead. The image this realization brought up displeased him and he hurried to put it out of his mind.

With a population of just under a hundred thousand, Worcester was the principal town in the Breede River Valley. Wild, difficult to negotiate mountains rose on either side of the valley, dominated by the two-thousand-meter plus Keeromsberg to the northeast. Here they would leave the steady traffic of the N1 to head southeast and then due east into the Little Karoo. Ingrid knew there would be no more accommodating automated roadways. She and Whispr would have to manual drive. That was partly the point. If anyone *had* managed to follow them this far, they would by now be wondering where the hell their quarry was going and why.

The road seemed to divide the landscape: greenery to one side, raw rock and scrub-covered mountain to the other. Whispr drove easily, more relaxed on the old winding pavement than he had been on the smooth-surfaced national highway. No howling police vehicles out here, he told himself. Pursuit of any kind, governmental or private, would have shown itself by now. He was starting to believe that they really had thrown any trackers off their trail. Probably as soon as they had boarded the flight from Miami. The roadster's scanner detected nothing behind them for at least half a kilometer.

Maybe, he told himself, he could even ease back and start to enjoy some of this journey. Leastwise the part before they tried to slip themselves into the most secretive of SICK's research facilities, where they would likely find themselves arrested or killed.

One more small town marked the turnoff to Sanbona. Many kilometers later they found themselves working to maintain their poise as the scanner attached to the terminal at the park's entry gate took its time examining their maniped identification. A seven-meter-high double electrified fence marched off to east and west as far as the eye could see. Ingrid was struck by the barrier's height and depth. From the brochures she had perused on the box she had some idea of what the fence was designed to contain, but it was far more impressive when viewed in person. The terminal's voice was cool and synthetic as it requested payment. Whispr expressed his surprise with a whistle and an epithet. As she had ever since they had left Savannah, Ingrid gritted her teeth and paid.

"The mobiads say this is a unique place, even for Africa. It had better be."

"They also say specific sightings ain't guaranteed." Whispr

gripped the 4×4's wheel. "I'll settle for a few of the usual and one special."

The methodical gate voice continued. "You acknowledge that you are entering a vast and largely undeveloped wilderness area that is home to a number of species that are potentially dangerous to Naturals and Melds alike? Each adult will please signify their understanding by voiceprint."

"I do," Whispr declared.

"I do," Ingrid added.

"You further acknowledge as consenting adults of sound mind that the SAEC Parks and Preserve Board bears no responsibility for any ill or injury that may befall you in the course of your sojourn in Sanbona Preserve, up to but not excluding the possibility of dismemberment or death?"

"Uh, yeah," mumbled Whispr.

"Please acknowledge by saying 'yes' or 'no.' If English is not your primary language please choose from the following . . ."

"I do," Whispr added hastily. Ingrid added her agreement after him.

"A variety of accommodations from tents to luxury rooms are available at Dwyka Lodge. All self-guiding visitors are required to check in at the main ranger station by nightfall on their date of arrival. Failure to check in will result in immediate expulsion from the Preserve and possible prosecution under SAEC's preservation code. No private travel is allowed in the Preserve before sunrise or after sunset. Removal of anything from the park, be it organic or inorganic, is a prosecutable offense. Removal of or harm to any fauna constitutes a felony punishable by a fine of not less than ten thousand rand plus prison time."

"Serious little bastard of an infochip, isn't it?" Whispr muttered under his breath. Louder he said, "Directions?"

"Please press a standard communicator or other recording device against the terminal." Beneath the scanner's translucent vandal-proof armor a green oval glowed brightly. Removing his unit from his pocket Whispr pressed it against the softly pulsing plastic surface. Seconds later a beep indicated that the transfer of information had been completed. He then handed his unit to Ingrid. The doctor touched it to her own more expensive handheld and the information was transferred a second time. Each of them now had access to everything they needed to know about the Preserve; its history, size, flora and fauna, facilities, roads, and more.

Slipping his device into the multistandard receptacle slot on the roadster's dash and voicing a request produced a three-dimensional heads-up display that showed the destination lodge and ranger station squinched down on the near side of a lush river valley. Unlike on the N1 there was no automedian here to take control of their vehicle and guide it to its destination, but by the same token it would be hard to get lost unless they deliberately went off-road. Its business concluded, the efficient terminal bid them a pleasant if emotionless farewell.

"Enjoy your visit to Sanbona. Remember the hallmarks of a successful visit. Take nothing but memories and leave no body parts behind. *Under no circumstances should you exit your vehicle anywhere within the Preserve except in areas clearly marked and fenced for that purpose.*"

Accompanied by a soft electronic chirping the tall gate in front of the visitors opened to admit them. Once their vehicle had advanced inside the first fence line the gate closed behind them. Only when it was shut and latched did the second inner gate open to finally allow them into the Preserve.

They drove slowly, letting the heads-up that had been downloaded from the entrance terminal guide them in the direction of the only place visitors were allowed to stay within the Preserve. There was no camping in Sanbona, and for good reasons. Watching her companion as they abandoned the last pavement and the supposed road became more and more difficult, Ingrid could see his expression slowly fall, his excitement subside.

"What's the matter? Isn't this what you wanted?"

"I thought—I dunno, doc." He waved a hand to take in their surroundings. Towering gray escarpments and scrub-covered plains now dominated the horizon in every direction. The high double fence had long since receded behind them. Though it was graded, the single-lane thoroughfare would not pass muster as a decent country road back in Georgia. "I thought there'd be jungle, or at least—what do they call the open spaces here with all the thousands of animals?"

"Veldt." She shook her head sympathetically. "That's all in East Africa, Whispr. And the jungle is in the middle part. Down here where we are—this is like Arizona, not the Congo."

"To come all this way . . ." Overflowing with disappointment his voice trailed away. "We might as well make a loop or turn around and get started toward our real destination." In front of the roadster clumps of lavender and yellow wildflowers splotched the otherwise dull terrain as if the rocks had been drizzled with paint.

Moving from left to right, a herd of shapes sprinted across the road in front of them. Some kind of antelope, Ingrid told herself as her heart raced a beat. Springbok, most likely, or klipspringer, or maybe even red hartebeest. She couldn't be sure. The time she'd spent reading about the place had been brief. Whatever they were, they were moving fast. Almost, she thought, as if something might be after them.

Something was, and it had been chasing the antelope toward its mate.

His jaw dropping, Whispr slammed the roadster to a gravel-scattering halt as something massive and muscular erupted from a cluster of boulders off to their right to smash into one of the fleeing springbok. The impact alone was sufficient to break the prey's neck.

"Holy Hell," Whispr yelled, "a white lion!"

Ingrid was staring, her mouth also agape. When she finally found her voice again it was to point out the stunningly obvious. "It's white, but that's no lion, Whispr."

The "one special" Whispr had hoped to see had more than justified their visit.

With the initial shock of the ambush over he was able to see how right she was. This was one of the sights they had come for but could not be certain of encountering in Sanbona's hundred thousand hectares, far less in such dramatic fashion. The rugged terrain and vast amount of open space, the lack of tourists who opted for more famous game parks like Kruger and Addo, made it ideal for the purposes of the gengineers who operated the Preserve's main facility. Sanbona was a place where the fruits of reverse genetic engineering could roam free and enjoy a privacy and seclusion unavailable to animals in more level, easier to negotiate preserves.

The *Smilodon* that had struck the antelope was not pure white but more of a mature pale beige color. As it lay panting on its belly with one massive paw resting protectively atop the dead springbok its mate, who had chased the herd into the ambush, appeared off to the left. Padding leisurely across the dirt roadway directly in front of the 4×4 and its awed occupants she yawned as she approached the kill. The razor-edged upper incisors thus revealed were more than a dozen centimeters long and pointed like knives. Both of the light-colored, spotted predators had stubby tails and were stocky of build, more like bears than cats.

The 4×4's electric engine made no noise, allowing Whispr and Ingrid to watch in fascination as the two hulking sabertooths tore into the fresh carcass. She could not have said how much time had passed since the kill before she finally murmured to her companion.

"Well? You wanted to see animals."

Whispr muttered something under his breath. "After this it's gotta be all downhill, and I don't mean the road." He nodded forward. "What now? Do we just drive around them?"

"I guess so." The kill, thankfully, had taken place just to the right of the graded route. "Unless you think they'll try to eat the car."

He didn't laugh. Thrust downward by powerful muscles, those saber teeth might conceivably penetrate a windshield. Fortunately the big cats paid no attention to the vehicle as it trundled silently past. Ingrid looked on with a physician's detachment as the apex predators efficiently ripped the dead springbok into sections, tearing off limbs and chunks while using their scimitarlike teeth to open up the belly and other soft parts of the kill. Only when the roadster had moved on and the bloody scene had vanished behind them did she speak again.

"Do you want to head for the lodge or keep driving? This is your big deal, your payoff for agreeing to come with me. So you'd better make the most of it."

He considered his options. A check of the sky showed that they still had a couple of hours until sunset. A broad smile spread across his narrow face. The rare expression made him look like an entirely different person and a childish enthusiasm infused his words.

"Let's go find some mammoths."

Having become skilled at melding their own species it was hardly surprising that some gengineers and biosurges with an interest in paleontology had chosen to devote themselves to the even more exotic efforts to reconstruct the megafauna of the preboreal Holocene. Working with DNA extracted from frozen and otherwise preserved creatures they had managed to reach as far back in time as the late Pleistocene. Restoring creatures who had gone extinct even more recently quickly became commonplace. Tasmania was once again home to free-ranging thylacines while New Zealand and Madagascar featured farms that flocked with giant elephant birds and moas. The moas' traditional ancient predator had also been brought back to life, but unlike its prey it was not allowed to roam free in the skies over Aotearoa. Since a Haast's Eagle could carry off a child as easily as it could a moa its range was restricted to the interiors of several gargantuan aviaries.

As soon as the science became viable the whole question of resurrecting ancient predators had been subject to serious debate. In the end it was decided that a sabertooth cat living in a nature preserve or park was not any more dangerous than a present-day lion or tiger, and in many ways less so since it was not as fast. Bringing the American cheetah back to the plains of Namerica to once again chase down its natural prey, the fleet-footed pronghorn, turned out to serve as a natural and welcome brake on the exploding cougar population. Previously extinct dire wolves mixed easily with their modern gray, Mexican, and timber cousins. But due to political pressures the more dangerous resurrected predators like *Smilodon* were not yet allowed in North America, Europe, or developed Asia. In contrast Africa offered plenty of sites well away from population centers as well as unrivaled experience in managing large numbers of megafauna.

Still, only in a few select locales could one hope to encounter the full range of once extinct Pleistocene and Holocene animals. Because of its rugged terrain and the cost of admission, among the largest and least visited of these was Sanbona.

Much to Whispr's obvious disappointment they didn't see any mammoths as they took their time wending their way to the lodge. They did encounter a small herd of woolly rhinoceros grazing in the river canyon. There was also a family of Irish elk led by a magnificent stag. Cropping grass close to the lodge itself was a herd of beautiful bluebuck. Occupying a similar plot of land on the south shore of the straight but slow-moving river, ranger station and visitor center alike sheltered behind curving double walls of the same high electrified wire that encircled the entire vast Preserve.

The lodge complex was more extensive than Ingrid expected from the information that had been provided by the mobiads. It boasted not only a variety of accommodations but several restaurants, multiple gift shops, and proper recharging stations for the use of private as well as Preserve vehicles. One of her principal concerns about following through on her promise to Whispr to see animals was that in a small park they might draw attention to themselves. No need to worry on that score here, she told herself. Even at a time of year that would be considered off-season the lodge complex was still playing host to hundreds of visitors.

It made sense to concentrate them all in one place, she told herself. That way they could be looked after, accommodated, kept track of, and provided for with a minimum of logistics. Each morning organized groups would set out either in their own transport or on Preserve vehicles to see the sights and look for animals. Nightfall required them to be safely back inside the lodge complex or outside the Preserve altogether. Such arrangements were not only efficient, they helped to ensure the safety of visitors and Preserve employees alike.

Especially, Ingrid thought later that evening as her ears picked up a faint distant howling that sent an atavistic shiver down her back, when park residents included among their number some of the most fearsome warm-blooded predators ever to tread the surface of the earth.

10

"I know your insides have been heavily maniped, but as a physician it's still hard for me to see how you eat enough to stay alive."

Scated across the small table from her in the lodge's quarter-full dining room, Whispr smiled across the top of his boiled egg. "It's not just the melding. When you live on the street and everyday existence is hand-to-mouth, you get used to making do with as little as possible. That applies to food as much as to subsist or anything else." Using a shaker taken from his backpack he seasoned the egg with one of his special powdered supplements, took a delicate bite, and chewed. "It's all about fuel. My body is slighter than most, so I need less of it than average. Don't compare my eating habits to those of a Natural."

"I wasn't." She slathered local jam onto a piece of toast. Like the rest of her substantial breakfast it stood in stark contrast to her companion's meal. "I was comparing them to those of a finch."

He chuckled as he continued to nibble daintily at the egg. "I'm a filch, not a finch."

One hand clutched the toast while the other made shushing motions. She looked around nervously. None of their widely scattered fellow early risers were looking in their direction, but still. . . .

"Let's not broadcast your antisocial affectations, okay? See that chunky guy two tables over? He looks like a cop on vacation."

Whispr barely turned, took a look, and shrugged indifferently. "He's got two kids and a wife with him. In a place like this he'll be lucky if he has time enough to remember what *he* does, much less worry about anyone else's professional preferences. Why don't you relax, doc? If I can do it, you sure can. We'll be swimming in a sea of suspicion and paranoia soon enough, as soon as we get near SICK's research facility." He took a larger bite of his egg, dumped enough salt on it to make Ingrid wince, and waved the half-demolished hen fruit in her direction. However, she noticed, he did lower his voice somewhat.

"Speaking of which, I'm wondering if maybe we shouldn't glom another biosurge before starting our final push north."

Her eyes widened slightly as she laid the last of the toast aside. "Another manip? Oh, no, I'm done with that, Whispr!"

He grinned challengingly. "You're just not used to them, that's all."

"And I have no intention of becoming used to them. I barely recognize myself anymore as it is."

"The biosurges have hardly touched you, doc. You're not even close to becoming a Meld. You barely qualify as a maniped Natural. It doesn't have to be anything elaborate. No collagen this time. Just the hair and maybe some putty work around the obicularus orbits. Narrow 'em down for a bit." He eyed her expectantly.

"You said the last manip was a good enough change to my appearance for the near future," she protested.

"And it is. But remember, you brought me along for my advice. So I'm giving it. We should change our appearance again while we still have the time and opportunity."

She nodded westward, back in the direction they had come, back toward Worcester. "I'm not letting anyone near my face who hails from a town with fewer inhabitants than the typical Savannah suburb."

"For an accomplished physician you're mighty disparaging of your foreign colleagues."

"I am when I don't know much about the colleague, let alone the country where he or she works." She shook her head. "Short of forestalling imminent death, this is the face and body I'm going home with."

"Assuming we get home," he murmured.

"What was that?" She eyed him sharply.

"Nothing, nothing. Just being my usual upbeat self." He waved at the rest of the dining area. "It's getting late in the morning for a game drive. You can tell because pretty much everyone else has already left." He pushed back from the table. As he did so the linen napkin that had been covering his lap was retracted into the table's central support pillar. It emerged a moment later stripped of organic debris and thoroughly sanitized by the u/v unit built into the center column, awaiting the next diner.

Though they could have stocked up for the forthcoming long road journey upon their return to the lodge, that evening Whispr convinced her to do so now. With everyone else out enjoying the scenery and looking for animals, the Preserve's food shop was devoid of customers. After neatly piling their purchases in the 4×4's trunk and activating its refrigerator, they were preparing to leave the compound when Ingrid suddenly began screaming.

"STOP, WHISPR, STOP!"

Startled, he slammed on the brakes with enough force to recharge half the regenerative system in one blow. "What, what is it, what's wrong?"

"Aren't they *precious*? Stop the car."

The times of day when most of the Preserve's visitors were out on game drives was when the lodge and park staff got most of their real work done. Three of them had been escorting a cart across the dirt-covered space between buildings when Ingrid had let out her frantic cry. She was out of the 4×4 and running toward the trio of employees before Whispr could decide whether to follow, get out himself, or drive on. He ended up pulling over and off the main driveway. After parking and securing the vehicle he followed in her wake, albeit with considerably less fervor.

The brace of kittens that the veterinarian and his assistants were transporting in the cart were certainly cute, he had to admit. But then all kittens were cute. It was a highly evolved survival trait denied to most humans. He himself was no stranger to cute. A universally popular meld, it was on ample display everywhere in Greater Savannah. The reclusive, late, and not especially lamented Yabby Wizwang had partaken of it to a large extent himself. As Whispr trailed behind his companion, who was now gushing like a schoolgirl, he had to admit that the pale, mewing, big-eyed kittens were cute even if they sported knives in their upper jaws.

The vet let her pick up one of the month-old sabertooths. Fussing and nuzzling, oblivious to Whispr's unconcealed unease, she cooed baby talk to the female cub.

"Who's a cutesy wuzzums, hmm? Who's a little stuffy-wuffy little furball?"

It yowled and swiped at her with downsized paws and tiny claws that would one day be powerful enough to fell a full-grown auroch with one blow. The camouflaging spots that covered its fur could not detract from the small curved, serrated blades that already thrust downward from its upper jaw. She was careful to avoid them as she petted and tickled and caressed.

This was the woman who hoped to infiltrate SICK's most secrecy-shrouded research center? This was the person to whose untried deceptive skills he was going to entrust his life? Whispr stood it as long as he could before dragging her away.

"But they're just so *darling*," Dr. Ingrid Seastrom burbled as her peevish companion urged her back toward their parked rental vehicle. She gazed longingly back toward the veterinarian and his trio of precious charges.

Other than being pitched an octave lower, Whispr decided that kittenish meows revived from the Pleistocene sounded little different from those he had encountered numerous times while slinking through the back narrows of Greater Savannah.

"Maybe they're darling to a dentist." He waited for the door to open automatically to receive the passenger and made sure she was inside before walking around the front of the 4×4 to resume his own seat. The rental started up smoothly and he sent it cruising at an accelerated pace toward the main gate. "The rest of us need to watch out. I've been scratched up pretty good by an ordinary alley cat. I'd hate to think what one of your darlings could do if it put its stuffy-wuffy little killer mind to it."

Swiveling the passenger seat so that she could glare at him without having to turn her head, she replied coldly, "You just don't want to have anything to do with anything soft or tender or gentle or loving. Do you, Whispr?"

He didn't look over at her, concentrating on the route ahead as they approached the first gate. "Excuse the hell out of me, doc, if I'm just focused on staying alive." Responding to their paid identification the high inner barrier opened to let them out. He pulled forward and waited for it to close behind them. Once it had shut, the outer gate began to slide aside.

"As for the abstract known as 'loving,' that particular contrary bitch and I got a divorce a long time ago. If it explains anything, she got my soul in the settlement."

She pondered his metaphor as they drove past the outer gate and once again found themselves alone in the rocky vastness that was Sanbona. But she didn't speak to him again for quite a while.

The road quickly became a track, giving her reason to be grateful that her dour companion had shown the foresight back in Cape Town to insist on renting a vehicle that was capable of traveling off-road. A floater would have been even better, of course, but the need to constantly refuel it prohibited the use of such vehicles for private travel. Unlike easily recharged roadsters, scoots, trucks, and buses, floaters ran on hydrogen. Taking in the vast, stony landscape before them and remembering the maps of the region she doubted there was a hydrofuel station to be found anywhere between the principal towns of Worcester and Barrydale. If there was one anywhere in the park it was doubtless reserved for the use of vehicles flown by the Preserve's rangers.

This would not affect them or their trip. Though they planned to take a roundabout route to their eventual northern destination, in the absence of a proper recharge station they could always top up the 4×4 at a private residence.

Despite her impatience to leave the Preserve behind and resume that journey she made herself relax and enjoy the scenery. Whispr's adolescent excitement was nothing if not contagious, and she had to admit that seeing so many animals, both resurrected and contemporary, was worth putting aside her obsession with the mysterious thread for at least a day or two.

One thing she didn't worry about was the safety of that sliver of strange metal which had kindled their journey. As it had ever since they had left Miavana it rode securely in her brassiere. Whispr's occasional and persistent requests that he be allowed to return it to the secret compartment located in one of his shoes were denied. As day after day passed in the company of her slender companion she had come to trust him more and more—but not to the extent of trusting him with everything. And certainly not with the irreplaceable thread.

They were not alone on the track that followed the river deeper into the Preserve. While it was not the high season at Sanbona it was still a popular destination for both local visitors and those from overseas. Since at this time of year the animals tended to congregate near the water, so did the tourists. There was enough room for everyone and it was far from crowded, but the sense of isolation she and Whispr had first encountered upon entering the Preserve was absent. As they came across other private vehicles and Preserve tour buses she realized how lucky they had been to have encountered the *Smilodons* and their prey without anyone else around.

Whispr badly wanted to go off-road and get away from other visitors. It was perfectly safe, he reminded her. The GPS apps in their own personal comm units as well as the one in the 4×4 would show their location at all times, and complete track and trail maps were among the data that had been downloaded when they had entered the Preserve. It was impossible for them to get lost, he insisted. His confidence and enthusiasm only partly mitigated Ingrid's concerns.

"What if we have mechanical trouble?" Gesturing toward the curved windshield she indicated their raw, unpopulated surroundings. "This isn't Cape Town. It isn't even Worcester. It's no place to break down, Whispr. Or have you forgotten about the predators we nearly collided with on our way in?"

"Just the opposite," he shot back, "I'm looking forward to seeing more of them." He spoke as if he was chiding an innocent child. "What are you so worried about? We've got three comm units; yours, mine, and the one in the rental's emergency drawer. We run into any trouble and one call brings a ranger in a Preserve floater out to us in five minutes."

She was gazing out the passenger-side window at the rugged scenery. "One of those sabertooths we saw could kill us in five seconds."

"Sure it could," he agreed readily. "All it would have to do is recognize that the car contains actual food, which goes against everything I've been reading about big cats, and then make the decision to chew through the composite roof or a door, which I bet would also go against all its predatory instincts."

The ongoing argument formed a backdrop to sightseeing as they trundled along the track that paralleled the south side of the river. The more distance they put between themselves and the lodge, the fewer tourists they encountered and the less anxious became Ingrid's protestations.

The mammoths Whispr hoped to see continued to prove elusive. As Ingrid pointed out when her companion again bemoaned the beasts' absence, the prevailing temperature at Sanbona was hardly arctic, much less Ice Age.

They did come across half-a-dozen mastodons browsing contentedly alongside their modern African cousins. Three-meter-long piglike *Toxodon* cropped the soft growths right at the water's edge, their basso grunts falling halfway between that of swine and hippo. Individual family groups of placid *Hipparion* grazed in the midst of a zebra herd while a single hulking bull *Elasmotherium* cropped grass in the shade of the tallest trees, the base of its conical two-meter-long horn covering nearly the entire upper part of its skull.

Except for its size it was almost impossible to tell the formerly extinct *Metridiochoerus* from the other warthogs that clustered for protection in its impressive shadow. Even more imposing than the mastodons was a herd of *Titanotylopus*. Nearly four meters tall, the giant camels plucked at leaves too high for any other browser to reach save the occasional giraffe. Formerly extinct antelopes mingled freely with gemsbok, bushbuck, steenbok, hartebeest, and eland.

Neither Ingrid nor Whispr being much of a paleontologist, the names and identifying details of the contemporary as well as resurrected mammals had to be supplied by the park guide app that had been entered into their comm units when they had first entered the Preserve. Activating the add-in and aiming the pickup lens of either device at any animal, plant, or geological formation would cause it to bring up an extensive description of the subject followed by a request for questions. The utterly enthralled Whispr seemed to have an endless supply of the latter.

Good, Ingrid thought to herself each time he excitedly queried his unit. Let him get his fill of the wildlife he came to see. Then maybe he would be able to focus entirely on the business they had come for. As their vehicle wound its way ever deeper into the Preserve she found herself wondering what her friends back home must be thinking. It wasn't like her to take off on a spur-of-the-moment trip, though if questioned every one of them would have agreed that she certainly deserved the vacation.

Turning the 4×4's wheel hard to the left Whispr headed off the main track and down a barely visible trail. Pausing in her sustained effort to wreak havoc on the contents of a box of cookies whose chocolate chips melted only when they came in contact with the heat and moisture found in a human mouth, she eyed him sharply.

"Where the hell do you think you're going?"

"Away from the river." His eyes remained focused straight ahead except for the occasional glance at the console readout that showed their constantly shifting position. "Away from people. Away from tourists."

Her heart beat a little faster. "I thought we were supposed to be trying to convey the impression that we *are* tourists."

"You know what I mean. There's no reason to linger in the vicinity of all these other visitors."

She used a cookie to gesture back the way they had come. "Maybe they're all back there, tour buses included, because that's where the animal action is."

"Maybe they're all there," he countered impatiently, "because people are sheep and follow each other blindly, and the tour buses are there because it's an easy drive back to camp that won't damage their precious expensive undercarriages."

Seeing she wasn't going to get anywhere with logic she concentrated on enjoying the cookies and said nothing further. The only way he was going to be satisfied was if she let him work out his adolescent fantasies. As long as they were back in camp by dark she supposed it didn't matter which way they went.

They drove most of the rest of the day without seeing anything but a few birds and small rodents, all of them contemporaneous, when she finally decided the time had come to insist that they start to retrace their route and head for the lodge. He would have complied except that on rounding a hillock composed of smooth granite boulders they chanced upon a herd of glyptodonts. Four meters long from head to macelike tail, the giant relatives of the modern armadillo were peacefully munching their way through a patch of wildflowers that bordered a shallow, shaded pool. As if the presence of the armored herbivores wasn't enough, Whispr excitedly pointed out a family of big cats that was resting nearby and enjoying the cool in the shade of the rocks.

"Look—more sabertooths!"

Ingrid had her comm unit out and aimed and was studying the readout. "They're *Homotherium*, not *Smilodon*. More properly called scimitar-tooths because the killing canines have a more pronounced backward curve." Lowering the comm unit she studied the dozing carnivores. "Interesting that the fur of the *Smilodons* was patterned like leopards but these are tawny and smooth like lions." She checked her unit again. "The guide says that's because the sabertooths are ambush hunters and scimitar-tooths are distance runners."

"There are cubs," her indulgent companion pointed out teasingly.

That revelation rendered moot any further immediate interest in scientific nomenclature on Ingrid's part. While the male and female slept, their trio of cubs cavorted in the grass, rolling and wrestling and play-fighting like typical kittens. Bored, two of them charged and challenged a juvenile glyptodont that had strayed slightly away from the rest of the slow-moving herd. It responded by hunkering down and retracting its head into its huge cauldronlike armored shell. Though the spikes at the tip of its clublike tail had yet to fully mature, they were still pronounced enough to break a cub's leg—or its skull—should one of the juvenile predators come too close.

Taking note of the increasingly dangerous play-hunting the female *Homotherium* lifted her head, growled warningly, and yawned to expose her huge serrated fangs. The cubs immediately came scrambling back to her.

The two Namericans stayed to watch until a beep from the guide declared even more insistently than Ingrid that it was time to be on their way. Automatically monitoring the time while calculating their position relative to the best available route it was reminding them that they now needed to start back to camp lest they be caught outside the fenced perimeter after sundown. Should they fail to make it back before dark the helpful guide app would automatically issue and record the appropriate heavy fine as well as alerting the park rangers to their prohibited position.

Drawing the interest of local authorities to their altered identities being the last thing Ingrid and Whispr wanted, they hurried to retrace their route. This time it was the doctor who was reluctant to leave. She could have remained parked in one place and watched the *Homotherium* family all evening. Even while the pride was asleep and motionless she found it hard to pull her gaze away from their exquisitely deadly forms.

"Well," Whispr murmured as the 4×4 struggled to cope with the difficult, out-of-the-way trail he had chosen, "was it worth the detour away from the river or not?"

She offered a histrionic bow in his direction. "I concede the astuteness of your decision," she confessed. "I guess I should know by now to trust you when it comes to finding our way around new places. My mistake. I thought your expertise only extended to areas that were urbanized."

"Getting off the beaten path was only common sense." Never a believer in false modesty, he readily accepted her compliment. "People like privacy, so do most animals. I figured that if we were going to see anything unique we had to get away from everybody else. Remember, when we ran into the *Smilodons* there was no one else around." He went silent for a moment, thinking. "I wonder where they keep the botched resurrections?"

She frowned. "'Botched'?"

"Yeah." He slowed down as their vehicle struggled to negotiate a steep slope. In the absence of a guide strip running down the center of the roadway the 4×4's built-in sensors strove to assist the driver by delivering power to the wheels in proportion to their respective position on the ground. "Surely not every one is successful. It's just like with human melding. Sometimes things don't turn out the way you expect. Arms and legs, for example. Or faces. It's gotta be the same with these animals."

She called up memories of the *Homotherium* cubs and of the sabertooth kits she had played with earlier. Whispr was doubtless right, she knew. Resurrection melding was an incredibly complex enterprise. It was absurd to think there wouldn't be any failures along the way. She tried to envision the cubs she had seen with distorted bodies and misshapen skulls, with eyes missing or legs twisted and crippled. Those resurrection melds wouldn't be on show in a place like Sanbona. And restorative, corrective melding was too much trouble and too expensive to bother with when newer, better specimens were always coming online. Instead of being treated, failures and mistakes would be—disposed of.

Definitely it was time for them to be on their way. Banishing the troubling images from her mind she sank deeper into the self-adjusting comfort of the vehicle's passenger seat.

THAT EVENING SHE ORDERED a second helping from the menu in the lodge cafeteria. The combination of the day's game drives, the brisk weather, and the excitement of not one but several extraordinary animal encounters had combined to give her an appetite that would have startled her friends back home. Whispr, naturally, was already more than sated by the meager amount of food he had consumed. Her continuing craving in the face of his contentment found her feeling slightly embarrassed. That did not prevent her from reordering, however.

As she waited for the food she had ordered to arrive via the delivery conduit that ran beneath the cafeteria floor and then rose through the gap in the center of the table, she had to listen to him plead for yet one more game drive tomorrow before they left the Preserve behind.

"Haven't you seen enough animals, both resurrected and contemporary, to last you a lifetime?"

"C'mon, doc." He smiled encouragingly. "You can't tell me you haven't enjoyed this as much as I have."

"I won't deny that it's been an enjoyable as well as necessary diversion." In the continuing absence of solid food she sipped steadily at her self-chilling glass of Roiboos iced tea. "But we didn't come here to play tourist. Only to prove to anyone who might be watching that that's what we are. Now we've done that." Her right hand passed meaningfully over the right side of her chest. Safe within the special compartment in her brassiere was the thread-holding capsule that literally never left her side. "It's time to move on."

"I know, I know. I'm not disputing that. And you've fulfilled this part of the bargain. I'm just saying that as long as we're leaving tomorrow morning we might as well see as much as we can on our way out." Removing his comm unit he inscribed instructions across the face until the device's tiny integrated projector generated a map of the Preserve above the dining table. With a forefinger that bordered on skeletal he traced a path through the glowing diagram. "Look. Instead of just retracing our steps we can head north. There's a park track that follows the Touws River northwest all the way to a service entrance near the N1."

She peered into the three-dimensional chart. Reaching out, she manipulated details with her fingers in order to study Whispr's proposal from as many angles as possible. Finally withdrawing her hand she indicated the vast area he had chosen to isolate.

"There's nothing up that way, Whispr. No park facilities, no proper roads, nothing for hundreds of square kilometers."

"I know." With a dismissive flick of one finger the glowing map vanished. "That's the point. The animals up there will be less used to tourists. There should be more of them, too. According to the guide app the central Touws River region is full of them. Except for flyovers not too many visitors get up that way."

Her second helping arrived. As she arranged it in front of her and began to eat she contemplated him over her fork. "Why do you suppose that is?" she wondered drily. "Could it be because there are no Preserve facilities and nothing for hundreds of square kilometers?"

"Please, doc. Ingrid. It's the chance of a lifetime. We both know neither of us is likely to ever get back this way. Except for possible floater flyovers we should have the region all to ourselves. There's no camping allowed in the Preserve so only guided tours get up that way. Individual vehicles can't get up there and back to camp in time to make the evening curfew. But we won't get caught out after dark because we'll be leaving the park via the little-used north gate. It'll just be us and the mammoths," he finished proudly.

"Mastodons," she corrected him. As she chewed reflectively on her second lightly breaded tenderloin of gemsbok she tried to ignore his imploring expression. It would help his cause, she thought to herself, if at such moments he didn't look so much like the painting by Munch. Unable to withstand his pleading, she finally gave in.

"Well," she conceded reluctantly, "at least we'll be heading north."

She feared the resulting cheek-to-cheek grin might split his gaunt visage.

"Thanks, doc! It's the last request I'll make on this trip."

"No it isn't," she replied confidently, "but we'll do it your way anyway." She jabbed her greasy fork in his direction. "You'd better make sure our rental is in perfect condition before we leave in the morning. I don't want to get stuck out there, have to call for help, and answer the inevitable awkward questions."

"I'll check everything out, don't worry." His boyish enthusiasm was unrestrained.

It was remarkable, she reflected, how much he had emerged from his self-imposed protective shell since their arrival in Southern Africa. The change of venue, not to mention continent, had done wonders for his personality. His brooding paranoia and interminable sarcasm had given way to a wary acceptance of the freedom they presently enjoyed and to a delight in ordinary everyday things that was a far cry from the hunted, apprehensive creature from whose back she had removed police traktacs in her office. It was amazing the effect a little wildlife viewing could have on a career urban malefactor. That, and being free of police surveillance.

She dug deeper into her second helping. All he was asking for, really, was part of one more day. She figured she owed him that much, considering that once they reached the Orange River and started into the Namib their lives would be seriously at risk. If anything—happened—at least she would know that she had been more than fair with her street-wise partner.

We're really going to do this, she found herself thinking. Try to sneak into one of SICK's most restricted research facilities. It was not too late to call it all off, she knew. Go back home, reconnect with her patients and her friends, pretend this was what until now it largely had been: nothing but a vacation, a break from routine, a getaway from everyday life. It would be easy enough to do. She could turn the mysterious thread over to one or more of her colleagues better equipped to study its baffling physical properties. Or she could hand it in to the government.

Unless, of course, the government had something to do with what was going on. In which case nothing more would be heard of what might be on the thread or the inexplicable metastable metallic hydrogen of which it was made. She could go on with her life as if nothing had happened.

Except—there was the less easily forgettable matter of the quantum entangled MSMH nanoscale implant she had removed from the head of fifteen-year-old Cara Jean Gibson back in Savannah, and the subsequent revelation that comparable devices had been found in the skulls of other adolescents throughout the world who had likewise required reworking of their bad melds. As a physician, that was knowledge she could not so easily put aside. Someone, some company, some organization, or some government somewhere was up to something. She would not be able to sleep comfortably until, like any good scientist, she found out the how and why of it.

Being the only place within the Preserve to get a cooked meal, even in the off-season the spacious cafeteria was busy at dinnertime. Intent on working out their itinerary for tomorrow the two visitors from Namerica paid little attention to their fellow diners. They ignored the nattering couple who occupied the table off to one side and paid no attention to the local family and its quartet of noisy children who occupied the other. They certainly did not inspect the room for interesting faces or visitors. Even the pair of Martian couples seated near the exit failed to attract any interest.

They certainly did not notice the little old man who sat off in one crowded corner, his presence shielded from them by a number of other talkative diners, and who only occasionally and surreptitiously looked up from his simple meal to gaze fixedly in their direction.

11

As it inevitably did, everything had fallen into place. This was not the result of accident or of luck, Molé knew. Accidents befell those who made mistakes and luck is an illusion loved by the incompetent. Everything he had achieved in his life, the sum total of his success, could ultimately be put down to nothing more mysterious than careful planning and hard work.

For example, he might never have found the thieving doctor and her indigent companion had he not maintained a regular watch on the competition. With the resources at his command this was not difficult to do, but many in his position and profession would not have bothered, choosing to rely instead solely on their own instincts and expertise to find their quarry. Molé wholeheartedly believed in accepting assistance wherever and whenever it could be obtained, be it voluntary or otherwise.

So when he had been informed of the futile attempt on the part of another organization's hirelings to penetrate the security of a local female witch doctor, he had followed up on it as methodically as he had dozens of other potentially relevant reports. All the others had been dross. But someone like himself needed to strike gold only once. In addition to reporting on the break-in, the local contact had also mentioned the earlier presence at the same sangoma's residence of two foreigners; one a near-Natural female, the other a lanky male Meld.

A broad-spectrum hack of every transportation outlet south of the Limpopo had produced supposedly private images of a traveling couple who had rented an off-roadster. Obtaining the vehicle's ident allowed him, with his sophisticated knowledge and experience of tracking, to further penetrate the rental company's network and obtain the broadcast code for the rented vehicle's emergency locator beacon. Implanted in the body of the 4×4 to counter theft and to enable it to be found in the event of an emergency, it would allow a police floater to track the vehicle anywhere it went. Equipped with an impressive assortment of illegal software, Molé had no trouble tracing the rental's signal himself.

More than a little to his surprise it had led him here, to this wild and expansive nature preserve. But then, the presence of his quarry in South Africa was itself a surprise. What were they doing here, so far from Namerica? The connection to the thread's rightful owner, the SAEC, naturally sprang to mind. But if they wanted to sell it back to its rightful owners there was no need to travel in person to the location of that powerful politico-economic conglomerate. Such a purely commercial transaction could have been carried out without leaving the shores of Namerica, or for that matter the doctor's home city of Savannah. She would have been far more secure exchanging sensitive communications and propounding industrial blackmail from there. Traveling to the SAEC's heartland exposed her to any number of dangers she would not have faced back home.

In the course of their single face-to-face confrontation she had struck him as stubborn but not particularly brave. Why then had she chosen to make this long, tiring journey, with all its attendant risks? Was it possible she knew something he did not? It was not unusual for Molé's employers to withhold sensitive commercial information from him. He did not mind. It was not his place to question why he was being asked to interdict specific individuals or recover certain items. A good house painter did not question why a homeowner chose chartreuse and puce for their color scheme. He simply brought out his sprayer and mixed up the requested combination.

Though he could not prove it, he suspected that the scrawny Meld she was traveling with might have something to do with their journeying to Southern Africa. Why an educated, respected member of the medical community like Dr. Ingrid Seastrom should be traveling in the company of an insolvent oaf like this Whispr-Kowalski person was a conundrum he had yet to unravel. It was not critical that he learn the reason, of course. Reasons were not his concern. His trade lay in recovery. While it would be nice to know why his quarry had come all this way, it was not necessary to the successful resolution of his task. Neither was killing them both.

However, while killing was not necessary, it was anticipated. This odd couple had caused him a good deal more trouble than he had expected and far too much of his time. He was an old man and had few lazy afternoons to spare. Additionally, the whole Miavana fiasco had made him look bad. This made him angry. Very angry.

Silently and out of sight of any of the other prattling diners he slipped a metal knife off the tabletop and bent it between two fingers. The strain helped to mitigate some of the annoyance he felt whenever he had occasion to think back to the botched confrontation in the Everglades. That should have been the end of this particular job. He should have finished it then and there and recovered his employers' property. Instead he found himself here, halfway around the world, in the heartland of the very concern that had employed him, chasing down two mismatched urban brigands.

That chase would soon be over. The realization was comforting. He made himself calm down, though anyone who had been watching him would have detected no change whatsoever in his outward demeanor. There would be no more slipups, no more mistakes, no more accidents. There was no meddlesome Alligator Man to come to their rescue this time, no pre-adolescent Meld master of intrusive stinging insects. Unaware they had been located, his quarry would be less on guard.

Observing them from across the dining room, Molé was not sure the good doctor was ever on guard. Perhaps that was why she had chosen to travel with the Meld. The stick-man was street-wise — he had already proven that. But at base he was an amateur now operating in the world of sophisticated international industry, a struggling sardine who had voluntarily squeezed his way into a shark tank. Just look at them, Molé told himself: the innocent and the overconfident. It was a miracle they had managed to evade him this long.

Now that he had found them again he was in no rush to end it. The termination must be carried out out of sight of any possible witnesses, if only because someone was bound to wonder at and follow up on the disappearance of a distinguished Namerican doctor. In his mind Molé had already made the necessary preparations. Having the luxury of a personal vehicle had allowed him to purchase and bring along a portable but commercial-strength biltong maker. Designed for turning select cuts of game meat into the local equivalent of jerky, it would reduce chunks of any dead protein to desiccated strips of dried meat tough enough to shingle a roof. Left exposed, this edible but utterly unidentifiable organic residue would attract scavengers who would finish the job. It was infinitely more thorough than burying a victim.

And besides, he was curious about the taste.

Unaware that they were less than a day away from their own deaths, his targets were finishing up their dinner. They had not so much as glanced in his direction. This ability to disappear into a crowd was one of the secrets of his success and his survival. Long-lived assassins were not made of massive muscle and brute force. Anonymity was not only a survival trait: as practiced by a professional like Molé it bordered on art. The thickly hewn (and often thick-headed) bodyguards and overmuscled minor athletes women flocked to and other men envied were quickly identified and easily cut down by their enemies. The smallest gun is more powerful than the biggest biceps.

He had seen some of them, employed by those who could afford no better. They would smile and make jokes at his expense behind his back. And it was true. They could boast of being younger, more muscular, more attractive. Whereas all poor Napun Molé could lay claim to was a continuing and comfortable existence.

He had come to the conclusion long ago that in place of good looks and friendship it was better to be able to buy women and be feared by other men.

He could have finished it that night. There was no need to wait for morning. Even a wary street slug like the Meld Whispr would not wake to Molé's presence as the hunter slipped noiselessly into their rooms. A single quick, kitten-paw slash of the knife he favored, the other hand over nose and mouth to stifle any outcry, and it would all be over in minutes. He could be on his way back to Cape Town before midnight.

Other than briefly contemplating the fanciful melodrama he

did not for a second consider actually carrying out such a scenario. While the actual killing would be quick and easy, the aftermath would take time. Terminating quarry while they slept in their beds was far too messy, too primitive, and downright insulting to someone of his skill. Also, there would be no biltong.

The mismatched couple who were the object of his professional attention had arrived in a rented vehicle; they would surely depart in one. The country surrounding the Preserve was nearly as empty as the park itself, its roadways almost as isolated and little traveled. He would follow them at a discreet distance, select an appropriate place, stop their vehicle, and then put a stop to them.

But first he would magnanimously offer to trade their lives for the stolen thread. Once his employers' property was safely in his possession he would then embark on a bit of local food preparation. This experiment in indigenous cuisine would be followed by a leisurely drive back to Cape Town and then a well-deserved rest, perhaps at one of the numerous local wine-country spas.

Knowing anything about Napun Molé and what he did for a living, what any other person would doubtless have found most remarkable about the stone-cold old executioner was how quickly and easily he could fall every night into a deep and completely relaxed sleep.

WHEN MORNING CAME, IT WAS plain that they were going to make it easy for him.

It was almost as if, he thought as he watched his quarry's rented vehicle pass through the double gate in the dusty wake of one of the big tour buses, that feeling guilty, a capricious Fate had decided the time had come to compensate him for all the unforeseen difficulties and delays he had been forced to deal with in the course of this particular assignment. Because as soon as it was outside the camp's security perimeter the 4×4 he was tracking turned right toward the interior of the Preserve instead of left along the track that would take it to the park exit. His victims were going on another game drive, or a picnic. Why they had chosen to drive deeper into the Preserve instead of leaving it did not matter. The end would be the same.

As if that was not enough they had obligingly checked out that morning, a fact he had already quickly and easily confirmed. According to the lodge's electronic register they had left no forwarding information or travel plans, had packed and taken all their belongings along with them, and to all intents and purposes appeared set on enjoying one more morning or day in the Preserve before continuing on their way.

It was most thoughtful of them, Molé mused with satisfaction as he prepared to follow in his own vehicle. He must remember to thank them before he killed them.

DRIVING DOWN THE LEAST-FREQUENTED off-road track that led northwest, Whispr settled in behind the wheel and was soon searching for animals. It quickly became evident that the farther they got from the tributary of the Kakoenshook River, the fewer and farther between the residents of Sanbona became. He resigned himself to the realization that they were unlikely to encounter larger animal groups again until they reached the Touws itself.

Not that the drive was entirely devoid of sightings. Grinding through a series of granite outcroppings they came upon a herd of grazing impala. Startled by the 4×4's silent arrival they exploded away in all directions, like so many bubbles from the mouth of a well-shaken bottle of champagne. There were also numerous colorful birds, from bee-eaters to rollers. A bonus appeared in the form of a family group of *Hipparion*. Emitting toylike whinnies, the partially striped pony-sized early horses bolted from the vehicle's approach like carvings escaping a carousel. But unlike on the previous day no mastodons, no rhinos, no resurrected megafauna crossed the car's path.

Looking out the open window Ingrid inhaled deeply of their rugged, rocky surroundings. The odors that clung to the passing terrain were vibrantly different from those back home. Savannah's air was loamy, damp, rich with the aromatic blend of healthy and decaying vegetation. Sanbona was dry but not a desert; typically Karoo. Possessed of a greater odiferous clarity because they were not overwhelmed by humidity, its fragrances were sharper and more immediately distinctive. She smelled grass shot through with flickers of musk, the tang of dry wood, thick essence of exotic scat, each one able to tickle the sense of smell in ways more subtle and far different from their southeastern Namerican counterparts. Though all wine to her senses, it was like switching in midmeal from shiraz to chardonnay.

When she mentioned it to Whispr there was little appreciation in his brusque reply.

"I came to see animals. Not parse stinks."

Her response was a scold. "You've seen plenty of animals. Why not expand your horizons, open yourself to some new sensations?" She was startled at how at ease she was, both with the bumpy trek and her freely offered criticisms. She had settled completely into a travel mode that was very different from sitting on the beach at Dubaia sipping margaritas with friends from her tower. A less civilized mode to be sure, yet somehow far more fulfilling.

"Don't be in such a hurry," he muttered. "We'll be exposed to plenty of 'new sensations' when we try to get past SICK security." He continued to scan the hilly horizon for signs of resurrected ungulates.

She sighed. "I guess your paranoia will never leave you long enough to let you enjoy life, Whispr."

He looked over at her. "I enjoy life, doc. Most of all, I enjoy having it. *Staying* alive is what matters. Everything else, including 'enjoying' it, is frosting. Some people don't think they're 'living' unless they have a lot of frosting. Me, I'm content with the cake."

She teased him. "But if you weren't interested in the frosting you wouldn't be here now, with me, trying to find out what's on the thread and if it's worth anything."

He refocused his full attention on his driving. "Hard to win an argument with a doctor, since they know everything, so I guess I'll shut up."

"You know," she murmured thoughtfully, "I keep thinking about the signal the thread puts out. You would think that whoever wants it back would be able to trace it."

He started slightly. He'd nearly forgotten about the minuscule transmission. "Didn't we decide that its signal is almost insubstantial? That it would take specially tuned equipment to pick up something so slight?" He found himself eyeing the landscape with fresh uncertainly. "I was having a pretty good time. Why did you have to go and remind me of that?"

"Sorry." Her smile was apologetic. "It just struck me. I suppose the answer to my own question is that the signal's not strong enough to be picked up at any distance. If it was, surely the thread's owners or manufacturers would have confronted us by now."

"Yeah." The tension eased out of him. "Yeah, that makes sense. But if it can only be picked up at such extremely short range, then what's the point of it?"

"I don't know. Maybe we'll find out when we get to Nerens." As she sat up a little straighter in the seat the responsive back struggled to conform to her new posture. "Are you sure you know where you're going?"

"I don't have a clue where I'm going," he replied cheerfully, "but the guide app does." He indicated the small, brightly colored projection that was hovering in the air midwindshield. Continuously updated and renewed from the downloaded material in his comm unit, it was watching over their progress as surely as any Preserve ranger. To reassure her he activated the 4×4's vorec. They were immediately enveloped by the quietly confident tones of a pleasant male voice with a scratchy Khoi accent.

"You are approaching the Umbiqui Hills. The track you are on will angle to the left approximately fifteen degrees and begin to descend a slight slope. In five minutes you will come to what appears to be a wide river. Do not be alarmed. This is not a river but a seasonal stream. Today's hydrologic forecast indicates that at the preferred point of crossing its depth should vary from two to five centimeters. As the vehicle in which I am presently functional is capable of safely fording active streams up to a meter in depth there is no reason to slow your progress. You have reached the turn. Proceed at a speed of no more than twenty-five kilometers an hour until you reach the crossing. At that point you will be ready to..."

Reaching over, Ingrid switched off the vorec. "Okay, okay, I'll quit worrying about where we're going, if not when we're going to get there." A quick look showed that the 4×4's battery pack still held nearly a full charge, with the vehicle's power supply constantly being topped up by its amorphous solar coating. Even if night suddenly descended they would have more than enough power to reach the N1.

As they rolled down the gentle slope whose location the guide app had accurately predicted she studied the surrounding landscape. This was truly rough country. "The Little Karoo," the maps called it. Sanbona Preserve occupied a good portion of the indicated region, an area from which small outposts and private homes had long ago been removed. All the better to give saved and resurrected animals adequate room in which to roam, she knew.

Why couldn't she just relax completely? As Whispr had pointed out with bothersome frequency they would be putting their lives on the line soon enough. In contrast there was nothing to threaten them here, far from potentially dangerous Cape Town. Big carnivores like *Smilodon* or modern lions would never attack a vehicle because it neither smelled nor looked nor acted like their normal prey. They would regard anyone and anything inside as part of the machine. She could and should consider herself safe and still on "vacation" at least until they crossed the Orange River.

Whispr peered sideways at the doctor as Ingrid leaned back into the responsive comfort of the passenger seat. Why couldn't he have fallen for someone in his own social, financial, and educational league? he reproached himself. She was too rich for him, too smart, too attractive. Not merely out of his league but off his planet. She had closed her eyes and finally seemed to be taking it easy.

He tried to keep his eyes on the dirt track ahead, but they kept darting back to the woman napping beside him. It wasn't enough that she was a respected and successful physician, he told himself. Oh, no. On top of that she had to have recently melded curves that now emulated the surrounding topography. Curves that thanks to the motion imparted by the 4×4 were tantalizingly less inert than the stony foothills through which they had begun to climb.

If she caught him staring at her she would freeze up. If he jerked around sharply from staring at her he would sprain his neck. He almost forgot that he was supposed to be looking for animals. Resolutely he turned his attention back to the passing countryside. A couple of *Osteoborus* went trotting by; canine in shape but with far more powerful jaws. A line of gemsbok crested a nearby ridge, strung out like spiky beads on a string of broken granite. A shape emerged, vanished, and emerged again behind them. . . .

It was not organic.

He sat up straight in the driver's seat and snapped a couple of verbal commands. The image in the 4×4's rear-facing pickup telescoped, tightened, and sharpened focus. For a moment he thought he had imagined what he had seen. For an instant he hoped that he had.

Hearing him voicing commands, Ingrid blinked and yawned as she looked over at him. Lulled by the clear air, the warm morning, and the gently cushioned rocking motion of the rental she had nearly fallen completely asleep.

"Something interesting behind us? Don't tell me we're being followed by a predator or something?"

Whispr divided his time between the rough track ahead and the scene to the rear. "Can't tell for sure yet. I only saw it once, and I'm not positive about what I saw."

She was interested now. "So it is a predator? What kind? Felid, canid, ursinoid—what?"

"The worst kind. Simian."

She sat up fast at that, turning in her seat to look back the way they had come. The view to the rear was very similar to what could be seen directly ahead: broken rock, big glacier-polished boulders, scrub, small trees, the occasional tiny furred shape rocketing between patches of cover. Certainly nothing to set off any alarms. She peered harder.

"I don't see anything."

"Good." Wiry fingers gripped the 4×4's wheel tightly. Had it been an illusion? A mirage? Hard to be certain of anything glimpsed to the rear of a moving vehicle jouncing its way through a landscape fraught with fanciful shapes. "Let's keep it that way."

MOLÉ MADE CERTAIN TO KEEP well back of his quarry's vehicle. There was no rush. He was enjoying the sights himself and in no hurry to commit murder. There was always time to commit murder. The abundance of remarkable creatures he had been privileged to see so far this morning were proving to be an unexpected side benefit of his task. Knowing that he might never come this way again and that there was no need to expend energy in the service of unnecessary haste, he had decided to wait to conclude the exercise until he and his target were in as isolated a part of the Preserve as possible. That was not yet. The Touws River still lay in front of them.

He did not look upon his decision to grant the condemned another hour or so of life as playing God. He was delaying for his own gratification, not for them. Certainly he appreciated their choice of this morning's sightseeing route. The more rugged and little-visited the section of Preserve they had unexpectedly set out to observe, the better for his purposes. In his line of work he was always grateful for the opportunity to take his time. Catching up to this pair of Namericans for a second time had cost him a good deal of extra effort. He fully intended to extract a certain amount of payback in kind.

It was so very good of them to come to a place where he could do so at his leisure.

"WAIT." HAVING SWIVELED HER seat a hundred and eighty degrees, Ingrid was peering hard out the back window. "I think I do see something. It's right at the limit of my vision." She waved loosely in her companion's direction. "Pull over and let's see if it comes closer."

He replied without taking his eyes from the track ahead. "For a doctor you sure have some annoying lapses in logic. If there's another vehicle that's been following us we don't pull over, we speed *up*. Can you tell if it's a private transport or a park vehicle?" He licked his lips nervously. He wanted a drink but given the increasingly uneven trail dared not take his hands off the 4×4's controls.

"Maybe it is park rangers on patrol and they're just checking up on us." She continued to search, hoping to get a better look at whatever was behind them.

Whispr was growing increasingly grim. "If it's Preserve rangers running a check they would've hailed us by now." .

"Then it's probably just other tourists like us, out exploring."

"Yeah," he muttered. "Tourists like us. Can't you see anything yet?"

"No—wait, yes, I see it now. It just came over a rise. It's another surface transport. Not a floater. Off-road terrestrial, like ours. I can't tell if it has any Preserve markings—it's still too far behind us." She glanced over at him. "I understand why you don't want to stop, but if you slow down a little I can get a better look at it."

"Make do with what you've got, 'cause I ain't slowing down. Not unless you identify it as some kind of official vehicle." His right foot depressed the accelerator and the muted hum of the 4×4's electric engine rose ever so slightly. "I'm going to pick up a little speed. Keep watching and let me know if it falls out of sight, maintains the same distance, or starts to close the gap between us."

Her eyes had widened slightly. "You don't think, Whispr, that we've been tracked all the way out here?"

"You're the one watching behind us, so you'll know before I do."

Her brief moment of relaxation had given way to uncertainty. "I still bet they're just adventurous tourists, like us."

"Possible," he conceded without taking his eyes off the track ahead.

"Maybe we should call for help, ask for some rangers to meet us at the river?"

"First off, you'd have to invent a plausible excuse for the call. Second off, if someone is following us with something other than sharing animal encounters on their minds, they're likely to be monitoring local transmissions. If they pick up a call for help they won't keep hanging back. They'll come after us with all intents blazing and for sure get to us before any park rangers can."

She swallowed. "So—what do we do?"

His voice was tight. "Just what we are doing. Keep acting like we don't know they're there, that we haven't spotted them. Hope we run into some patrolling rangers. I'm thinking that's not likely out here, so we bide our time until we find a better place to make a run for it. If they're in a terrestrial off-road like you said then we might be able to stay ahead of them until we can get to an outpost. Or at least the presence of witnesses."

She sounded crestfallen. "It's SICK, isn't it? One or more of their operatives?"

He responded with a bitter laugh. "What happened to 'adventurous tourists'?" He accelerated a little more, ever so slightly and hopefully at a rate that might be overlooked by whoever was following them. "Don't be so quick to agree with me. I've been known to be wrong before."

They continued climbing into the rocky foothills, the track becoming narrower and more difficult to follow the higher they ascended. In places the usual electronic ping posts were even replaced with ancient, painted trail signs. They had reached a very remote part of the Preserve. A truly apt place, Ingrid realized, in which to carry out a termination.

"Where is it now?" Whispr's naturally high voice had risen fretfully into soprano range. "Still behind us?"

"I think it's gone!" It took only another couple of seconds for Ingrid's excitement to vanish. "No, it's still there—and I think it's closer." She turned in her seat. "Whispr! What are we going to do?"

"Same thing I'd do if I was being followed in Greater Savannah. Which I was, not too long ago. Run like hell." He studied the image on the rear-facing pickup. The vehicle that was trailing them did not look any more sophisticated or capable than their own rental. Unless their pursuit was experienced in and knowledgeable about Preserve conditions they were likely to be on an equal footing when it came to driving. That possibility offered better odds than he was used to, and he had beaten difficult odds before. His foot shoved down on the pedal. The request for maximum acceleration was answered, with an electrically powered vehicle torque was instant, and the rented off-road leaped forward.

"We'll try to get to the Touws River." He glanced only occasionally at the rearview. "If we're lucky we'll find some rangers there!" He didn't really believe that. According to the guide app they were unlikely to encounter anyone except perhaps a few other backcountry tourists until they reached the N1. Could they stay ahead of those who were tracking them until then? Even if they managed to make it safely to the main highway it was still a long way between towns. But on the principal roadway between Cape Town and Joburg there would be road trains, he told himself, and witnesses.

Ingrid let out a scream and he jerked his foot off the accelerator—too late. Missing a tight turn on the winding track the rental soared over a pile of crushed rock. They hung in the air for what seemed like minutes but was only a second or two before the

4×4 slammed into the slope below. The solid, cushioning wheels were designed to compress considerably before they reached the point of material failure. The real threat lay in damage to the multiple independently riding struts that attached them to the rest of the roadster. If any of these were bent or broken the 4×4 would become unmaneuverable. That they remained intact despite the pounding they were taking was a tribute to the vehicle's manufacturer and its engineers' knowledge of the unforgiving South African terrain. Reinforced for off-road travel, the chassis and wheels held together.

Though fully intending to berate Whispr for his driving, a shaken Ingrid held off. She could yell at him later. Right now the last thing he needed was to be distracted or have his confidence undermined.

Repeatedly swiveling her seat so that she could switch her attention between the view ahead and the one to the rear she struggled to identify the following vehicle and to count its occupants. Despite her most strenuous efforts this proved impossible. Their own 4×4's continuous jouncing and banging made it difficult for her to keep her seat, much less pick out details within a trailing transport.

Screw Whispr's warning, she told herself. Anybody following them at this speed through this kind of terrain had something on their mind other than wildlife watching. And if it turned out that the trailing vehicle was full of nothing but a bunch of wild-eyed teens intent on throwing a scare into some unsuspecting tourists, then she wanted to be able to tell them what she thought of them. Either way she'd had enough of Whispr's paranoia-driven life-threatening driving. She pulled out her comm unit.

Whispr took his eyes off the trail ahead long enough to notice what she was doing. "Hey, remember what I said about any calls being picked up by whoever's behind us?"

"I don't care!" *You're not panicking,* she told herself. *You're just voicing your anxiety.* "I've had enough of this!"

Checking to ensure that the vorec control was on she shouted at the pickup. "Sanbona Preserve main ranger station! Emergency!"

A faint and perfectly incongruous musical tone chimed softly as the communicator complied. A couple of seconds passed before a voice responded. It was disconcertingly mechanical.

"The number you are trying to reach is unavailable at this time."

"Again, try again!" Ingrid wiped furiously at her face. Despite the fact that it wasn't hot within the 4×4 or outside either for that matter, she was perspiring profusely.

More music, further demurral. "The number you are trying to reach is—"

Without taking his eyes off the track ahead Whispr interrupted. "If you're gonna do this in spite of what I say, try the lodge!"

She eyed him blankly, completely out of her depth. In a medical emergency she could make quick decisions. This part of the world required experience she did not have.

"What department?"

"Any department!" His exasperation overroad any attempt at politeness. "The front desk, the dining room, janitorial center—anything! Just get somebody online."

She tried every possible call signature she could think of as Whispr fought to keep them level while driving wildly over and around immovable rocky relics of Gondwanaland. To his horror he saw that no matter what he did and in spite of the dangerous chances he took, the machine behind them was now beginning to close the gap between the two vehicles. And they still had no idea who its occupants represented or what their goal might be. Worse yet, every one of Ingrid's electronic shout-outs produced the same indifferent synthesized response. A coldness began to spread within him.

"Try Cape Town. Try—try the company office where we rented this sled!"

She stared at him, her communicator held tightly in her right hand. "Why? What good would it do even if...?"

"*Just try it!*"

Though bewildered by his request, she did so. After several failures she even tried entering the request manually on the unlucky chance that the comm unit's vorec firmware or software was malfunctioning. Unbidden, she then tried to contact first the rental company's district office, then its main office. She tried the hotel where they had spent their last night in the city. She tried the Cape Town Visitors' Welcoming Bureau. She tried dialing her own codo.

"The number you are trying to reach is unavailable at this time. The number you are trying to—"

"*Block.*" Whispr stole one of his rare glances at the rearview. He could not make out any visible antennae on the following vehicle but that was hardly conclusive. What was irrefutable was that none of Ingrid's outgoing calls were going any farther than the immediate vicinity.

Holding on to the wheel with his left hand as they careened down a narrow straightaway between lines of huge boulders interspersed with low conifers, he used the other hand to pull out his own comm unit.

"Universal access four-six-five!" he barked at it.

"Acknowledged, Mr. Kowalski," the compact unit replied immediately.

With a nod he passed it to Ingrid. "Here—I canceled secure ID. It'll work for you now. Try it."

She did so—with the same disheartening results.

"They're blocking us," he explained bleakly. "Using an ether-either blanket or else a directional disseminator." He chewed his very thin slip of a lower lip. "If it's the first method then there's nothing we can do except keep trying to outrun them. If it's the second, then if we can put a ridge or something else big and solid between us, our gear should work again and you should be able to call out. Keep trying!"

She did so. He instructed her to keep at it not only because she might suddenly be able to make contact but because it gave her something to do and thus kept her mind off the fact that someone was trying to run them down.

Who had the resources and the tenacity to have found them here, in a remote South African game preserve? SICK itself? Or was it the opportunistic criminal consortium that had been behind the attack on Ingrid's elderly physician friend? Or maybe an entirely new entry into what threatened to become an expanding field of thread-seekers?

It didn't matter, he told himself. If whoever was pursuing them caught up to them, they wouldn't have much leverage out here. No witnesses for sure. No curious onlookers to dampen the anger or the avarice of whoever was on the hunt. He was certain now that they could not, must not, stop until they succeeded in meeting up with other humans, be they Natural or Meld or off-worlders.

He still didn't know exactly what kind of vehicle was darting in and out of the rearview. Was it tougher than theirs? Faster? If the latter it seemed as if it should have caught up to them by now. If its off-road capabilities were *less* . . .

They weren't having any luck losing the pursuit by keeping to the established trail. The guide app on their communicators would keep track of their position no matter which way they went. Reaching a decision, he wrenched the wheel hard to the left.

If not for the highly responsive passenger seat that reacted by wrapping itself gently around her shoulders and side, Ingrid would have gone flying. As it was, the ensuing jolt as Whispr took them fully off-road nearly sent her head crashing into the roof.

"What the hell are you *doing*, Whispr?"

"Trying to avoid hell, for one thing."

He had taken aim at a narrow slot canyon. Rocks and boulders and talus closed in around them. Deliberately he began letting the 4×4 skid from side to side, allowing it to make contact with the narrow walls. Dislodged by the recurrent impact, first small rocks and then larger ones came tumbling down. With luck the mini-landslides he was creating just might be enough to impede or even disable their pursuers' vehicle before Whispr rendered their own inoperable. Still holding her communicator a wide-eyed Ingrid sat staring straight ahead.

The only other time in her life she had been this frightened was in her first year of medical school when she had been asked to take over from a paramedic fighting to restart the heart of an accident victim. As Whispr sent the 4×4 airborne once again she found herself hoping she wouldn't have to perform a similar procedure on him.

Or on herself. . . .

MOLÉ WAS DIVERTED. NO, he told himself. More than diverted. He was—amused. How utterly delightful! His quarry was trying to outrun him.

It was only to be expected, of course. By now they surely would have discovered that he had made it impossible for them to call for help. Their solar-rechargeable vehicle would keep going unless it broke down. That was becoming more and more of a possibility, he mused as he watched his quarry's vehicle repeatedly slam up against the sides of the increasingly constricted canyon.

Enjoying himself, he still felt no overriding compulsion to overtake his victims. Having memorized their enhanced dossiers, by this time he knew both of them as well or better than did their nearest living relatives or best friends. As Archibald Kowalski had very few of either, he felt that he knew Dr. Ingrid Seastrom a little better than he did her lanky, worthless associate. Certainly she was the more interesting of the two. She was intelligent enough to by now have learned more about the company property she had stolen than he had.

This lack of knowledge did not trouble him. It mattered not one whit to him whether she was carrying the secret formula for a new weapon, a new medicine, or information with which to blackmail unsuspecting politicians. He had been charged with getting it back. Knowledge of the actual contents was immaterial to the fulfillment of his obligation.

By this time he was confident he could overhaul them whenever he wished. The one who called himself Whispr was an enthusiastic but plainly inexperienced off-road driver. Molé had once participated in and finished third in a downhill race that began at the crest of the Andes and finished at the town of Tacna on the Pacific shore. Not a bad result for a nonprofessional off-road driver. Keeping up with his current target hardly compared to rocketing downhill in an uninterrupted sprint that from start to conclusion boasted a vertical descent of several kilometers.

He knew that he was wasting time. He did not see the harm in spending a little of it on a personal divertissement. Certainly after pursuing his quarry across a good chunk of southeastern Namerica and now all the way to the southern tip of another continent he had earned the right to some entertainment. He could bring down the curtain at any time. Close the distance between the two vehicles a little more and he could easily disable the one in front of him with a single shot. Assuming they survived the resultant crash, spend a little more leisure time with the Natural and the Meld. Perhaps leave one alive but unable to move so they could watch as their companion was shredded and turned into biltong.

The more he pondered this option, the more it appealed to him. Leaving most of both of them here would be his contribution to the Preserve's wildlife. Napun Molé was nothing if not an ardent conservationist.

Just not of his own kind.

12

Whispr could be slow about many things. Reading too much always gave him a headache, and try as he might he could not get the hang of crosswise gaming. Women he would never understand, and language held mysteries that extended beyond the mere meaning of words. But certain things he knew not only from experience but viscerally.

Such as the fact that no matter how hard he tried he was not going to be able to lose whoever was behind them.

Certainly he had given it his best effort, to the point of nearly crashing several times. Trying to disable their pursuer by knocking rocks from canyon walls and into his path had not even slowed the other vehicle down. Following that failure Whispr had sent the roadster struggling up a winding streambed without even knowing if it had an exit. The guide app on their comm units had been vague about that particular bit of local geology. Fortunately, there had been a way out.

Climbing out of the rocky wash at the first available low spot he had once again flattened the accelerator in hopes of losing their pursuer. But whoever was behind the wheel of the trailing vehicle was no tracker on foot, to be thrown off course by such an obvious maneuver. Instead of continuing on upstream their pursuer had rolled out at the same access point. Once again he was directly behind them.

Directly, Whispr thought frantically. Maintaining a proper distance. Why didn't whoever it was try to close the rest of the intervening space? Instead, they didn't fall back and they didn't make a move to draw alongside. Why?

It finally dawned on him that whoever it was, was playing with them. Drawing out the game. Postponing the ending. The realization was alarming. It implied complete confidence on the part of their pursuer. The knowledge that he could call "game over" as soon as he or she or they became bored.

Whispr did not inform his already terrified companion of this chilling epiphany. Better she should keep busy trying to send messages that could not get through. He would endure enough silent panic for the both of them. It was plain that they were on the losing end of an equation.

He had to find some way to change the numbers.

Over the course of the preceding hour of mad flight and insane driving their vehicle had acquired several insistent internal complaints that had begun to grow noticeably louder in the past five minutes. Any moment now any one of them might graduate from an aural irritation to a declaration of mechanical hara-kiri. Much as their pursuer might want to string out the chase, if their 4×4 broke down that would probably bring an end to it—as well as to Whispr and the doctor. His expression tightened. His whole life had been predicated on not succumbing helplessly to seemingly overwhelming odds. He would not be a wimp to Fate.

Also, and quite unexpectedly, he thought he smelled lion fat.

A gap loomed ahead; another small canyon like several they had already traversed. Accelerating yet one more time, he headed directly for it. Only this time he would not drive down into it. Dirt and gravel flew from the 4×4's rear wheels. With luck it would be thick enough to obscure their pursuer's vision, if not his vehicle's radar. At the last possible instance Whispr singled out a large, smooth boulder that sloped slightly upward. A fleeting glance to his right showed that the frightened Ingrid was still making futile demands of her communicator.

She did not look up until they were soaring through the air. When she finally did, she was too stunned to scream.

A *few more meters*, Whispr thought frantically as the 4×4 reached the top of the short arc and began to descend. *Just a couple more meters.* Seen through the windshield, yellow and ochre stone splotched with the dull green of tough Karoo brush loomed larger and larger. Unfortunately it did not loom quite large enough quite soon enough. In an instant that was less than eternity but sooner than insight his view was replaced by blackness.

Notwithstanding the swirling dust that did indeed obscure his vision, Molé did not follow his quarry into the open air over the drop as Whispr had hoped. As the assassin's radar screamed a warning he slammed on the brakes and sent his vehicle skewing wildly sideways. Despite the speed of his defensive reaction it did not quite stop in time. As it toppled over the rim of the chasm he fought with the wheel to stabilize the descent. The wall of the shallow canyon where the two Namericans had achieved all too brief liftoff was not perpendicular, but it was very, very steep. Only for someone of Molé's skill and experience was it even marginally negotiable.

Straightening out his machine he applied the brakes intermittently, alternating them with precisely coordinated and carefully gauged taps on the accelerator. Down the canyon wall he plunged front-end first; dodging an upthrust boulder, skewing around a dark slash that was a heavily eroded tributary ravine, the bottom of the canyon and the river that flowed through it coming ever closer, closer...

The angle of descent became unmanageably precipitous even for him. It was steeper than the tough off-road vehicle could hold. He fought to guide it to the right, angling to gain a less acute slope. As he struggled with the wheel he could feel the roadster rolling; slowly, slowly, turning turtle as if in slow motion. Proof positive that in the end, he reflected without bitterness, gravity always wins. His seat automatically enveloped him as the 4×4 began to tumble, rolling over and over, banging and smashing and groaning as if he were trapped inside a kettledrum at the last hurrah of Respighi's triumphant orchestral legions.

When finally all motion ceased and the sounds of splintering composite gave way to the nearby gurgle of fast-moving water he quickly determined that he was not dead. The protective carbon fiber plate installed in his skull just under the skin and bonded with the bone had, as designed, cushioned and protected his brain. Though the world now appeared distorted and strange he knew it was not because he had suffered damage to his perception: his vehicle had come to rest upside down.

Extending an arm he shoved at the driver's-side door. Partially crumpled, it would not budge. Irritated and impatient, he shot whiplike tentacles from one hand, wrapped them around the cracked barrier, and yanked. Pieces of the already stress-cracked door came away in his tendrils. A few more rips and tears enlarged enough of a gap for him to pass through. A touch on the emergency release freed him from the protective embrace of the 4×4's seat. His body dropped toward the roof, which was now the floor. After one more check to make sure that everything important was functional, he crawled out.

In unsurpassed physical condition for someone his age he rose immediately to his feet and took stock of his surroundings. His vehicle was a total loss. Both its integrated comm unit and his own portable were smashed and useless. Unless he could somehow commandeer a ride he was going to have to find his way out of this wilderness on foot. Fashioned of tougher material, the small pistol he had purchased in Cape Town to replace the weapons he had been compelled to leave behind in Namerica in order to board his commercial flight remained intact. A quick check revealed that it was still in working order.

At that moment he would have given vent to his frustration and fury if not for the sight that greeted him when he turned his gaze downstream.

Being carried away by the fast current but beginning to show signs of sinking was the off-road vehicle he had been following. Like his own it was also upside down. Kneeling on its upturned underside an unnaturally slim figure was struggling to pull a woman from the water.

Molé allowed himself a small smile. One had to admire the audacity of his quarry, he told himself. Or perhaps in taking such a desperate step the wretched stick-man had simply been acting out of hopelessness and desperation. Whatever his motivation it would come to nothing. Going through his clothing Molé found that at least some of the equipment that he always carried with him had survived the crash intact along with his skillfully melded assassin's body.

Starting out slowly to confirm that his lower body was functioning properly he headed downstream. Though not wide, this substantial tributary of the Touws ran swift and deep. Deep enough to carry away his quarry's upturned 4×4. More than deep enough for him to explore how long the stick-man could survive with his hatchet head held underwater.

This time of year the midday temperature was mild. Thick brush and occasional trees shaded his progress from the southern sun. Feeling good despite the loss of his vehicle, he lengthened his stride. Sooner or later, and probably sooner, the river would push his quarry's broken and crumpled vehicle ashore. Or it would ground itself on some projecting rocks or be caught up in a small rapid. Or the exhausted, worn-out couple would abandon it in favor of swimming or walking to dry land. Whatever happened Molé would come upon them eventually. Their end was as assured as if they had died in the plunge into the canyon. But he was glad they had survived.

On top of everything else, now they were going to have to pay for the damage they had caused to his clothing.

"Do you see anyone?" Whispr asked.

Lying on her back on the unyielding underside of the ruined off-road vehicle as it drifted rapidly downstream, Ingrid's respiration was slowly returning to normal. As she gradually dried out beneath the morning sun she was in no mood to sit up, much less engage in any strenuous searching back the way they had come. That was the sort of thing she expected of her companion. Besides, her vision was trained for close-up work.

"You tell me."

Using her right index finger she dug something thin and dull green out of her back teeth and made a face as she examined it. Though insufficiently sanitary to pass muster in her office or her tower's hospital, it was probably harmless. Out here in the absence of towns and people the watercourse down which they were being

carried was probably free of bilharzia and other interesting indigenous parasites.

Demonstrating remarkable agility Whispr not only managed to
stand up on the overturned 4×4 as the current carried it downriver,
he maintained his balance while shading his eyes from the sun as
he scanned upstream.

"I can't see any movement. As I climbed out the window after
we landed in the water I saw it come over the ledge, drive down
about halfway, and then flip and roll. It must've slowed down before it went over. Maybe whoever it is is still trapped inside." There
was grim satisfaction in his voice. "If they are I hope they're good
and busted up. So they'll still be alive when the scavengers find
them. The guide app says that there are some *Percrocutas* in the
Preserve. Resurrected hyenas as big as lions."

His words all ran together in her head. She sat up. The last time
she had taken a leisurely boat ride was when her sometime para-
mour Rajahn had treated her to a relaxing cruise on board the
replicated sternwheeler *Abelmare Queen* for a romantic jaunt and
moonlight dinner up the Savannah River. Her present situation
was neither relaxing nor romantic. Her companion was neurotic,
paranoid, and possibly a borderline psychotic. Chasing them were
one or more unknown individuals who, if nothing else was known
about them, were certainly not borderline.

A sudden thought made her raise her right hand. Her fingers
carefully probed the fabric near the top of her left breast. Only
when they encountered a barely perceptible bump did she let herself relax. The hidden compartment was intact and so was its precious cargo. She was not worried about the capsule's integrity.
Though thin-walled, it was made of industrial-grade material. Her
body might shatter but the capsule would not. But if the security
compartment's seal had been broken in the crash then the small

capsule and its irreplaceable contents could easily have been washed away. Small as they were it was unlikely they would ever have been found again.

Confirmation of its presence on her person and the absence of any discernible pursuit were the only good nuggets she was able to mine from the crash. Her comm unit and Whispr's were both missing; swept away by the churning force of the river. The rest of the 4×4's electronics were accessible but useless, waterlogged beyond reboot. On impact with the river the off-road vehicle's rear hatch had popped open. All the supplies they had purchased from the lodge shop and carefully packed for the rest of their journey had been whirlpooled out. As she sat contemplating the disaster an assortment of local fish were no doubt dining happily on the lost food. They had bought enough to sustain them all the way to the Namib. Now not so much as a dehydrated doughnut remained.

But—they were alive. And if Whispr's ongoing observations of the river behind them were to be believed, finally safe from whoever had been trying to track them down.

"You know," he told her as he swayed like a lone cattail atop the upturned, slowly drifting vehicle, "this has its upside."

She gaped at him as she fought to wring water from the hem of her shirt. "Really? Upside? Pray enlighten me."

Given their present circumstances he was unaccountably cheerful. She would have stood up and punched him except that she was afraid of falling into the river. His brain might not be better than hers, but his balance was.

"Whoever was after us no longer is. If their backer or backers run a follow-up they'll find their minion's vehicle wrecked by the riverbank and, hopefully, the body or bodies of whoever they hired. When they come looking for us, all they'll find is this derelict 4×4."

She brooded silently for a moment. "If they're as persistent as whoever they hired then they'll look for our bodies, too. For confirmation. Even if they don't give a shit about finding us, they'll take a long hard look for the thread."

He was smiling like a penniless Meld who'd suddenly found an unopened prepaid enhancement package abandoned on a park bench.

"Don't be so quick to give them that much credit. They're just as likely to believe we drowned and that our bodies got trapped on the river bottom or eaten by scavengers. Hyenas or crocs or fish. As for the thread, they might assume it was consumed along with the rest of us. Or if it got swept away separately that it fell to the bottom somewhere back near the crash site." His brow furrowed as he tried to remember geographical details from the Preserve guide.

"The Touws becomes the Groot River, which dumps into the Indian Ocean." He spread his hands. "If SICK or whoever's been after us here comes to the not unreasonable conclusion that we're dead, and that the thread is irretrievably lost in the river, then—no more people trying to kill us. And if they're not looking for us anymore, the better our chances of getting into this research place."

Though she could not refute the basics of his logic she was unwilling to share what she regarded as his premature glee.

"This isn't like you, Whispr."

Resting his hands on knoblike knees he bent toward her. Silhouetted against the almost cloudless pure blue sky all he needed, she thought, to be the splitting image of a well-known character from a classic children's book were a few strands of straw poking out of his collar and ears. As it was, he looked as if a stiff breeze could carry him away.

"What isn't like me?"

"Optimism. It's atypical. Not like you at all. I'm not sure how to handle it."

He straightened and looked back downstream. "For the first time since you popped those traktacs out of my back in your office I feel like no one's chasing me. Unless you've spent the better part of your life feeling like someone's always chasing you, you can't imagine how that feels." He moved toward one of the roadster's up-turned wheels.

She frowned at him. "What are you doing?"

"We're going the wrong way. The Namib is in the other direction. We have to get off this wreck and go back the way we came."

Days ago she would have said nothing. Several near encounters with the homicidal hirelings who had been chasing them had made her bolder. Whispr ought to have been proud. Reaching out, she grabbed a leg of his pants to hold him back.

"How do we know the maniacs who were chasing us aren't sitting around their wrecked vehicle waiting for their own rescue? It would be worse than merely ironic if after surviving the crash and finally getting away from them we were to just walk into their camp."

He shook his head confidently. "Trust me, doc. If any of them could walk they'd be following us as fast as they could. I'd have seen 'em by now. I know the type. They don't give up until they're dead, or so busted up they can't move." With a thin forefinger he traced an arc in the air.

"We'll land on the opposite bank from where we went into the river and make sure we hike a ways inland before retracing our float. Besides taking us in the direction we want to go, on the off chance that someone did survive their crash they'll be looking for us to keep floating *downstream*, just like the 4×4. And they'll be on the opposite bank from us, looking for footprints. So we have multiple reasons to get off this piece of drift trash and start back the way we came. Besides," he added encouragingly, "upstream is where we're most likely to run into other visitors, or maybe a patrolling ranger vehicle."

She stared at him. "Now I know something's wrong with you, Whispr. You must have hit your head. You're making too much sense."

He grinned and looked away. "Where my own future is concerned I'm always thinking ahead. Maybe I'm not an intellect like you or your friends, doc—but I'm a survivor. Stick with me and you will be, too."

She was not entirely sure she agreed with him, but neither was the only real alternative especially enticing. Drifting downstream until their ruined vehicle beached or grounded itself held little appeal. And as the river continued to widen on its way to the sea it was likely to provide a home for more and larger wildlife. Hippos, who killed more people in Africa than any other animal. Crocodiles. So...

With the thread safe under her shirt she joined him in swimming ashore. Helping one another they ascended the far bank and started walking northwest. The still-rising sun was warm enough without being overpowering to finish drying her and her clothes. Occasionally she caught him looking over at her and realized that until it was dry, her outfit was going to cling to her. She plucked at it repeatedly in hopes of accelerating the drying process. But she did not touch herself when he was looking at her.

After an hour of hiking beneath what was a relatively benign African sun and having had nothing to eat but some wild berries that Whispr found, she no longer cared what she looked like.

IT WAS VERY THOUGHTFUL of his quarry, Molé felt, to come back to him instead of continuing to try to run away. Almost touching. Perhaps they had seen too many ancient entertainment vits where the pursued intentionally walk backward and attempted to circle around behind those who are after them. Or, depending on what if any of their travel gear had survived their crash into the river, they had realized that help and civilization lay much farther away downstream than up.

Their decision to reverse course and hike against the flow of the river was understandable, even sensible. Normally it would have been difficult to impossible for anyone to detect the two fugitives as they made their way upstream while keeping well inland from the tributary itself. But then, a pursuing Natural would not have been alerted to their negligible presence by the visual alarm that appeared on the inside of Napun Molé's wholly melded left eye as it picked up a trace of their slow-moving but unmistakably human infrared signatures. He tut-tutted softly.

Previously they had made it difficult for him, and now they were making it too easy.

Monitoring their progress, he waited until their heat signatures had moved upriver well past his present position. Then he crossed. A medium-sized croc, no more than three meters long, coasted toward the strange figure to investigate. The maniped fast-twitch muscle fibers in Molé's legs went to work, enabling him to outdistance the curious reptile.

Emerging dripping wet on the far shore he scrambled up the slope and settled into a comfortable practiced stride that would allow him to keep pace with his quarry. He was in no hurry to catch up to them. The likelihood of them encountering other travelers or rangers before nightfall in this remote corner of the Preserve was slim. It was a chance he was willing to take for the pleasure of waking them from what they would be confident was a secure sleep. He could not keep from smiling as he envisioned the look of horror and confusion that would wash over the stick-man's face when he awoke to see the muzzle of the small pistol centimeters from his head just before Molé blew his left ear off.

Though the pistol made little noise it would probably be enough to wake the good doctor Seastrom. He would not blow her ear off. He would take his time with her. As he indulged himself he would every so often ask her to provide him with formal medical descriptions of the procedures he planned to carry out. In between operating he would reduce her shrieking companion to dehydrated trail food. He hoped the local scavengers who would find whatever he left behind of the two bodies would appreciate the time and effort he intended to put into providing them with a late-night snack.

One of Africa's innumerable species of bloodsucking flies landed on an exposed part of his right forearm. It had a heavy soot-gray abdomen and a brilliant metallic green thorax. He looked on with interest as its hypodermiclike proboscis pierced his flesh. The pain was sharp but insignificant compared to what he had lived through in years gone by. It was an excellent stimulant. He felt recharged, alive, and freshly angered.

From the middle finger of his left hand a thin metal tendril whipped out to crack like a whip a couple of millimeters from the banqueting insect. The miniature sonic boom the snap generated shattered the fly's head. Retracting the tendril Molé reached over and flicked the now headless and blood-bloated body off his arm.

Everyone, he reflected, had their own way of connecting with Nature.

INGRID WAS TOO TIRED to do anything but concentrate on the way forward. Fortunately the vegetation inland from the river consisted largely of low grasses interrupted occasionally by clusters of trees or the weird local succulents. This was dry country;

not desert, but far from veldt or jungle. There was plenty for both contemporary and resurrected browsers to eat, which was one of the reasons the government had expanded Sanbona to encompass much of the Little Karoo.

From time to time small four-legged creatures scampered out of their way or hopped frantically clear perpendicular to their path. From reading the Preserve guide she knew these would all be modern species. Bringing back and successfully maintaining the ancient Pleistocene and Holocene megafauna was difficult enough, but it did have one thing in its favor. It was hard to lose track of large animals. For that and many other reasons, some of them patently obvious, resurrecting extinct rodents was an idea whose time had definitely not yet come.

"Do you think it'll be like this all the way to the N1?" she asked tiredly.

Whispr did not seem to walk so much as flow forward. "Hard to say. We don't know the country. If I remember the app right it's at least eighty kilometers from where we went into the river up to the highway, and that's in a straight line. I'm hoping that as long as we stay close to the water we'll eventually run into some other travelers." He jerked a thumb skyward. "Guide app says that park floaters regularly track animal movements. We just need one to see us and help'll be on its way. Or someone somewhere running an idle satellite search might see two unequipped people out walking in the middle of nowhere, get curious, and make a report." He smiled encouragingly. "One way or another we'll get out of this okay."

"Of course," she commented sardonically, "it doesn't improve our chances for rescue that we deliberately didn't file any travel plans because we didn't *want* anyone to know where we're going." Stumbling on a loose rock she nearly turned her ankle and proceeded to curse everything within view. Whispr eyed her in mock surprise.

"Why Doctor Seastrom—I don't think I've ever heard you use such unprofessional language."

"Better get used to it," she snapped. "The longer we have to walk, the less professional my bedside manner's going to become."

"May I say that I find it charming?"

"You may not. In fact, why don't you shut up for a while?" She surveyed the surrounding grassland uneasily. "All we need is for one of the big cats to hear us plowing through the brush."

He slowed until he was once more walking alongside her. "I wouldn't worry about that."

"Oh, wouldn't you? And why not?" She glared up at him.

"Because," he explained amiably, "a *Smilodon* or a leopard or a lion is likely to smell us long before they hear us."

Her expression twisted. "I can always depend on you for reassurance."

His tone turned somber. "You can always depend on me to be realistic, doc. I told you that a long time ago."

And I wish I'd seen the back of you, she thought dourly, *a long time ago.*

A barely perceptible bulge against her left breast, the capsule holding the thread was a constant reminder as to why that would not have been a good idea. But it did not keep her from wondering where she would be and how she might be doing if she had simply left him behind in Miavana.

13

Unexpectedly, they found a wonderful place to spend the night. The jumble of house-sized, water-polished boulders that edgy eons had spilled into the river extended all the way from the water's edge to the crest of the ridge where they had been birthed. The result was a level three rapid flanked by shards of mountain like cracked hard candy. Though open at both ends and not properly a cave, one enormous stone raft cantilevered at a forty-five-degree angle offered complete protection from the elements. Surveying the interior of the temporary shelter as she sat on a smaller stone, Ingrid decided that if the skies opened up and it poured they would still stay comfortable and dry beneath the impenetrable overhang. Of course, the sky was not likely to open. This was the Little Karoo.

Whispr seemed reluctant to join her. "What's the matter?" she teased. "Afraid of the dark?"

"One, it isn't any darker under that big rock than it already is out here. Two, I'm fine with it. It's a really nice shelter. Three, really nice shelters usually attract critters who are in need of them. Something similar in Savannah would stink of dogs or cats or rats. So I would expect a great place like this to also attract dogs or cats or rats. I dunno about the local rats, but I do know that some of the dogs and cats run bigger than the average. You smell anything? See anything suggestive? Like maybe gnawed bones with the marrow leaking out?"

Startled by the suggestion she rose from where she was sitting and peered back into the deeper reaches of the overhang. The sun was still up and there was enough light to see into the farthest recesses. To her relief her gaze encountered only dirt and rock.

"It *looks* empty."

He joined her but carried out his own inspection as he did so. Wary eyes flicked from one potential place of concealment to the next. He would have reacted exactly the same had they been back in Savannah, except that there he would have been looking for two-legged predators. But the doctor's eyes were good and her judgment sound. The semicave showed no signs of recent occupation.

With all these big broken rocks around there are probably lots of equally good hiding places, he told himself. And a predator would prefer to make a den higher up, away from the river. Not far from where he stood the rapids thrown up by the boulders that had tumbled into the channel gnashed and gurgled like caged raptors, the tributary impatient in its rush to join the Touws.

The temperature was starting to drop along with the sun. They might have to huddle together to keep warm, he mused. Would she concede to the inevitable or would she prefer to shiver rather than lie beside him? He was nothing if not hopeful. Meanwhile another concern manifested itself.

"I'm *starving*," she whined.

His tongue pushed into one cheek. "I'll just get on my comm and ring up the nearest mobile fastfood bot. What would you like? Fried chicken? A burger? Sushi? Köfte?"

"Shut up!" She glared at him. "Anybody ever tell you there's no sustenance in tempting imagery?"

"Not really. The folks who inhabit the circles I move in don't use words like 'sustenance.'"

Her frustration and anger gave way to curiosity. "What about you? You're not hungry?"

He rested a hand on the lower portion of his nearly concave midsection. "Had a NEM put in long time ago. Nutrient extractor and maxi—"

She cut him off. "I know what a NEM is. I've had patients who had them put in."

He nodded amiably. "Then you know that I don't have to eat much, and that what's left of my digestive system can process pretty much anything." He turned serious. "Though I'll need my supplements eventually. But gut-wise you're a miserable unmaniped Natural, so we'll have to see if we can find you something to eat besides roots and berries."

He turned away from her and toward the overhang's opening. The stone-circumscribed vista revealed more rocks, an assortment of the hardy trees and scrub that somehow managed to make a living in such hardscrabble terrain, and cephalopod patches of some thick green vine. A fair number of the vines terminated in pale-green-and-white bulges the size of footballs.

Stepping out from beneath the shelter he walked over to the nearest eruption. The vines spilled from a gap between two boulders that was higher than his head. *Fecund little suckers,* whatever they were, he decided. Bending, he rapped the nearest globular extrusion with the bony knuckles of his left hand and was rewarded

with a hollow sound. Following some strenuous tugging and twisting accompanied by suitable invective, the vine surrendered the
oval shape.

He presented this to her, if not quite triumphantly, at least with
a certain self-satisfaction. She eyed it dubiously.

"What is it?"

"How should I know? It's something that didn't come vacuum-
wrapped in plastic and delivered to your codo door. I think it might
be some kind of wild melon."

"You 'think' it might be?"

He shook his head pityingly. "For someone with so much education you sure as hell are pretty goddamn helpless in the face of
the real world." He started searching their immediate surroundings. "Wish I had a knife."

Finally settling on a pointed rock that was sticking out of the
ground, he walked over to it, raised the maybe-melon high, took
careful aim, and slammed the globe down on the point. A second
attempt was sufficient to split it in half. Rather neatly, he thought to
himself with pride. The juice that spilled from the interior was aromatic, the seeds small and black.

"I'm not as helpless as you think," she protested crossly from behind him. "Higher education counts for something. For example, I
read somewhere that if you're lost in the jungle you can tell what's
safe for your system by watching what the monkeys eat."

"Crap, and here we are fresh out of monkeys."

She said nothing. Just ground her teeth in silence.

Taking one half of the melon he dug out a piece with his fingers
and tentatively popped it into his mouth. Engineered to extract
nutrients from anything short of raw wood, his NEM shouldn't
have any difficulty processing something that actually looked edible. But despite the bravado he had paraded before Ingrid he knew

nothing about what he was eating, and there always existed the possibility that the innocent-looking fruit harbored unknown toxins.

Going by what she had said he expected her to wait until long after he had finished to see if he experienced any aftereffects, but she was just too hungry. All but wrenching the other half of the split melon from where it balanced precariously on his spindly legs, she shoved her face into it and began chewing furiously. When she was halfway through he found himself having to repress a chuckle.

She noticed anyway. "What are you laughing at, stick-man?"

He restrained himself with an effort. "You've got melon juice running down your chin, pulp all over your face, and seeds in your nice new melded hair."

She paused a moment, then nodded agreeably. "It's all good. Maybe you can find another one of these? It's actually—delicious."

"Sure." Tossing the empty rind outside the shelter, he rose to his feet. Beyond the massive overhang the last flickers of daylight were following the sun over the horizon; yellow streamers from Apollo's chariot. "They're all over the place."

They chowed down on two more of the unidentified but wonderfully refreshing melons. Ingrid could have consumed another couple all by herself, but she was wary of overeating. Her digestive system had not yet fully processed the strange fruit and the last thing she needed or wanted was an upset stomach, or worse. But the hunger was gone. She would be able to sleep.

Tomorrow they would run into some other Preserve visitors, she told herself. Or a park floater would spot them and call for help. One way or another, surely they wouldn't have to hike all the way to the cross-country highway. Equipped now with a full belly her body was able to fight off the creeping chill of evening. Finding a flat place she started to settle down for the night.

"Wait." Watching her, Whispr shook his head pityingly. "You

really don't know anything. Do you have any idea how many nights I've had to spend on the street, sleeping in city parks or alleys?"

Without waiting for a response he pivoted and exited the shelter again. When he finally returned it was bearing an armful of leafy vines. Spread out on the patch of dirt she had chosen they made a crude bed. She looked up at him.

"Whispr, I—thank you. What are you going to sleep on?"

He indicated the pile of inviting greenery. "There's more than room enough for tw—"

She was on her feet and moving past him. "Thanks for the chivalrous gesture, but I think it's my turn to get the vines."

He put out an arm to block her while being careful not to make contact. "Never mind. I'll go get some more." Pain showed in his expression. "Even though I'll just rip them up and you'd probably remove them with surgical precision."

"Whispr, I'm just not—"

"Forget it, forget it." He was already out past the overhang, walking fast.

She followed him as he headed toward the nearest clump of vegetation. Was she being unfair? He was keeping her alive, tending to her needs. How far, how much, did that obligate her to reciprocate? She deliberated, quickly came to a conclusion.

She would reciprocate fully—once they had unraveled the secret of the thread and were safely back home. She had money, he needed money. She would do right by him, and comforted herself by imagining the look on his face when she handed him the reciprocation she calculated would be fair and just.

She didn't know him at all.

Whispr did not grumble to himself as he set about gathering a second armful of soft green bedding. Griping never did any good. When life is nothing but a steady succession of disappointments one soon grows inured to the repetition. While ever hopeful, he had received nothing more than the response he had expected.

Still, there was time yet. It was a long way to the Namib.

FROM HIS VANTAGE POINT just below the crest of a line of rocks Napun Molé watched as the preposterous but persistent stick-man struggled to wrench a couple of stubborn vines from their rocky moorings. Behind the willowy Meld the renegade physician was lying prone beneath the outthrust granite overhang. From a distance it appeared that she was already asleep, or nearly so. In twenty minutes it would be dark and both of the stranded visitors dreaming soundly of softer beds and the delights of climate-controlled lodging.

Molé glanced upward. The three-quarters full moon would give him plenty of light with which to finally finish off this particular bit of unexpectedly time-consuming work. Not that he needed the moonlight. His exquisitely engineered artificial left eye allowed him to see comfortably by starlight alone. But he welcomed the moonlight for the shadows it brought with it. He was very fond of shadows. Among other things, they reminded him of himself. Cold, silent, impenetrable, and to many people who happened to sight them unexpectedly, slightly unnerving. If he could have done so he would have dispensed with his clothes and dressed wholly in shadows.

While he marked the passing of the hours he lay back against the rocks, put his hands behind his head, and regarded the moon while listening to the nocturnal birds of the Little Karoo. This was a beautiful part of the world and he was pleased that he had been able to experience it on an expense account.

Following the conclusion of tomorrow's business he would start the long hike back toward the lodge. The closer he got, the more likely that he would encounter a tour bus or an official Preserve floater. When asked by the authorities what had happened he could reply truthfully that he had missed a turn and crashed his vehicle. He would be dutifully apologetic. By the time anyone thought to broach the possibility that he might have crashed because he had been traveling at an excess rate of speed, he would have taken his leave.

Closing his left eye left him with only moonlight to steer by. Opening it activated a plethora of internal sensor mechanisms that allowed him to see as clearly as if by daylight, albeit daylight tinted a pale green. As a last unidentified warble faded into the night he rose from his resting place, drew his pistol, checked to make sure it was active, and started down from the top of the ridge.

He did not head directly for the cavernous overhang. Instead, he angled toward the river. He would approach from that direction. While comfortable in the water, swimming was not one of his specialties nor was he especially fond of the activity. Where water was concerned he preferred to avoid intimacy unless it was contained in a glass. None of his many distinctive manips included melds designed to put him at ease in lakes or oceans. Or rivers. So on the wild chance that the stick-man or the doctor might be a better swimmer than he and might try to break for the tributary in hopes of making an escape, he chose to block that route, just in case.

Pistol gripped firmly in his right hand he was soon circling back toward the rear of the overhang and his prey. Clumps of boulders he went around, individual rocks he clambered noiselessly over. He was near enough now to view the overhang in its entirety. His heart did not accelerate and his blood pressure did not rise as he found himself closing in on the end of what had been too long a pursuit. Reaching down, he sought a grip on one of the last rounded boulders that lay between him and the cavelike opening.

All that remained for him to decide was whether he was going to wake the stick-man by shoving the muzzle of his pistol into the other man's mouth or into an ear.

Which was when Fate's handmaiden Irony stepped in, and the thrust of "rock" he had clutched to support his purchase turned out to be an ear.

Shaking off the tiny two-legged creature that had roughly disturbed its rest, the *Megatherium* rose up on all fours. In that stance it was as big as an elephant. When upon hitting the ground Molé fired instinctively at the monster that now loomed before him, it rose up bearlike on its hind legs to blot out not only the moon but much of the night sky. It was, of course, only a ground sloth whose species had, like so many in the Preserve, been resurrected.

Except that unlike its placid and far smaller modern brethren, *Megatherium* was four tons of ground sloth. With claws like scythes. Who did not appreciate being roused from its nap by a violent tug on one ear and a reflexive follow-up slug to the shoulder.

Shrugging off the bee sting the infuriated sloth glared down from its six-meter height and swung a right arm the size of a scoot at what it rightly perceived to be the source of its rude awakening. Only Molé's maniped muscles allowed the old man to roll clear in time. Robust enough to decapitate a grizzly with one blow, the enormous claws on the end of the huge hand gouged parallel grooves in the ground where Molé had been lying an instant earlier.

Swinging its left arm as it lurched forward, the sloth reduced to kindling the trunk of the small tree behind which Molé had taken shelter. As he continued to retreat he fired a second time, and a third. Of sufficiently large caliber to kill a human outright, the shots only further enraged the massive mammal that was lumbering toward him. From its throat came a bellowing like the mother of all hogs.

The repeated bursts from the silenced weapon did not wake Whispr, but the thunderous bawling of the *Megatherium* shook the air around him sufficiently to make him sit bolt upright. Sprawled on her bed of vines it took the dog-tired Ingrid a moment longer to rouse from dreamland. When a second nightmare roar rattled the semicave she abruptly found herself as awake as her companion.

"Mother of...what *is* that?" Her eyes were wide in the near darkness.

Having scrambled hastily to the edge of the overhang Whispr was peering out into the moonlight. "It's close, but it doesn't sound like a cat. Not that I'm any kind of expert on cats, contemporary or resurrected." The bellowing shook him again. "Sounds like a herd of cattle being squished together. I can't see anything and I'm not really interested in identifying species right now." He looked back at her. "I know you're exhausted, doc. I'm tired, too. But on the off-chance that this place might be a temporary den for whatever it is that sounds like it's trying to take down the moon, I think we'd better move." He looked up. "There's enough light for walking. And it's nice and cool. We can sleep during the day."

Brushing greenery from her arms she came up beside him. A mixture of fury and pain, the horrific bellowing continued. The unknown source was somewhere behind their shelter. "What if it comes after us?"

In the dim light her melded companion was more of a phantom than ever. But if his silhouette was uncomfortably spectral his words were determined. "I don't know about you, doc, but I'd rather have some open ground between me and whatever it is that's making that racket than take a chance on being cornered in here." He stepped out into the moonglow.

She stared at him. "You'd leave me here, wouldn't you?"

"In a southern-country minute. You coming? Or are you gonna

try and go back to sleep?" He was looking not at her but in the direction of the roaring that if anything had grown louder and more terrifying.

She hurried past him.

FINDING HIMSELF BACKED INTO a crevice Molé held off letting loose any additional shells. The ones he had already pumped into the giant ground sloth had been about as effective as spitballs against a rhino. If the monster would hold still long enough for him to get a clear shot at an eye, a bullet so directed would likely penetrate the *Megatherium*'s brain and kill it. But it was remarkably agile for so massive an animal. Instead of its head it was the flailing, girderlike forelegs and their disemboweling claws that commanded most of his attention.

He didn't think it could reach him this far back in the narrow cleft in the rocks. While he could not line up the killing shot he needed neither could it grab him to rend him limb from gut. He steadied himself. He was safe and his options were improving. Either it would grow bored and wander away, allowing him to make a dash for safety, or it would eventually lean in for a better look, in which case the next thing it would see was a bullet on course for a pupil. Periodically switching the pistol from hand to hand so that his fingers would not get cramped he waited for the hulking, previously extinct mammal to declare its intentions. For the first time in quite a while the thoughts at the forefront of his consciousness were not of his human quarry.

There was, however, a third option that he had not considered, and it soon presented itself. Molé possessed an impressive command of a wide variety of knowledge, some of it as arcane as it was deadly. He was not, however, conversant with the capabilities of the resurrected species called *Megatherium*. One of these abilities now made itself known to him in a manner that left no doubt as to why the monster was classed in a group loosely known as ground sloths.

Employing all of its considerable strength, the *Megatherium* began to tear the assassin's rocky sanctuary apart stone by stone.

WHISPR WAS RECITING AN endless string of four-letter words as they ran. Struggling to keep up with the muscle-maniped, long-legged Meld, Ingrid barely had enough strength to keep moving while voicing a plea.

"Take it easy! I can't even hear it anymore."

She looked back the way they had come. Bathed in pale silver moonlight the rocks behind them seemed to glow from within. Nothing moved save a gang of hyrax. The tiny relatives of the elephant were as equally panicked by the *Megatherium*'s sudden eruption as the two fleeing humans.

"Can't slow down." Thin puffs emerged from between nearly nonexistent lips. "It's him."

She blinked at her companion, who despite his insistence had reluctantly slowed from a sprint to a jog. "What? It's 'who'?"

"The shunt who tried to kill us in Florida. The stocky assassin. The old Mole—'Molé.'" Eating up the terrain with long, lanky strides, he jerked his head back the way they had come. "When we came out of the shelter and started toward the river I looked back and I saw him. He was moving away fast from what looked like one of the bigger boulders—one that was really hairy and really angry."

Still struggling with the aftereffects of having been so roughly awakened, Ingrid found herself having to deal with this new revelation. Their remorseless hunter was *here*?

"What was after him—another *Smilodon?*" Her tone indicated that she was as hopeful as she was curious.

Whispr shook his head, his reply terse. "Something bigger. *Much* bigger."

She tried to recall her minimal university paleontology. "A mammoth? But there probably aren't mammoths here. At least, we haven't seen any. I'd think the summers are too hot. There are just mastodons."

"It was as big as an elephant, but it wasn't an elephant. This thing was moving on two legs. And it was no gorilla. Way too much hair, way wrong skull shape." He grimaced as his legs continued to eat up the meters. "Whatever it was, it isn't apelike."

"Carnivore or herbivore?" she asked him.

"How the hell should I know?" he replied irritably. "I have a hard enough time telling cats from dogs—never mind the melded ones. I saw enough to know that I don't want one of whatever it is coming up on me in my sleep—regardless of its diet."

She looked over her shoulder. There was nothing chasing them but moonbeams. "He must have surprised it while he was watching us. Maybe it'll eat him."

"I'd settle for it giving him a warning slap. From what I saw that'd be enough to take his face off." Raising both hands, he held them nearly a meter apart. "I swear, its claws were *this* big."

"Then that's for sure no cat, modern or resurrected." She could not keep from wondering what kind of animal it was that had shocked them awake and was confronting Molé. She could only hope that it would kill or incapacitate him.

Because while with his long maniped legs Whispr might be able to outrun the shorter assassin, she knew she could not.

●　　●　　●

Morning dawned inconclusive as well as overcast. There was no sign of Molé or the creature that had challenged him. Occasional droplets of tepid rain helped to keep them awake until they couldn't run anymore.

It was amazing, she thought as she let herself collapse to the ground, how quickly one becomes enamored of even the slightest of comforts. She found that she missed her bed of vines. But not enough to try to make another one. Sensibly, she feared what might come upon them if they stopped to rest. One of them would have to keep watch while the other slept.

She was unable to stay awake long enough to ask Whispr if he would do so.

After what seemed like days but had only been hours a pungent aroma woke her. Her companion was seated on a nearby rock. Something small, quadrupedal, and much too cute was cooking over an open fire. Dripping fat sizzled as it oozed off the body and made contact with the flames. Thankfully he had removed the head and most of the fur. What remained of the latter had been seared black and would provide crunch.

To her utmost disgust, it smelled wonderful.

Aching from sleeping on the bare ground and fighting to slough off the last vestiges of sleep, she felt gingerly of herself. Miraculously, everything still seemed functional. She nodded wordlessly at what appeared to be a broiling bunny.

"Found it sleeping in the grass. Came up on it and bashed its head in with a rock before it woke up and saw me." He grinned. "Usually I'm sneaking up on prey with two legs. But the hush-walk works on animals, too."

Staring fixedly at the incipient meal she swallowed hard, her mind at war with her stomach. "How—how did you skin it?"

"Sharpened a stick with my teeth. Took a while. Kept twisting the head until it came off. Once you get the skin started at the neck and begin peeling back, the rest of it comes off pretty easy."

The image thus conjured might have caused the average listener to puke up their guts, but not Ingrid Seastrom. More than most, she knew what a body looked like with its epidermis removed.

"What about the fire?"

"Used the same stick. Found another couple of pieces that had been sheltered from the rain and started twirling. Amazing what you can pick up watching entertainment vits." He nodded at their rapidly browning breakfast. "As far as the actual cooking, I learned how to do this from having to live on roof rabbit when I spent a year in Charleston."

She looked uncertain. " 'Roof rabbit'?"

He smiled. "Rats. Capybara is much better, but it's hard for the cops to overlook somebody roasting a capy in the middle of a city park." Lifting the stick off the fire he examined the smoking result with a professional eye. "I think it's done. You want a drumstick?"

She gulped. Observing and analyzing such a phenomenon with academic detachment was one thing; consuming it quite another. In the ensuing argument her stomach won out. She accepted her portion gratefully, but she ate with her eyes closed. It was surprisingly tasty.

Even better, by the time they had finished there was still no sign of their uncompromising pursuer.

"You'd think he would've seen the smoke." Whispr was kicking the coals apart. "Sure it's a small fire, but that squint bastard Molé is an enhanced Meld. He should have seen it."

"Unless he got himself eaten or killed."

The continued absence of the assassin gave Ingrid cause to

hope. Surely if their nemesis had survived the encounter with the night monster he would have caught up to them by now. That didn't mean he was dead. He might be alive but injured. The prospect brought her to her feet. The mystery protein she had consumed had revitalized her. With Whispr's street skills to rely upon they might survive long enough to reconnect with civilization. Raising her arms high, she stretched.

"I'm full of rat and feeling fine. Let's get moving."

They would head north, following the new tributary. Very soon it should flow into the Touws River where, if they were lucky, they might run into some other adventurous tourists.

"Even if he's limping," she said as she started off, "I don't want to give Molé a chance to get close to us."

Whispr nodded agreement, took a last kick at the dying embers to ensure they would not get a grip on the nearest grass behind them, and broke into a brief jog to catch up to the newly determined doctor.

"You're learning," he told her approvingly.

It was later in the day when she finally gave voice to a recurring concern.

"How did he find us? We've disguised our appearances not once but twice. We're continually revamping our identities. He has no idea where we're going. We've made a good show of being nothing but ordinary tourists. Yet he *keeps finding us*."

Lowering her head she shook it uncomprehendingly. As her eyes encountered a pudgy dark green beetle crossing her path she found herself wondering what it would taste like. Bitter, probably. Like much of what had happened to her since Whispr and the damnable wonderful thread had come into her life.

Even if she wanted to she couldn't make things go back to the way they had been. Couldn't simply step on a plane and slip back into the comfortable, conventional life she had left behind. She still had the mysterious thread. Napun Molé and his employers, whoever they might be, still wanted it. If she just turned it over to the assassin, would he be satisfied with that and leave them alone? Let them go? That was not the attitude he had displayed in Florida. It was more likely that he would kill her to ensure that she would never speak to anyone else about what she had discovered. Or maybe, she reflected with a shiver as she thought back to that horrific final confrontation in the Everglades, he would kill her just for fun.

No—she was stuck with the thread and the unquenchable desire to know where it came from, how it had been fashioned, and what, if anything, was contained on it. Since Molé was as likely to kill her whether she returned the thread or not, she might as well keep on going.

Keeping going would be a lot easier, she told herself, if in addition to the thread she also had possession of a sandwich. Any kind of sandwich. Or even one of the small wild melons Whispr had harvested the previous night. Raising her head she scanned the horizon. The valley through which they were walking had flattened out. There were no melons in view, no nut-carrying trees or berry-bearing bushes. There was only grass, and whatever her resourceful companion might be able to catch with rocks and sharpened sticks. And it was still a long way to the national highway.

At least when the intruder appeared it took her mind off the emptiness in her belly.

Whispr, naturally, saw it first. Shielding his eyes against the afternoon sun, he had stopped just ahead of her and was staring northward into the distance. Panting, she came up alongside him and squinted in the same direction. Not for the first time in such circumstances, she saw nothing.

"What is it?"

"Not sure." His eyes strained to resolve the object. "It's coming toward us, though." He hastened to dampen any expectations. "It's not a vehicle. Animal of some sort."

She considered this. "Just one?"

"Near as I can tell. Getting closer." He lowered his hands. "Getting bigger, too." Seeing the look on her face he hurried to add, "It's not a cat. I can tell that much. The general shape is all wrong. I suppose it could be one of those big hairy things like the one that saved us last night." He nodded in the direction of the oncoming creature. "Moving at a steady pace but not fast. Could be a bear, I suppose, though it would have to be one hell of a big bear. Or maybe a rhino." He studied their immediate surroundings, which were disconcertingly flat. There wasn't a suitable tree to climb and the hills behind them and off to the southwest were a disconcerting distance away.

"Might as well wait here until we have a better idea what we're dealing with. If it is some kind of predator and we run, it's a lot more likely to come after us, even if it's not hungry. The last thing we want to do is set it off."

"Maybe if it catches our scent it'll turn away," she opined hopefully.

He shielded his eyes anew. "If it has then it's either not worried or it's taking its time." He paused a moment. "It's still coming this way."

She was edging to her left. A downed tree wasn't much of a hiding place. If whatever was coming toward them decided to attack, the weather-worn wood would not provide much of a deterrent. But it was better than standing straight as a power pole on flat ground in the middle of the dry Karoo. Whispr joined her behind the big disintegrating log. Lying prone on his belly he looked a lot like a fallen tree himself. Huddling side by side they peered through the gap between the earth and the underside of the log. The advancing shape soon resolved itself.

The elephant appeared to be an old bull. Both tusks had been broken off, leaving little in the way of protruding ivory. His skin was a geology of thick gray folds, the heavy creases packed with dirt, dust, and scratches. To Ingrid he looked like a badly layered shipment of used gray rugs perambulating on four pillarlike legs. It made sense that the solitary visitor was an old bull, she knew. Nature vits about such creatures often made mention of the fact that bulls, and especially senior ones, lived alone.

"I don't think he can smell us down here," Whispr murmured. "Probably he'll just keep on going right past us."

He did not. Slowing to a halt the aged pachyderm stopped just to the right of their hiding place. As Ingrid tried to dig herself in deeper beneath the log, the elephant turned long-lashed eyes to gaze directly at them. She was certain it was staring straight at her. Then the huge bull turned its head forward once again, raised its trunk, and began sampling the air.

As soon as this process was completed, a hatch opened in its belly and a man got out.

14

He was slightly shorter than Whispr, with skin the color and texture of fried pork rinds. His eyes were blue as those of a Swedish movie star's ghost and his hair short, kinky, and mostly soot-gray. He wore long pants, no socks, brown sandals on the verge of disintegration, and a sleeveless beige vest open almost to the waist. Instruments and devices of unknown purpose flowered from the vest's numerous pockets. His muscles were those of a basketball player or swimmer; long, lean, heavily veined, giving a defiant finger to time. In his arms he cradled a flashy long-barreled chromed rifle that tangoed with the sun even as it screamed high-tech danger.

It was pointed in their direction.

"*Goeie middag, sawubona*—good afternoon, you funny people." The gleaming muzzle of the rifle did not move as the man raised his gaze to scan the surrounding country. "What you doing out here like this, on foot in the Sanbona Karoo? Don't you know is dangerous to be out here like this?" He grinned, revealing teeth that were perfect and white except for one incisor that periodically and unsettlingly rotated from gold to silver and back again like a tiny orthodontal carousel. "This is Sanbona Preserve, not Cape Town Zoo. Animals here feed themselves."

Whispr and Ingrid exchanged a glance before rising from behind the log. The man seemed friendly enough, and his method of transportation was more than intriguing. Still, there was the small matter of the rifle pointed in their direction.

"We're just tourists," Ingrid explained blithely. "We had an accident."

The man nodded. "I bet-say you had an accident. You didn't walk here from lodge. Where your vehicle?"

Whispr jerked a thumb back the way they had come. "In the river."

Their interrogator frowned. "River not easy to miss, even in dark. How so-come you end up in the water? Truth no auto-strips here, but even so. . . . You both asleep at same time? You wafting on drugs? Drunk-o?"

Ingrid looked over at her companion. In the realm of excuses Whispr was easily her master. He did not disappoint.

"We were following a herd of antelope, got lost, and were in the river before we knew it."

"Ah-hum. What kind antelope?" The oldster was eyeing the much thinner man intently.

More than content to play dumb, Whispr spread his hands in a gesture of helplessness. "How should I know? We're tourists."

"We lost our communicators and everything," Ingrid added sorrowfully. Though she was not a pro at it she was perfectly capable of instinctive coquettishness. She did not quite bat her eyelashes. "This all happened last night and we've been walking for the better part of the day. I'm Inez Sparrow and this is my friend Arthur

Cotswold. Can you give us a ride back to the lodge?" She tapped a shirt pocket. "I still have my primary credcard. I'd be happy to make a subsist transfer as an expression of our gratitude."

"No gratitude necessary," the man replied without hesitation. "First we go in my transport." He indicated the artfully constructed pseudo-pachyderm. "We find your vehicle. See if some things valuable are salvageable. Then I must kill you."

Even the usually unflappable Whispr looked stunned. Overwhelmed at last by the combination of exhaustion, lack of proper food, and now shock, Ingrid simply fell to her knees and dropped her gaze to the ground.

"You're working for him." Whispr's tone was resigned and accusing. "Or with him."

"What?" Their interrogator looked perplexed. "What you talk-talking about, branch boy? Josini Jay-Joh Umfolozi work for nobody but himself."

Now it was Whispr's turn to look confused. "You're not working with a professional man-tracker named Napun Molé? You're not working for SICK?"

"Me, working for SICK?" Inclining his head sharply to one side, the older man spat sharply. Thick moisture stained the dust. "I hate SICK! SICK people would kill Umfolozi if they could, py damn. Or at least put me out of business and lock me up for long time. Why you crazy stick-man and about-to-cry pretty lady think I work for SICK?"

From where she was kneeling in dirt and despair, Ingrid looked up at him. "Why else would you want to kill us?" She spread her arms to take in their empty, semi-arid surroundings. "Why else would you be out here by yourself?" She indicated his highly distinctive transportation. "Why else would you be out here in the middle of nowhere in a crazy contraption like that?"

"Yeah," Whispr added. "Why are you using something like that to get around instead of a proper vehicle or a floater?"

Umfolozi cackled. "Because I would be seen, and being seen would be identified, and being identified would be killed or arrested, like I just told you, py damn. You really are ignorant of this part of world, ya? You really no got way figure it. I am a poacher."

Ingrid gaped at this admission, but Whispr just nodded knowingly. The faux elephant made sense now.

"That explains the camouflaged transport. It fooled us. I guess it would fool a patrol floater, too." He scrutinized the clever construction. Tellingly, it had not moved a muscle ever since Umfolozi had emerged from its belly. "Having now met its owner I'm surprised you didn't put the doorway in the ass. It would match your crappy sense of hospitality."

Ingrid tensed—but their captor laughed uproariously. "Oh-hoh, cheap shit stick-man makes jokes on deathbed! I like you, Arthur—if that your name. I still going to kill you, but I like you. You make this hard for me—but not impossible." He gestured at Ingrid with the end of the rifle. "Pretty lady get on your feet. We walk back to river and you show me where your vehicle make like frog. Then we look for salvage. Then I kill you."

"Could—could I have something to eat first?" she stammered, licking her lips. "I haven't had anything to eat since half an overcooked rodent and I don't think I can make it back to the river without some kind of nourishment."

Umfolozi pushed out his lower lip and nodded to himself. "One makes jokes, other asks for last meal. Both can be accommodated."

Whispr stepped forward. The gleaming rifle immediately came up to confront his midsection. "We can't go back." He nodded southward. "Someone's trying to kill us. I mean, someone besides you. He's been following us for a long time. He was going to kill us last night but he ran into something big and hairy that sounded like a cow giving birth to quadruplets. It might have killed him, or crippled him, but we can't take the chance of going back to find out. If he survived, then he's still on our trail." He met the older man's gaze without flinching. "If he finds us together he'll kill you, too. He's not the kind of shunt who leaves loose ends lying around."

"Sounds like he go to dancing with *Megatherium*," Umfolozi supplied helpfully. "Too bad I not there. Illegal *Megatherium* pelt is worth thousands of rands. Claws alone are worth thousands. Tastes pretty good, too, but the meat would be just for me and my family. I got three aunties, four uncles, one great-uncle, eight children…"

By the time Umfolozi had finished delineating the members of the extended family who depended on him for sustenance Whispr had developed a certain amount of sympathy for their new captor. Bearing in mind, of course, that he had announced his intention to kill them.

"Why this *isilima* want to kill you?" The old man's gaze narrowed. "You tell-say you just tourists. Nobody come out here all this way and trouble just to kill couple of ordinary tourists." He examined Whispr closely. "You say he been following you a long time. Why he been following you? Why SICK want you dead?

"You know what I think? I think you both more than just tourists. I think you full of secrets you try to keep from old Josini. Well, that okay. I got plenty secrets myself." To Ingrid's amazement the death-dealing end of the rifle came up and Umfolozi proceeded to place the narrow butt on the ground. The slender metal rifle, she noted, was taller than its owner.

"Say maybe I not kill you. If SICK, Inc. want you dead, then you my friend. Better still, you say you can pay me."

Weak from heat and hunger, Ingrid staggered to her feet. "Yes,

yes, I can pay you! Whatever you want, Mr. Umbolazi, I can pay you! Just please help us!"

His free hand made calming gestures. "It 'Umfolozi.' But you call me Josini. Is better. Especially coming from pretty lady I maybe now not going to kill."

Whispr eyed him suspiciously. "*How* many wives did you say you had?"

"I am old, stick-man—but not dead. Calm yourself. I have enough wives already. Wives easy to get—money not so easy." Turning back to Ingrid he flashed a bewitching smile. Or at least, she mused, it would have been bewitching if not for the rotating front tooth. She had the crazy thought that it might be capable of playing music.

"I take you back to the lodge, you pay me. Is plenty time to agree on a sum satisfactory to both."

"Okay, sure." Ingrid's relief was unfettered. "And some food. And water, if you have it."

"No water." He was deeply apologetic. "Only cold beer."

"We'll manage." Whispr spoke without a hint of irony. "But we can't go back to the lodge. We, uh—when he doesn't find us out here this Molé will look for us back there."

Umfolozi pursed his lips, ruminating. "Now I think of it, you not walking toward lodge when I first telescope you. You walking away from it. Upstream toward way *I* come. Either you bad lost or—you got other reasons for picking way less traveled. Maybe while we beat hell out of here you tell old Umfolozi why you walking away from lodge. Maybe you also tell me your real names." He smiled anew. "If we going to be in business of hired transportation it only fair and just we know each other's rightful names."

Whispr didn't like being caught out. "How do we know that you've given us *your* real name?"

"You don't, but I did. If I was not going to kill you I would have made up a good name." He shrugged. "Doesn't matter now. Too late to take back truth."

A reluctant Whispr gave up his real name. For all he knew their potential savior was carrying a truth sensor along with all the other gear that was spilling out of his vest pockets. If he and Ingrid told another lie or two the old man might decide they weren't trustworthy enough to do business with. Then he *would* shoot them.

Umfolozi turned expectantly to Ingrid, but she wasn't looking at him. She was gazing back the way they had come. Whispr was beside her in an instant.

"You see something, doc?" His voice was tight.

"I—I don't know. I thought maybe—it could have been blowing dust." Extending an arm, she pointed. "Up near the top of that low ridge."

Whispr nodded, squinted in the indicated direction, then looked back at the old man. "We'd better move. This son of a bitch is kind of like you: old but tough. I'd still like to think he's *Megatherium* chow, but knowing this squint I wouldn't be surprised if the sloth came out on the short end of the fight. We do know that he's on foot, however. Depending on the speed your 'vehicle' can make without attracting the attention of Preserve authorities, we should be able to outdistance him easily. But just in case he's still alive, let's finish this conversation while we're on the way out of here."

"You awfully anxious. You sound like nervous poachers. I think maybe you two are pilfer something also. Maybe on way out of Preserve you share interesting information with a bored old man." Another smile. "Just for friendlies sake." His voice rising to a near shout he hefted his rifle and pointed it at the ridge Ingrid had picked out.

"I am Josini Jay-Joh Umfolozi! I am half Afrikaan and half

Zulu. That is a meld by Nature. I fear nothing but sand cobra in bed and ancestors in dreams! Only thing in this country tougher than me must be made of wood or metal—and not so sure of that!" Pivoting on one heel he gestured for them to follow as he lowered his voice. "But no reason to stand here in afternoon sun. Plenty of time to talk while moving."

Ingrid and Whispr followed him toward the waiting elephant. "Are you sure you're still not going to kill us?" she asked plaintively.

"You pay me, I not kill you." He tucked his rifle under his left arm. In his aged but powerful clutch it was an echo of the spears and guns that had been raised at Isandlwana. "You don't pay me, I kill him (he gestured at Whispr) and sell you." Big smile. "Otherwise everything fine and we friends forever." He halted with one foot on the lowest step of the stairs that had descended from the vehicle's belly. A slightly rattled Ingrid noted admiringly that it even smelled like a real elephant. The illusion was as complete as science and semilegal engineering could make it.

The ultimate perfectly camouflaged 4×4, she thought.

Whispr was not shaken by their host's offhand response. In the shadows of the antisocial segment of society in which he had grown up, certain facets of business were sacrosanct. He and the doctor might be thousands of kilometers from home, in an alien land and a difficult country, yet despite their awkward situation it was some relief to learn that these qualities did not differ greatly from their set-in-stone equivalents back home.

Familiarity, even when murder was being discussed, was a comfort.

THE BANDAGE MOLÉ HAD improvised from the same kind of vines and leaves that had cushioned Ingrid Seastrom's sleep the previous night were stained dark, but the serious bleeding

seemed to have stopped. To worry the assassin the bleeding would
have to be profuse enough to threaten his mobility. His left leg had
been mangled but not broken. A long gash ran down the right side
of his face where just the tip of a single claw had barely made contact. Had he been a second later in ducking, the rest of the *Megatherium*'s giant paw would have removed his head like a cork from
a bottle.

Neither Molé nor his monstrous, hirsute assailant was dead.
While capable of dispatching targeted representatives of his own
species with a single bullet, the pistol he carried was insufficient to
affect the lumbering giant ground sloth. Unable in the darkness to
line up a potential killing shot, he had sensibly opted for flight.
Having overcome its outrage at being awakened from its beauty
sleep the sloth had eventually given up the pursuit, deciding that
the fast-moving, jittery, sting-carrying primate was not worth the effort it would have taken to bring it down.

It had taken Molé most of the night to regain some of his
strength and bind up his wounds. While it was true that everything
from head to toe worked, it was also true that everything in that
vicinity was sore. His muscles protested when he heaved his body
upright at the first sign of daylight. They screamed louder when he
insisted on following the path taken by his target. That they had
used the opportunity presented by his inadvertent encounter with
the *Megatherium* to put distance between them and himself was
obvious from the nature of the trail they had left. Longer than usual
strides plus the depth of their footprints showed they had taken off
running. Surprisingly, they had headed upstream and not back
toward the lodge. Perhaps they felt that he would expect them to flee
in that direction and by heading for a different point of the compass
they could shake free of him. He shook his head sadly. It was hurtful
that even after all this time they thought so little of his abilities.

He always looked at the evidence, not at the expected. And the evidence clearly showed them heading north.

For the first few hours of walking he had relied for support on a crude crutch he had fashioned from a tree branch. Eventually he had cast it aside, disgusted at the picture it presented. The longer he pushed on without pausing, the stronger he became. His only fear was of infection. The medical kit that was one module on his still largely intact work belt contained only basics. Though an anti-bacterial spray was included, it was not designed to cope with the exotic parasites to be found in the Little Karoo.

No matter, he told himself. He could tell from the footprints and other signs he had been following that the gap between him and his quarry had been shrinking for some time now. If he maintained his current pace he should catch up to them within the hour. His only regret was that now he would not be able to linger over his work as he had planned. Present circumstances and a lack of supplies dictated that he reclaim his employer's property and dispatch those who had stolen it with efficiency rather than enjoyment. Upon rendering recovery and termination he would immediately have to start the long hike back to the lodge to ensure his own safety and survival.

He did not expect to see them when he topped the rock-strewn rise. Far less did he expect to see them in the company of others, even if only a single stranger. He ducked out of sight behind a protruding boulder. Neurons welded to nanoscale wiring caused the superfine optics in his left eye to zoom in on the trio. There was the exasperating stick-man Whispr, next to him the moderately attractive physician Seastrom, and striding along just in front of her a lanky local of indeterminate ancestry and name unknown. At this distance Molé could not tell if the unexpected newcomer was Natural or Meld. Not that it was important. What mattered was that the stranger appeared to be conversing amiably with Molé's targets. Such conviviality did not bode well for the hunter's intentions.

More peculiar still was the unnatural composure of the elephant standing nearby. It was virtually motionless. Squeezing highly trained muscles in his left eye, Molé zoomed in on the solitary quadruped. It looked real enough. Its true nature only became apparent when a narrow set of stairs descended from its underside and the intruder and probable owner led the two Namericans up and into its stomach. Plainly it was a superbly camouflaged vehicle of some sort.

Having no transportation of his own save what his battered body and injured legs could manage, the determined Molé drew his pistol and took aim. No matter how slow the elephant-transport he did not doubt for a minute that it would leave him in the dust.

There was no need to mount a scope on the weapon. Circuitry imbedded in the gun made wireless contact with equally minuscule receiving equipment in his melded left eye while the right one closed in a lethal wink. Crosshairs appeared in his field of vision. Wherever his eye focused the muzzle of the gun would aim. Suitable fine adjustments were entered into the weapon to compensate for distance, wind velocity, and other properties that might interfere with a bullet's trajectory.

From atop the ridge he could see his targets clearly. The barrel of the pistol lined up on the back of the stick-man's head. But the pale red warning that appeared on the inside of his eye above the crosshairs as he pulled the trigger could not be denied.

DISCHARGE ABORTED: TARGET OUT OF RANGE

His frustration knew no bounds. He needed a rifle. Or a small launcher. Or a self-propelled explosive seeker. He had brought none of these with him, believing the newly purchased pistol more than sufficient to conclude his business. As it would have been, had they not tricked him into crashing by deliberately wrecking their own vehicle. As it still would be, if the present distance between them could be halved. Rising, refusing even to wince at the shooting pain in his badly injured left leg, he pocketed his weapon and started down the far side of the stony slope as fast as he could limp.

He had not descended twenty yards through the talus and brush when what he feared most happened. With its human passengers safely inside, the "elephant" returned to life, turned elegantly on its four massive legs, and set off northward at a fast trot. Its destination was unknown but its speed could be estimated. Even at his best Molé could not have kept pace with it.

The elderly assassin could only totter downhill and curse. The pachyderm-driving stranger might give his two hitchhikers a lift for an hour, for a day, or for longer. Attempting to keep up in the heat of the open Karoo would be foolish, perhaps fatal. As much as he hated to do so Molé knew it would make more sense for him to start back toward the lodge in hopes of being picked up. He was tough but not invulnerable, determined but not obdurate. His body needed medical attention and he knew it.

It was *infuriating*. By the time he was in any condition to resume the hunt his quarry would probably have acquired swifter and more modern transportation. By the time he could resume formally tracking them they were liable to be anywhere. Since he did not know their intended destination they could vanish anyplace, even out of the country. Unless he could quickly reestablish contact he would practically have to start all over again.

At least he didn't have to worry about them going to the authorities. If that had been their intention they would have done so in Savannah.

He had been so close to finishing it. To completing the assignment. What made the recent series of events almost unbearable was that his failure had been due not to human interference but to a wholly accidental nocturnal encounter with one of the Preserve's resurrected mammals. Better the giant herbivore whose sleep he had inadvertently interrupted should have stayed extinct, he told himself as he turned reluctantly westward.

As he hobbled off in the direction of the distant lodge he decided that he should not be so hard on himself. The great majority of his work took place in cities, in civilized surroundings. He was not used to the country. He did not seek out the company of nor did he much care for animals. He liked them even less now that one had tried to kill him, even though the creature's reaction had been only natural.

A proper reckoning and recompense would occur only when he finally caught up to his quarry. Regrettably, there would be no experiments in biltong-making. Not that he couldn't avail himself of a choice nibble or two. For the sake of tradition. The vision gave him strength. He would begin with a select bit of the good doctor Seastrom.

And in keeping with his original plans he could still make her wretched, irksome meat-string of a companion watch.

THE INTERIOR OF THE inimitable four-legged transport provided comfortable space for one. With three packed in, it was crowded even though Whispr did not take up much room. Watching as their host piloted the heavily automated vehicle Ingrid could not help thinking that as opposed to other occasions, this time the problem was not the elephant in the room but the room in the elephant.

Moreover, it stank.

Though their agreeable host opened every available vent, the steady flow of air was unable to counter the overwhelming pong of uncured pelts, hastily removed skulls, awkwardly extracted claws, and slabs of plastisealed flesh that were packed into the rear of the single compartment. While much of this highly illicit bounty belonged to resurrected Pleistocene mammals, some of it was contemporary. Flanked by hand-cut wedges of spray-frozen springbok, a kudu skull with its magnificent twisted horns had been crammed into one high corner. Several glittering birds stood posed exactly as they had been when shocked by the poacher's preservative. A whole *Smilodon* glowered from the back of the improbable vehicle, looking even in death uncomfortably ready to awaken and pounce.

Studying the collection, Ingrid remarked on the absence of ivory or modern cats.

"Nobody want to buy conserved leopard or lion when they can have a sabertooth." A cheerful Umfolozi addressed his guests from the driver's seat in the elephant's head. "Is very unexpected good luck for such modern kitties, py damn. Fortunately all resurrected sabertooth and scimitar-tooth cats reproduce well. *Smilodons* live in prides and screw like lions. Preservation is assured." He indicated the menacing presence stored behind the doctor. "You take out one big male, another immediately steps in to assume his place and make sure all the females get good and impregnated. Original cubs suffer, is true, but the pride lives on."

"How do you squeeze something like a *Megatherium* skeleton in here?" Speaking from Ingrid's left Whispr had bent and twisted himself like a contortionist in order to fit into the seemingly nonexistent remaining space.

Umfolozi made a face. "Can't fit whole skeleton. Sometimes I'll take a skull and the claws. The pelt I also take because there is big demand. One sloth skin carpets a whole room. I got a suction setup removes all the air from fur. You be surprised what you can pack into a small space once all the air is remove from it. But only works with pelts, not bone or keratin."

The elephant gave a sharp lurch to the left. Ingrid yelped as she was dumped into a pile of something warm and pungent. Whispr voiced a strangled protest.

"Sorry." Their host ran his fingers over a couple of controls and the ride steadied. "We crossing a stream and climbing opposite bank. I could make ride smoother still, but then this elephant would not look like an elephant. And I can't risk that. A Preserve floater might home in on the discrepancy." He smiled apologetically. "I'm afraid I going to have to close the vents now. Just for little while. We have to cross the Touws River here."

Whispr stared. "This thing is a boat, too?"

Their host chortled at the assumption. "No, no—is an elephant!" Looking back, he eyed his guest critically. "You not know that elephants are good swimmers?"

"My error." Whispr struggled to find a more comfortable position atop his makeshift couch of salvaged animal parts. "There's an ongoing shortage of elephants where I come from."

"You will note with interest," Umfolozi continued, "that air supply for us is by same method as would be for real elephant. Except our trunk has no-pass membrane and filter installed."

Once safely across the river Ingrid felt that they could finally relax. Even if the relentless Molé was somehow still on their trail he would not be able to get across the major, croc-filled waterway unless he paused to build a raft or a boat. Knowing what she did about the assassin it was probably unwise to think that a little water would stop him, but she preferred a false sense of security to none at all. Anyhow she was too exhausted to worry any longer.

"Could we—do you have any food, Josini? My friend and I haven't had anything to eat in a long time."

"Food? Sure! I got food—and I give you good price." Leaving the elephant to navigate on its own he turned in his seat and reached down to open a storage bin built into the upper jaw. As Ingrid's eyes grew wider with each successive withdrawal he extracted apples, bananas, mangoes, self-chilling bottled drinks, and strips of what appeared to be antique wall siding.

"Biltong," he explained to a curious Whispr. "My Aunt Sophie make it herself."

Handed a strip of the brown material, Ingrid eyed it dubiously. "What's it made from?"

"Whatever's handy and dead," Umfolozi explained with a smile. "You are holding some eland. That the best, I think. Mr. Whispr, you have some duiker and some giraffe."

Ingrid swallowed. "You eat giraffe?"

Their host looked at her in surprise. "Meat is meat. Especially when it has been turned into biltong, py damn. Try it."

Whispr bit down tentatively on his strip of duiker, strained his jaw muscles mightily, then removed the curled brown strip of desiccated protein and examined it thoughtfully. Very little seemed to have vanished.

"Where's the laser you use to cut it with?"

Umfolozi nodded encouragingly. "Just keep chewing. Eventually it come apart in your mouth. Then you can swallow. Or else you pass out from the effort. Either way, your hunger go away."

As they lumbered northward they were able to view their surroundings through pinhole pickups concealed in the pores of their transport's synthetic skin. They strode unchallenged through herds of giant camels and other extinct ungulates. The matriarch of a group of mastodons made a couple of fake-charges in their direction but her heart clearly wasn't in it. Quickly perceiving that the strange-smelling modern visitor posed no threat to her juniors or their offspring she allowed the intruder to pass in peace.

"Modern elephants mix comfortably with their resurrected relatives." Now that they were nearing the northern boundary of the Preserve Umfolozi had eased back in the driver's seat. "Not so with many other species. Lions and *Smilodons* will fight over territory."

"What about the giant sloths?" Ingrid was eyeing a herd of waist-high ancestral horses as they galloped across the vehicle's path like so many painted toys escaped from a girl's playroom.

"Nothing big enough to challenge them," their host explained. "Even elephants give way." He sighed. "I dream that one day they put some *Indricotherium* here even though would be hard for me to smuggle out anything bigger than the teeth."

They exited Sanbona through a restricted-use supply gate whose electronic seals Umfolozi had hacked. As they continued to move northward Ingrid could not help but wonder how far they were from the N1 highway. Wouldn't the sight of an elephant outside the Preserve's boundaries draw notice? North of the Little Karoo lay the Swartruggens, which according to the map she remembered was even more empty than the protected region they had just traversed. Once there they ought to be safe from unwanted attention. But surely a pachyderm spotting on the country's main highway would be cause for an excited exchange of communication on the part of passing drivers. She said as much to their elderly driver.

"Of course it would, but we not going to cross highway in this. You see very soon."

The big cross-country truck was parked on the dirt pull-out with its back door down. As they drew near Ingrid was able to see via one of the elephant's internal screens a single well-built young man waiting by the gaping opening. His unnaturally thick legs and arms marked him as a hardworking Meld. Operating a remote he deployed a sturdy loading ramp. Without hesitation Umfolozi drove his camouflaged poaching machine up the waiting platform, into the belly of the truck, and parked the elephant. As they descended the belly stairs and walked outside Ingrid and Whispr gratefully inhaled the fresh, uncontaminated air. Halting before the young man their host introduced them to his nephew Vusi.

"This is a family business." The nephew chatted amiably as they made their way toward the front of the truck. "Everyone helps out and everyone shares in the profit."

"And you run the business." Whispr was always interested in such matters.

"No," Umfolozi corrected him. "*I* run the *family*." He smiled at the thinner of his guests.

After the cramped, smelly quarters inside the elephant, the truck's modern climate-controlled cab was a veritable mansion. Boasting vit projector, two inflatable beds, opposite-facing massage chairs up front, and much more, it was a veritable traveling apartment. The tinted windows allowed driver and passengers to see out while being screened from the view of passing travelers.

"Vusi makes the triangle run on a regular basis between Cape Town, Durban, and Joburg." Umfolozi enlightened his guests as he waited for the truck's automated food server to mix his favored libation. "Sometimes he go to Maputo, sometimes as far as Nairobi."

"One time I took a cargo all the way to Jeddah." The nephew spoke as he guided the nearly silent big rig down what looked like nothing more substantial than a goat track. "Stopped on a pull-out halfway across the Fagal-Mayyun bridge to watch the boats."

With some real food in her stomach and a growing conviction that their nightmarish pursuer was now far behind them, Ingrid's mind had begun to ponder other matters again. Open country trekking in the elephant had alternated between uncomfortable and dangerous. In complete contrast the cross-continent truck was modern, clean, comfortable, and designed for long-range travel. And hadn't Umfolozi said that it was part of a family business?

Still, the day was nearly done before she felt sure enough of herself to broach the idea.

"We'd like to hire this truck and its most congenial young driver. If they're available, that is."

Reaffirming Umfolozi's claim to be head of the family business, the younger man looked wordlessly at his senior relative. After a moment's consideration the old poacher gestured his acquiescence.

"Uncle says it's okay, so sure, I can take you. But wherever you're going you'd probably get there faster in a normal rental from the Cape."

Whispr stepped in to explain. "We already rented a vehicle at the Cape—and crashed it. I'll bet all the rental companies in this part of the world are just like they are back home: linked together to share information. It would look more than suspicious if we tried to rent another vehicle without returning the first one—it would set off alarms throughout the industry. Also, as we told your uncle, there are some unpleasant people looking for us. If we don't rent transportation they can't track us through nonexistent records. And the last sort of transport they'll expect us to be traveling around in is a big rig like this one."

"Just give us a price," Ingrid coaxed the younger man. "I can pay you through indirect electronic satellite transfer."

Four handshakes sealed the arrangement.

The high and wide front window offered an uninterrupted view forward as they pulled into a small village late that afternoon. Neat, compact houses lined the unpaved main street. It was a tranquil, rural scene. A few oldsters sat chatting on screened-in porches while a younger couple crossed the thoroughfare hand-in-hand. There were no children in view. Most likely they were in their homes, Ingrid suspected, attending to school lessons transmitted via private boxes.

Vusi ran a finger across one greasy control screen and the truck turned sharply to the left. As it slowed to a stop outside an oversized prefab barn, several men and women appeared as if out of nowhere. All of them waved excitedly at the cab while moving quickly to the big rig's stern.

As they unloaded the elephant and carried the product of Umfolozi's poaching into the barn, the truck's driver swiveled his seat to face his uncle's guests.

"Now then my new friends: we still need to discuss where is it you wish to go? If not back to Cape Town, then maybe to Joburg? Or perhaps farther north? Gaborone? Harare?"

"North, yes, but much more to the west," Ingrid explained. "A little place in the Namib, called Nerens."

How Umfolozi had kept a personal weapon concealed for so long and so invisibly on his aged person not even Whispr could explain, but it loomed very large as the old man now pointed it straight at the center of his guest's startled face.

15

The nephew's own handgun made its appearance seconds after that of his uncle. With a barrel the size of a drink container it was much more impressive than that of the older man, though a startled Ingrid had no doubt that in their respective fashion each could accomplish the same lethal end. Expecting Whispr to respond, she was more than a little flummoxed when instead of objecting to the disquieting appearance of all the hardware her street-wise companion shrank back against his seat and said nothing. The look in old Umfolozi's eyes indicated that one of them had better say something, and fast, or the offer to hire his nephew's truck would be rendered swiftly and violently moot.

"You are with SICK!" The old man's voice was heavy with accusation. "You are here undercover to take down my family and our livelihood!"

"What? We're nothing of the . . ." Ingrid choked, regained her voice, and started over, struggling to maintain her emotional balance. "Be reasonable, Josini! I don't know what I said to set you off, but if I'd known that it might have provoked this kind of reaction then I wouldn't have said it, now would I?"

Their abruptly less than hospitable host hesitated. The muzzle of his pistol wavered. Ingrid's gaze flicked to her left. She was more worried about the nephew. It was a medical fact that rational action in the human male is inversely proportional to his age. Plainly unsettled, Vusi's attention kept switching between his uncle and the two passengers.

After a moment that had begun to stretch into eternity, the old man relented. The pistol disappeared into his vest and his smile returned. It was as if the frightening confrontation had been a fleeting bad dream, like a sharp pain shooting through the skull that for a few seconds causes everything to go black.

"*Uxolo*—I am sorry, my friends." His tone had gentled, but the gaze he focused like a laser on Ingrid had not. She supposed she should have been flattered. In a country still fraught with custom, challenges and queries would traditionally have been directed at her male companion and not at her. In defiance of convention Umfolozi was enlightened enough to address his queries to the more intelligent of his guests. He glanced over at his nephew.

"Vusi! What's the matter with you? Put that gun away."

"Yebo, Uncle, but you..."

"Put it away." The old man indicated the ebb and flow of the excited human tide that was lapping at the sides of the big truck. "Go and help your brothers and sisters and cousins with the goods. I will be out in a moment."

The younger man eyed the two visitors uncertainly. "Are you sure you will be all right, uncle?"

"Yes, yes, of course!" Turning away from his nephew, he smiled anew at Ingrid. "I make a little mistake, that's all. Weeks alone in the Karoo will do that to a man. Especially if he is living all the time in the belly of an elephant, py damn! Everybody make mistakes, yebo?"

"Sure. Sure." Still wary, Whispr peeled himself off the back of the transporter cab. "I've made plenty."

"I still don't understand." Ingrid's confusion was genuine as she watched Vusi exit the truck. With the door open and the integrity of the vehicle's advanced soundproofing violated, the carnival laughs of women and children filled the cab. "What did I say to set you off? What's wrong with wanting to go into the Namib?"

Having shoved a gun in her face only moments earlier, their host was now all smiles and chuckles as the door closed behind his nephew. "You said you wanted to go to Nerens, in the Namib. First of all that is little bit of a redundant request. The Namib is already nowhere. Oh, I forget—no Afrikaans in Namerica. 'Nerens' is old Afrikaans word meaning 'nowhere.' So what you asking Vusi is to take you to Nowhere in the nowhere."

"Okay." Whispr nodded his understanding. "I can see why the request would produce some giggles at our expense. What I don't see is why it would bring forth guns."

Umfolozi's laughter faded away. As quickly as a classical Greek tragedian swapping masks he turned deadly serious. "Nerens is a SICK company town. Nobody but vetted employees allowed near it, much less inside. Not many people even known there is anything there."

Having survived multiple encounters on the street by learning instinctively that the best defense is a good offense (except for the offenses that get you killed), Whispr asked challengingly, "Then how come *you* know about it?"

Their elderly host took no offense at his guest's insinuating tone. "Is part of my business to know about places others do not know about. I have never been there myself, but I have heard stories about it. I trade in many things, including information."

Ingrid quickly forgot all about the guns that had been waved in her face, about the grueling past few days, even about the shocking and near-fatal appearance of Napun Molé in South Africa. The sangoma Thembekile's information notwithstanding, this was the first confirmation that the destination they sought actually existed. That it was a real place and not just a few buildings on a satellite map.

"What kinds of stories have you heard about it? Tell us, Josini! Don't omit even the smallest, seemingly most insignificant detail."

"That will not be a problem, pretty lady, because I have no details. Nerens is not the sort of place that readily relinquishes details about self. What I do know is very inconsequential and very general." Seeing that she would not be denied, he proceeded to relieve himself of what little information had come his way.

"All I really do know, if story can be believed, is that Nerens is a research facility for SICK. Very important place."

Whispr sniffed derisively. "We already knew that."

"Then, smart fella, you probably also know that it is more than a hundred kilometers from anywhere, the nearest anywhere being the little town of Orangemund near mouth of Orange River. In olden days was a crossing point between two countries, Namibia and South Africa, that all now part of SAEC. Is still crossing point—into Sperrgebeit."

Ingrid was nodding eagerly. "The restricted diamond area."

Umfolozi's tone grew more solemn than ever. " 'Restricted' is exceedingly polite word. Except for the small park section, Sperrgebeit is like separate country, separate even from rest of SAEC. Has own internal administration, police, customs, everything. You found there without authorization, company security can shoot you for trespassing. No questions. Maybe in twenty years you family's lawyer wins case for unjustified homocide. Does *you* lot of good, py damn." His gaze narrowed as he shifted his attention to his slender male passenger. "You two maybe hoping to look for illegal diamonds? Many talk the talk. Those who walk the walk end up dead the dead."

"No." Whispr spared a glance for his companion. "You won't believe this—I don't always believe it myself—but we're trying to find an explanation for an inexplicable phenem—phenomenon." He fought hard to maintain a serious mien. "It is, um, a matter of scientific curiosity."

Umfolozi drew back, his expression one of exaggerated surprise. "Oh, so? You scientists?" He turned to Ingrid. "*You* maybe I can imagine as scientist. This one"—and he gestured dismissively at Whispr—"I see maybe as subject of experiment, but not as experimenter."

The slender subject of the slur did not react. Being persistently underestimated by others had been a key to his survival since childhood. The more people who thought him stupid, the better his chances of surprising them when he revealed that he was not.

"Whispr's telling the truth." Ingrid shifted her position on the transporter seat. "Our journey is all about science."

Leaning back in his swiveling seat Umfolozi stroked the white bristle that sprouted from his chin. "But not straight authorized academically all right-and-proper legal science, I think. If that were so I think maybe you would indulge your curiosity through proper channels and journals. Not by risking your life on the ground in places like Sanbona or the Namib. Because if you try to go to Nerens that for sure what you will be doing."

"Look, *can* your nephew take us there?" With an encompassing gesture the increasingly impatient Whispr took in their immediate surroundings. "We could fill the truck with some kind of cargo. That'd make a great cover for why we're in the area, and he could sell it later and pocket the subsist."

"Is a good idea," Umfolozi seemed to agree, "except is not possible. Are no roads to Nerens. Is only one ancient stinking-bad dirt track running north–south in all of the Sperrgebeit, from Orangemund to Lüderitz, and needless to say but I say it anyway it does not go through Nerens. Even this terrible road that doesn't go where you want to go is closed and guarded. No gypsy cargo truckers allowed. No tourists. No scientists. No nobody."

"How does the research station get its supplies?" Ingrid's mind was working furiously. There *had* to be a way in. "Maybe we could slip inside the same way?"

Their host frowned. "I imagine a lot of supplies, including personnel, come and go via heavy-lift floaters. Really big stuff probably uses private dock at Chamais Bay." His tone had turned sympathetic. "Listen to me, pretty big-brain and other nice parts lady. You try to drive in, they blow your car off the road. You try to fly in, they blow your aircraft out of the sky. You try to sneak in with boat, sensitized radar and other detectors pick you up and you find youself swimming with the white pointers. Maybe you can fake youselves. They still find and kill you ass." He gave this unpromising assessment time to sink in before sitting up straight and concluding importantly.

"Now, for small fee I can have Vusi or one of my other nephews or nieces take you safe back to Cape Town. Is rough ride but not so far from here. From here to nowhere, where you want to go is, I say off top of my old head, a thousand kilometers or so. As the *ig-wababa* flies."

There was silence in the soundproofed cab of the transporter. Outside, relatives of all ages were busy stowing the results of their patriarch's illegal activities deep within the capacious barn. It was beginning to grow dark.

Ingrid Seastrom looked long and hard at her companion. Torn as usual between common sense and innate greed, he said nothing. No words passed between them. She turned back to their host.

"We've come a long way to get this close. We've been through a lot. A good friend and mentor of mine was nearly killed by un-known parties seeking the same things that we are. Both of us have nearly been killed, twice, by a professional assassin we left behind in the Little Karoo, and we don't even know if he's dead or still coming after us." She leaned toward the old man and her voice un-characteristically hardened. The most stalwart of her patients would have been taken aback by the change in her personality.

"There are things, Josini Jay-Joh Umfolozi, that I need to know. There are questions I have that require answers. My friend is inter-ested in their financial potential. I'm not. But I am no less driven or determined because of that. Science is as powerful a motivating force as money. A thirst for knowledge can motivate people as powerfully as the desire for money. You poach some animals be-cause you have to. I intend to poach some information because I need to. *Will you take us?*"

Leaning forward sharply and without warning, Umfolozi kissed her square on the lips.

As she drew back, startled, and wiped at her mouth, the old man threw his head back and filled the transporter cab with a de-lighted cackle. Confused and flustered, Ingrid glared at him.

"That wasn't funny!"

"Oh, I dunno . . . ," a muted voice off to her left started to comment. She whirled on a grinning Whispr.

"You shut up!" Her head snapping around, she glared at their host. "If you agree to take us, that childish little imposition is coming off your fee!"

As he slapped his knees with both open palms, Umfolozi's laughter faded like steam from a kettle that had been taken off the fire. "Okay, pretty lady. Calm down. You not appear to be in much pain. We settle on value of kiss later when we finalize price."

Some of her outrage slipped away. "So you *will* take us?"

His satisfaction at having surprised her now gave way to unavoidable reality. "I am sorry, but Vusi cannot take you to Nerens. Is simply not doable. Not possible for Vusi, not for me, not for anybodies, py damn." He eyed her evenly. "But carrying cargo as disguise and rationale is good idea. Nearest town-place we could get you where cops would not hassle non-SICK visitors on sight is also only town in southern Namib. Orangemund is at delta mouth of Orange River and so is longtime historical recreational place. Even ordinary tourists must have special pass to get into town and stay there, just to play seeker or bird-watch or lie on beaches. I can get necessary permits faked and box-transferred from Pretoria." He smiled hugely. "Extra cost, of course."

Ingrid looked for help to her advisor in such matters.

"We'll take the permits," Whispr replied, "and if necessary we'll use 'em, but it would be better for our purposes if Vusi or whoever takes us up there can get us into town without our having to check with local security. Even though we'll be traveling under assumed idents, and even if those looking for us haven't managed to snag those details, there might be a country-wide alert out for a Namerican man and woman traveling together."

Umfolozi shrugged. "I would not worry about that. Is a description could fit thousands of tourists. Even if a special corner is set up in the SICK box to weed out all possibilities, is still unlikely would single-search you down to a place like Orangemund."

"Nevertheless," Whispr insisted, "it would still be better for us if we could slip in quietly."

Their host sighed heavily. "You are even more mistrustful than old Umfolozi when he is making business in the box. I salute your paranoia." He slapped a hand down on the upholstery, which immediately tried to conform itself to his spread fingers. "I promise Umfolozi will make this happen for you!" His attention shifted mischievously to Ingrid. "Was pleasure knowing you, pretty intellect lady. If you somehow survive and find yourself come back this way, know that poor old scavenging man Josini still has room in his house for one more wife."

"I'll keep the opening in mind," she told him dryly. Her gaze dropped to her trail-worn attire. "We could do with some new clothes and we need to replace the supplies we lost in the Karoo, but we dare not go back into Cape Town to go shopping."

Umfolozi raised an open hand as if bestowing a benediction. "No problem. My first wife Sara and her girls will take necessary measurements and requests. You stay as guests for a few days. They will go into the city and make necessary purchases. No one will question them." His confidence was infectious. "Not to worry— they will use aliases also. I will make everything good for you. But first you must answer one question for me."

Ingrid tensed. "What is it?"

"Say my family get you safely to Orangemund. South of Orangemund is hundreds of square kilometers of nothing. East is nothing but river and more nothing. West is only cold ocean. To north is the

Namib, which is less than nothing. How you think you going to get to Nerens without being observed or killed? And even if you get there, how you going to get inside?"

She took a deep breath. "We don't know."

"Haven't a clue," Whispr added moodily. He'd been down this speculative road with his determined but naïve companion before.

Their host considered this response before nodding understandingly. "I think I have decide I like both of you. Glad not have to kill you. I think you even crazier than old fox Umfolozi." Spinning his seat around to face the dash he ran a finger across the console. The passenger-side door of the big truck hummed as internal motors eased it open. Noise from the busy barn filled the cab.

"Now come sit and have some Rooibos tea with a tired old man and we will discuss the ways you are likely to die—py damn."

EVEN WITH FOURTEEN-WHEEL drive Ingrid was still astonished how effortlessly Vusi wrestled the big rig over the numerous narrow, unpaved tracks that led steadily northward. Cruising through the isolated Roggeveldberge at what seemed to her to be near suicidal speed their driver relied on the truck's advanced computerized shock and strut system to compensate for both the uneven terrain and his high rate of travel.

"No one will track us out here," he told them conversationally. Secure in his driver's gravity harness he could not turn to look back at them, but his words reached them clear and strong thanks to the transport's impeccable soundproofing. If they crashed, Ingrid reckoned, they might not hear it.

"We are traveling parallel to but far away from the main north–south roadway, the N7," he explained. "That's the road everyone uses. By the time we turn west at Calvinia to join it we will be far,

far away from where my uncle found you—and far, far away from anyone who might be looking for you."

Whispr broached a puzzle that had been bothering him ever since they had left the extended Umfolozi family compound. "You say this N7 off to the west is the main north–south road. But it still doesn't go anywhere near Nerens?"

Their young driver laughed without turning. "The N7 runs parallel to the coast but not right along it. And when it starts to get closer to the Namib it gets frightened, just like everyone else is frightened of the Namib, and so it turns inland before swinging back north again to reach for Keetsmanshoop. Even roads avoid the Namib."

"Like your uncle said we should." Gazing out the right-side window Ingrid was doing her best to enjoy the view.

"Like any sensible person should. But you must have your reasons or uncle would not have asked me to take you to Orangemund."

Whispr's thoughts were churning. "Thanks to your uncle's help we'll start out with new packs and proper supplies, but there's still a couple of things I'd like to look for the next time we hit a real town."

Vusi chuckled and shook his head. "Sorry. There are no more real towns. This isn't Europe, where there's a nice little town every ten kilometers. We can try to find what you want in Calvinia, or maybe later in Okiep, but the last real towns are to the south of us now and falling farther behind with every 'k.'" A hand emerged from the driver's seat to indicate the view through the windshield. "From Worcester north are only tiny farming communities. No shopping. People order everything they need through the box and have it sent up. Cheaper than driving to the Cape."

Whispr went quiet until Ingrid thought to query him.

"We went over all this with Josini's wife before she went to Cape Town on our behalf. What did we forget? What else is it you want?"

He gazed out the cab's heavily polarized window. "I'd like to have another battery pack for the gun she bought; for charging the shells in case the original in the grip fails."

She sighed wearily. "We've been over this, Whispr. You need to arm yourself with curiosity and care and stop worrying so much about weapons. If we end up in a fight we'll never get inside Nerens."

He offered a wan smile by way of reply. "Old habits die hard. The more caliber I can carry, the more comfortable I feel."

She did not try to hide her annoyance. "Keep that in mind if we find ourselves on foot again. Every extra gram is going to feel like a kilo after we've been hiking for a while."

"*If* we have to hike," he reminded her.

"Yes—if."

Now that they were drawing comparatively near to their goal they could no longer put off wondering how they were going to get inside the secretive research facility. Whispr's innate desire for ever more ordnance notwithstanding, they needed to begin concocting a suitable narrative. Ingrid was convinced that only subterfuge would gain them admittance. Her profession offered a starting point for a story that might provide a means of entry, but if they chose that tack she was going to be hard-pressed to pass Whispr off as her assistant.

They still had time, she told herself. They would think of something. They had made it this far. She had dealt with extensive security at a number of medical centers, and Whispr had already demonstrated his mastery of other potentially useful skills. But before story or skills could be brought into play, first they had to get to Nerens, and to get to Nerens they had to go through Orangemund.

At the moment, Whispr was brooding on other matters.

"He'll never give up, you know."

"What? Oh, you mean Molé. We don't even know if he's still alive." Staring out the window she watched increasingly barren hills and mountains rush past. Despite a road that in places seemed to disappear completely the big rig's automatic leveling system kept the ride remarkably comfortable. "That giant ground sloth might have killed him."

Whispr was not as easily convinced. "One thing about hunters like Molé: they don't die easy. Our assassin is an old assassin, and professional assassins don't live to be old unless they're very, very good at what they do. This is twice now that we've been lucky with him." One corner of his small mouth turned upward. "Both times we've been saved by the intervention of animals: first in Florida and now here. Almost makes me want to get a dog."

"Yeah, that's what we need now," she murmured sardonically. "A dog."

"Or something. Considering how critters have come to our aid, even if unintentionally, a superstitious type would start thinking of them as good luck charms."

"Thanks for the thought, but I'd prefer to continue relying on common sense, sound preparation, and your skills, Whispr. I do have to agree with you on one thing—Molé is not only scary, he's relentless."

Her companion was nodding knowingly. "I know guys like him. Not as good as him, but like him." He crossed his arms over his narrow chest. "They never give up. They're like machines. You've seen Molé, you've heard him. He'll get us or he'll die trying."

"I know, I know," she agreed worriedly. "That's why I'm hoping the ground sloth got him. Molé, he's almost like an alien or something."

"Or he's one hell of a meld job," Whispr muttered.

She was quiet for several moments. Then, unexpectedly, she leaned toward him. One small but strong hand came to rest on his bony right knee.

"*You're* one hell of a meld job, Whispr. No matter how much subsist was at stake a lot of guys would have given up by now. On this quest. On me. Don't think I don't know that."

He looked down at her hand. It was a doctor's hand, clean and sure. Much more important, it was her hand. Though the touch was light, it burned.

"Yeah, well, money is a great motivator. I figure this is my one chance at something big. And even a slug like me can hope that there might be more at the end of this razor-edged rainbow than just subsist." He stared into her eyes meaningfully.

As if suddenly aware of where it had strayed, she withdrew her hand. "I don't know what to say, Whispr. I thought I'd already made my feelings clear about—that. You're not my type."

"There's no meld for hope." The truck's cab seemed to shrink around him, the air to grow hotter despite the almost oppressively efficient climate control. "Even a false hope is better than no hope at all. Don't try to tell me that it's not. I've spent my whole life dealing with false hopes, but I never give up. Call it a mental narcotic and me a hopeful addict. You wouldn't deny me that little thing, would you, doc—Ingrid?"

She exhaled heavily. "All right, Whispr. I promise that I won't deny you any false hopes."

The smile that resulted spread across the majority of his narrow face.

"What more could any man ask?"

16

The Orange River was a lot bigger than Ingrid expected, and the town much smaller.

How the river had acquired its name she could not imagine. Anything but orange, it was brown and muddy and turbid with pieces of Africa that had been washed all the way down from the center of the continent. For millions of years it had also carried diamonds among the dirt. Picking the gem quality stones up from the river's mouth the chill Benguela current had flicked them northward to be deposited on the ocean floor, the beaches, and the marine terraces of the Sperrgebeit.

In that Forbidden Zone modern technology had allowed mining to continue. New technologies such as spray-foam sea walls allowed the Namdeb corporation (a division of SAEC Ltd.) to keep the hungry sea at bay. Solar- and wind-powered pumps kept the ocean from seeping in to flood the vast excavations. Melded workers whose skin had been maniped to cope with the searing sun of the Namib labored in absurdly light clothing to maintain the activity around the clock. Even more than tourism and fishing, the support of diamond mining was the main reason for Orangemund's continued existence. The town contained no support facilities for the research center at distant Nerens and there was no road linking the two SAEC enterprises.

Having turned off the autoroad at Vloolsdrift, Vusi had been intent on the task of hands-on driving ever since. Now he guided the big truck across the bridge that spanned the Orange. After the endless kilometers of Namaqualand and the southernmost Namib, the sight of the river's broad, steady flow was a shock. So was Orangemund itself. Centered on historical structures that had been saved from the heyday of mining, the New Town was a disappointing sprawl of architecturally and culturally inconsequential single-story structures linked by climate-controlled pedestrian pathways. The village of several thousand was wholly utilitarian and unbeautiful. Like rain-fed streams in the desert, paved roads petered out and disappeared into long, flat stretches of sand and gravel. As far as Ingrid was concerned the area's only real attraction was the air itself, which was clearer and purer than any she had ever inhaled.

There was a nervous moment or two as they checked in at the community guard post. While the old town itself was faded and historic, there was nothing outdated about the weapons the guards brandished nor the technology they utilized to check visitors' idents.

Vusi parked his truck. Under the watchful eyes of a quartet of armed men and women, the three arrivals were escorted into a nearly windowless white building over whose double climate-sealing doors arched a sign that proclaimed "Welcome to Orangemund." Originating from and terminating in thin air, the image of a miniature Orange River flowed in three dimensions through the arch, gurgling cheerily. To Ingrid the animated holo looked much cleaner and more inviting than its eponymous namesake.

The fortyish official seated behind a simple desk had no hair, dark maniped skin, and only one eyebrow—an odd fashion trait. He accepted their idents without offering a welcome. One by one these were inserted into a reader while a visual scanner played over their bodies, illuminating them lightly.

"What is your purpose in coming to Orangemund?" It was hot outside. Ingrid felt it was rapidly growing warmer inside.

"I've got a cargo of fruits and veggies from the Karoo." Vusi affected the casual air of someone who had done this a hundred times before and who fully anticipated doing it a hundred times again. "From my cousin's farm. I had a week between contracted loads and both of us figured we could make a small killing by taking the time to sell it in as remote a place as we could find."

The official grunted understandingly. "You sure did pick well. Piet van Hendrik and Damali Nongoma manage our two main markets. I'm sure they'll be glad to take your cargo off your hands. Probably bid against each other." His voice had lost some of its initial official bite. "You bring with you any pineapples, maybe? I haven't seen a pineapple in two months."

Vusi grinned. "I'll leave a couple with your name on them at one of the markets. So that proper agricultural clearance can be conducted, of course."

The official smiled thinly and nodded. "Always got to make sure nobody brings any bugs in," he agreed, disregarding the fact that there wasn't a fruit or vegetable field at risk of infection for a couple of hundred kilometers in any direction. That bit of unofficial customs business concluded, he turned serious again as his attention shifted to the idents of the driver's companions.

"Namericans? We don't get so many Namericans here."

"We're just tourists." Ingrid offered her most engaging smile, musing as she did so if this was to be the ultimate result of all those years of study and medical school. "We happen to like visiting out-of-the-way places."

"And traveling by ourselves, away from other tourists, by non-traditional means." Though considerably less engaging than that of his now red-haired companion, Whispr offered up his own smile. "If you travel by tour bus or train or floater you never meet anyone interesting or learn anything about the local culture."

"Like I say to your driver, you pick correctly."

As the official studied the readout on the privacy screen in front of him, Ingrid found that she was sweating despite the cool air that filled the room.

"We're especially here to see the birds," Whispr added, unable to let well enough alone.

In spite of her determination to appear as indifferent as possible to the formal entry procedures Ingrid could not keep herself from glancing warningly at her companion.

"Really?" Suddenly interested, the official eyed the exceptionally slender visitor more closely. "Well, this area is famous for its birds. Because of the river, of course." One at a time he methodically slid their idents beneath a scanner that electronically embedded them with the necessary visitors' permits. "I was only going to admit you for a couple of days, but if you are birders then you may need more time." He chuckled to himself. "Nothing personal, but from what I have seen it is clear that all birders are more than a little crazy. Will two weeks be enough?"

Ingrid tried hard not to betray her relief. "Two weeks should be more than sufficient, thank you."

"You are welcome. You may go now." He peered up at Vusi.

"Either market is okay to leave the pineapples. Everyone shops everywhere here."

Once back in the truck Ingrid turned angrily on her companion. "Tell me something, Whispr—what would you have done if that man had asked you what *kind* of birds we were here to look for?"

He shrugged. "I didn't think he would. Like he said, even on the street in a place like Savannah everyone knows that birders are crazy. You see them out in the swamps and the drowned territories, sitting in small boats glued to their synoptics and getting eaten alive by bugs. Anyway, what are you so upset about? He bought it, and everything's fine."

She turned away from him to stare moodily out the window on her side of the truck cab. "I just wish you'd discuss strategy with me first. There are enough surprises on this journey. I don't need to have to deal with any extras from you."

"Then don't," he responded sharply.

They didn't speak to each other as they helped Vusi dispose of his cargo of fruits and vegetables; produce that was always welcome in the isolated community despite the presence of several well-stocked Namdeb corporate stores.

"The company keeps us pretty well supplied," explained one store manager, "but they have no control over the weather or supply scheduling from the Cape or the east coast. It's always a bonus when we can lay in extra goods." He eyed a stack of transparent plastic corkscrews full of tomatoes. The containers would keep their contents in stasis, ripening them only on command.

After the last of the cargo had been sold and unloaded the three visitors had lunch at an outdoor café near the western edge of the sprawling community. A freshening breeze from the ocean mitigated the temperature. Vusi tucked into the remainder of an oversized sandwich whose contents Ingrid was unable to identify. Nor was she sure she wanted to.

"My uncle says that you two are bound and determined to get yourselves killed."

"Yeah. We're real single-minded that way." Whispr chugged Tusker beer from a self-chilling container.

"We are not going to get ourselves killed."

A glance at their fellow diners told Ingrid that no one was looking in their direction or paying them the least attention. While she and Whispr were not the only authorized tourists in town, their counterparts were not numerous and were widely scattered. Ironically, at this time of day many were out bird-watching on the river or hidden in blinds along the shore. Orangemund was one of many remote underdeveloped communities that received encouragement and support from the government to develop its local tourist industry as a way of diversifying an otherwise limited commercial base. It was not the government's fault nor for lack of trying on the part of the locals that hardly anyone wanted to go there.

Vusi inhaled the last of his sandwich, chased it with what remained of his own beer, and pushed back from the table. "Well, best of luck to you. It's likely I'll never see you again, whether dead or alive."

His former passengers remained seated and silent. They were in no rush to proceed. Or as Whispr would have put it, in no hurry to get killed. The usual brief and polite words of farewell were exchanged, and then Vusi was gone. The doctor and the deadbeat were on their own again, Ingrid thought. On their own on the southern edge of nowhere, wondering how they were going to get from their present location to Nowhere incorporated.

The tourist industry was sufficient to make going concerns of a couple of small hotels. One was full of backpackers, more than a few of whom were full-time desert lovers. This was evident from their specialized melds: elongated skin flaps to protect the ears, protruding brows to shade the eyes, permanently altered melanin content in their skin, splayed feet with hardened desensitized soles for walking unshod on sand, esophageal reroutes that enabled them to keep their lungs extra moist, and fleshy epidermal catchments to allow for the recycling of perspiration. Where other Melds and no Natural dared not hike without special clothing and equipment, they strode boldly.

Wouldn't last a week in Oslo. Ingrid looked on as a young couple that had been so modified headed toward the river without hats or packs and a quantity of water that between them would not have sustained her in similar circumstances for more than twenty-four hours.

Grudgingly resuming conversation out of necessity, she and Whispr spent the next couple of days establishing an identity in the minds of the locals as a pair of unexceptional tourists; lying on the river beaches above the crocodile fences, visiting the mouth of the Orange, shopping for knickknacks they had no intention of taking home, and pretending to record vits of themselves standing in front of each of those locales and more. After the first two days they continued their faux touristic pursuits, except that from time to time Whispr would stop to engage in conversation with newly-made acquaintances whom he deemed to be less than upstanding citizens of either Orangemund or the wider SAEC.

It was on their third night in town as they were eating dinner at a café that overlooked the river that Ingrid, while having found her appetite, nearly lost her patience.

"Are you sure you're talking to the right people, Whispr? We can't keep this up forever. Someone's bound to track us here eventually. It might be the people who attacked my doctor friend. It might be the SAEC government, or recovery people for the agency whose rental we didn't return, or an entirely new group with an interest in the thread." She sounded glum. "It might even be that horrible degenerate Molé, if the sloth didn't kill him. No matter how out of the way it is we can't spend weeks in a little place like this."

Whispr gazed across the table and shook his head. "You're better off leaving the doom and gloom to me, doc. I'm much better at it and I've had a lot more practice. I'm doing my best." He leaned toward her and lowered his voice. "What d'you expect me to do? Walk up to a local official and say, 'I beg your pardon but my companion and I have had enough of bird-watching and what we'd really like to do is visit the super-secure SAEC research facility at Nerens up in the Forbidden Zone. Do be a good fellow now and arrange transportation for us, won't you? That's a nice bureaucrat.'"

She growled back at him. "There's no need to be so snide. It's just that after where we've come from and all we've been through that we're so *close* now."

"Don't you think I'm impatient, too?" He scrutinized the other diners. Neither comments nor looks were aimed in their direction. "Listen to me, doc—Ingrid. I've seen it before, what happens in situations like this. This is when people slip up. This is when they get themselves found out: right when they're close to their goal. Right when everything seems within their grasp. That's when the cops arrive, the bullets burn, and the excrement impacts the air compressor. That's when you have to move more slowly and carefully than ever. The time to watch your step is when you only have one or two left on your path."

At which point their waitress, a young woman whose complex cosmetic meld consisted of desert snakes in place of hair, leaned toward them and murmured softly, "I hear you two are trying to get to Nerens?"

Whispr replied before Ingrid could respond with anything more than a startled gasp. "Who says that we are?"

"Sandword says. In a town this size you can't talk to anyone without someone else eventually finding out about it." Ingrid noted that the waitress's eyes were a bright golden hue, with slitted pupils. Whether her hissing of her "s" sounds was due to an epiglottal manip or a conversational affectation the doctor was unable to tell.

Ingrid didn't care if the girl spat her "p"s. "Suppose we are? Suppose we've heard that there are rare species up that way which we could add to our birding lists by going there. Can you help us?"

"Who, me?" The young woman recoiled, while her Medusan coiffure simply coiled. "Are you insane? In this town just talking about helping someone get anywhere near Nerens is enough to get you hauled in for interrogation."

"Then why," Whispr inquired reasonably, "are you talking to us about it?"

"One, because if anyone helps you to get up there it's not going to be me, and two, because you haven't paid the bill yet—or left a tip."

Ingrid sighed. Some cultural constants never changed, not even when changing continents. "Tell us what you can."

Leaning over the table the young woman let two of her serpentine coils deliver the old-fashioned plastic bill. "Corner of Francis and Rico streets, third house toward the sea. A friend of mine is renting it to a transient who might be able to help you."

"You expect us to believe that some bum has information on how to get to Nerens?" Whispr was openly dubious.

Slitted eyes focused on the stick-man. "The 'bum's' name is

Morgan, and he *is* information. According to my friend, until recently this guy actually used to work at Nerens."

Beneath the table the excited Ingrid reached across to grasp and squeeze Whispr's hand. So stunned was he by the unexpected contact that he did not mind the pain. He was also careful not to squeeze back.

"Francis and Rico," she repeated carefully. "Third house from the sea. How will he know we're not police or SICK security?"

"Slap the center of the door twice, then kiss it."

Ingrid frowned. " 'Kiss it'?"

"Tactile response entry."

Whispr did not try to conceal his impatience. "You think he'll agree to see us?"

"I'll make sure the word gets to him that you're clean and to expect you." The waitress accepted Ingrid's credcard and ran their bill. "You'd do well to start there now. It's dark, and tactile door security or not, from what I've heard after eleven o'clock I don't think this guy would open up for Jesus."

Ingrid rose from her chair. "Thank you so much for the information, and the help!"

A snarl of hair hissed in her direction as the waitress responded with a professional smile. "Thanks for the big tip."

The doctor blinked in confusion. "I haven't totaled or signed off on the final bill yet."

Their waitress and informant smiled, as did her coiffure. "I believe in being proactive."

FROM THE OUTSIDE THE house in one of the nondescript developments on the edge of town was uncompromisingly ordinary. Illuminated by the moon that floated in the transparent Namib sky it appeared identical to the second house toward the sea, and the fourth. Beyond the last building lay open desert. There were no walls, no hedgerows, no landscaping to commemorate the changeover. After the last yard in back of the last house at the end of the last road, civilization halted and the ancient desert took over. Though laid side by side they were two different books whose contents had nothing in common.

Having taken the precaution of having their autocab drop them several blocks away, Ingrid and Whispr had walked the remaining half mile down paved streets alive with nearly silent automated vacuums. Like giant silvery beetles the automatons were engaged in the never-ending task of slurping up the sand that blew in from the surrounding desert. For the utilitarian street robots their Sisyphean task was to keep the Namib from reclaiming the rows of neat little homes and their incongruously colorful, heavily maniped gardens.

The two Namericans did not linger to inspect their surroundings in greater detail lest someone happen to see them turn up the short winding walkway that led to the door of their intended destination. As they made their way to the front of the house each successive paving stone they stepped on illuminated from within. Without hesitation Ingrid twice slapped the center of the one-piece white barrier with her open palm and then leaned forward to buss it firmly. For the first time in his life Whispr found himself envying a door.

After a pause a deep voice issued from the door's speaker grid. "Are you the two tourists who wanted some information about desert birding?"

Ingrid replied immediately. "Yes, that's us."

Within the door something clicked softly. Instead of opening inward it retracted into the ceiling: a suburban portcullis.

The interior of the house was neatly laid out and decorated in muted colors to match the surrounding countryside. A vit wall in the den presently displayed a tactile alpine scene that emitted cool air, birdsong, and a faint scent of edelweiss. Morgan Ouspel was waiting for them. His eyes kept searching the entryway behind them, as if he expected their meeting to be interrupted at any moment. Of average height with a blond crew cut, his features were fine and almost feminine. He wore secondhand clothes and the look of a man designated to substitute for the fox in the hunt. Recognizing a kindred spirit, Whispr liked him immediately. That did not mean that he trusted him immediately.

"So you've worked at Nerens?"

"Quiet, quiet!" Holding a small rectangular instrument out in front of him their agitated host proceeded to nervously pace the circumference of the room, paying particular attention to the one small, heavily curtained window that faced the street. There was no need for a large picture window, Ingrid realized, as it would only look out on the house across the street while forcing the residence's climate control to work that much harder to keep the home's interior comfortable.

Only when he was satisfied did Morgan slump into a chair and beckon for them to seat themselves on the couch opposite. While the responsive furniture strove to make them as comfortable as possible their host leaned forward to regard them with an intensity that verged on the fanatic. Though unsettled by his stare, Ingrid knew enough to know that he was not mentally unbalanced: just jumpy. Still, his rapid eye movements and physical twitching added an edge to the conversation that she could have done without.

"I'm told that you want to go to Nerens. I find that not only amusing but ironic because I want to go anywhere *but* Nerens. You need information, I need money. Maybe we can help each other."

His attention kept shifting rapidly back and forth between his two visitors. "Why do you want to go to Nerens?"

"Why do you want to get away from it?" Whispr refused to let their host dictate the conversation.

"Because I've been there." Though the rest of him appeared Natural, Morgan's eyes were open so wide that for a moment Ingrid thought they had been maniped. "Because I've seen things there. Things that made me break my contract and my sworn obligation and leave without being officially discharged." He threw another glance toward the window. "They're after me, I'm sure of it. Just to check on me, maybe. But I don't want them checking on me. I don't want them asking me questions. Not after what I've seen."

This was not at all what Ingrid had expected. "What things? What have you seen?"

"I've seen the Big Picture. It's real, and it moves. I've seen the Painters of the Picture, and they move, too. They are not of God. They are . . ." He paused as if catching himself. "If I tell you any more you'll think I'm crazy and we won't have a deal and I won't get the subsist I need to get away from here so I'm not going to tell you. Once again: why do you want to go to Nerens?"

"None of your business," Whispr replied promptly.

Their host rose from where he had been sitting. "Nice meeting you. Don't worry about the door: I'll close it behind you."

"Calm down, calm down." Ingrid shot Whispr a poisonous glance. The stick-man shrugged as if to say, "Just doing my job," but held his peace. Turning back to Morgan she conjured up a pleasant smile that bordered on the flirtatious. Practice, she thought, was making her better at this, even though it was not a subject she had studied at university.

It occurred to her that he might be an undercover operative for

SICK. It also occurred to her that if they tried to dicker with him or tiptoe around the truth they would get no more second chances. He would throw them out without a moment's hesitation. They had come too far to risk that happening. In fact, ever since they had left Savannah life every day had been all about risk.

She felt unreasonably and unnaturally exhilarated.

"We have in our possession a small device that's made of a kind of metal that shouldn't exist. Our own personal research suggests that SICK may be the manufacturer. I want to find out how it's possible to manufacture such metal while keeping it stable and also to learn its purpose." She gestured at Whispr. "My companion's interests are less lofty. What interests him is the subsist that might be gained from learning the answers to these questions."

Morgan absorbed all this, listening quietly and occasionally nodding slowly. When she had finished he pursed his lips thoughtfully. "Learning the answers to those questions might also get you both killed."

"We have some understanding of the dangers involved," she told him. "We've already had to deal with a few. We're prepared to go to the limit to learn these secrets." Next to her Whispr muttered something unintelligible under his breath.

"If I tell you what you need to know," their host murmured tightly, "you must swear not to mention my name in context with your proposed 'visit,' no matter how strenuously and persistently you're asked."

"Sure, we swear." Unlike the doctor Whispr had no money to offer their informant, but his capacity for making meaningless promises was boundless.

Morgan glanced at him, turned away as if the slender Meld didn't exist, and locked eyes with Ingrid. "I'd never tell anyone else what I've seen—and I've seen a few things—but convincing *them* of that would be hellishly difficult."

"Yeah, you told us. 'The Big Picture.'" Whispr was unimpressed. "'Painters.'"

Morgan didn't even look in the other man's direction. "So I just left," he told Ingrid. "Fast, unofficially, without signing anything, and notably without undergoing the decommissioning physical they give to everyone who's retiring or leaving for any other reason. I'll tell you what I can and what you want to know, which is how to get there, for..." He named a figure.

Whispr stifled a laugh. Ingrid stiffened, but nodded agreement. Satisfied, their host took out his communicator and extended it toward her. As Ingrid removed her credcard Whispr moved to intercede, smiling at their host as he did so.

"Huh-uh. Information first, then subsist."

Morgan looked as if he was about to object, then nodded reluctantly. Ingrid withdrew her card. "Give me both of your comms," he told them. She passed hers across, followed by Whispr. Their host made some rapid adjustments to his own device, then pressed the necessary contacts first against her unit and then Whispr's. After a final check to make sure the transfer had gone through he sat back and looked satisfied.

"I've conveyed to your units all the information and details on the best way to get from here to Nerens without going through official channels. On the *only* way to get from here to Nerens without going through official channels. I know it's the only way because as far as I know I'm the only one who's ever managed it. The crossing will take more time than the actual distance suggests because you'll have to go on foot. It's rough in places but it's all negotiable. I know—I just did it myself." He indicated Ingrid's comm unit. "The trail mostly follows gullies and ravines. That helps you to stay out of sight as much as possible. Safe sources of water are marked on the maps. There are enough perennial waterholes so that you'll be able to travel without having to carry too much."

Delving into the files Morgan had downloaded onto his communicator Whispr was furiously checking every detail as fast as he could. Searching for blatant inaccuracies, he could find none.

"Why do we have to walk?" Ingrid was not looking forward to the prospect. Not after the hot, arid trek they had been forced to make in the Sanbona Preserve.

Their host explained patiently. "Because the facility's security is always scanning for intruders. It's never down. Additionally, there are three overlapping layers: the one operated by the research facility, the park's, and the one belonging to the diamond mining concession. This being the Namib, their personnel are trained to expect any unauthorized visitors to arrive by mechanical means: floater, aircraft, heliarc boots, ground vehicle, boats, scuba—any way except on foot. Even so, they have security out watching for hikers also, but it's not as intensive or as well monitored. At least, not according to the security people I got to know. I made it out. By the skin of my arse, but I did. Who knows? Maybe you'll make it in." He appeared to wrestle with himself for a moment before leaning toward her again.

"Can I—see this device you say you've got, whose attraction is powerful enough to bring you to the point of risking your lives to learn about it?"

She looked over at Whispr. He was still intent on validating the information their host had provided to them. The decision was hers.

Reaching inside her shirt she gently squeezed the concealed pocket containing the hidden capsule. Reading her touch the compartment unsealed, allowing her to remove the tiny transparent cylinder. Intact and undamaged, the metallic thread gleamed within its storage container. It had been a while since she had actually looked at it. As she started to pass it to Morgan he reached out to take it . . .

And recoiled from it as if she were trying to hand him a live cobra. His eyes grew wild. The alarm in his voice was enough to make Whispr instantly look up from his communicator.

"Oh, *shit—*a *distributor!*"

A startled Ingrid looked down at the capsule that contained the thread. To her eyes it appeared as harmless as ever.

"You know what this is?"

"It's a distributor! Goddamnit—chances are it's still loaded."

"'Loaded'?" Whispr's thin brows drew together. "Loaded with what? It's an information storage thread."

"Is that what you think? It's *not*. It looks like one, but it's not." His anxious gaze returned from the capsule to Ingrid. "It's full of implants!"

"Impla . . . ?" She gaped at him, looked down at the thread, over at Whispr, then back at their host. "It's a storage thread. It's made to hold information, not surgical components."

Morgan's eyes were hard. "You already admitted you don't know what it does."

She contained her exasperation. "Look, this is impossible. Even if someone, somehow, somewhere, managed to figure out a way to put surgical implants on a storage thread, the ones I'm interested in were quantum entangled. There's no way to preserve them on some kind of faux storage medium in a state of permanent stasis where . . ."

She stopped herself. Where the thread and the implants were concerned, "impossible" was a descriptive term that had long since outlived its application. She hesitated, then looked over at her companion. The stick-man stared back blankly and shook his head, desperately aware that he was well out of his depth.

"You know, Whispr, it might explain why neither my lab nor the Alligator Man nor Yabby Wizwang could figure out what's on the thread. If what Morgan is saying is the truth, the contents are probably security screened. A normal thread reader looking for information might see only a blank. In the usual sense there wouldn't appear to be anything on the thread." She peered down at the hair-thin piece of glistening, tantalizing, impossible metal. "If the thread's been engineered and security-screened to contain something other than information, even an advanced data decompiler is going to see the content as empty."

"Empty, yeah." Whispr turned to their host. "You say there are implants on the thread. What kind of 'implants'? What do they do?"

Morgan continued to stare at the thread as if mesmerized. "I don't know. I don't know. I don't *want* to know. I only know that they come out of the facility stored on the threads and that they're sent away, and that no diamonds or gold or government secrets ever were moved from one place to another under tighter security. I only learned enough to know that these implants are transported on the thread, not what they actually contain. It was a freak encounter that enabled me to learn that much, and I was lucky I wasn't shot on the spot." His gaze went again, briefly, to the window and then to the front door.

"I've told you everything you deserve to know and more than I should." He indicated the capsule. "Put that back where you got it and don't show it to anyone else ever again. Don't even hint that you have it." His eyes flicked back and forth between them. "You're never going to find out what's on the distributor, but it's not my business if you're determined to try. Pay me my money."

Ingrid checked again with Whispr. This time he nodded. As soon as the transaction had been completed and verified, their host rose from his chair. His tone was solemn.

"You were never here. You never heard of me. With luck and if I can arrange events in the right sequence I'll be on my way out of here and out of Africa by tomorrow morning. I'd advise you to do the same." A pause, then, "If you don't, and you're determined to go ahead with this, make sure you take plenty of food concentrates with you. As I said, you'll find plenty of potable water along the way, but there's precious little to eat. The Namib is the world's oldest desert and it's no more a bulging larder now than it was a million years ago."

Ingrid nodded her understanding. "It's a lucky thing we were able to make contact with you."

For the first time since they had entered the house his attitude seemed to soften a little. "You think I'm the first employee who's quit the facility? Plenty retire, on good pensions. Others can't take the isolation and just tender their resignations. What's different is that I had a top security clearance. As soon as I saw what I saw and learned what I learned I knew that if I wanted to get out I was going to have to do so fast, before I learned too much, and without official approval. And no way was I going to go through their medical decommissioning procedure." He lowered his voice.

"Like I said, plenty of people retire. But above a certain grade there are none of the usual personal box sites for ex-employees. No way to make contact, no way to have a friendly chat. They just disappear." He straightened. "If I was going to have to disappear I damn sure wanted it to be in my own way and on my own terms." He surprised Ingrid again, by reaching out and taking her left hand in both of his.

"You seem like decent people. As a favor to me and as a last caution, before you start out pay a visit to the Boot Shop under Market Square."

She eyed him blankly. "The walking shoes we have are still in good shape."

Their host was almost amused. "It's not that kind of boot shop. Ask for Nokhot and ask her to run a boost trace on the signal from the thread." At their expressions of surprise he smiled. "Yes, I know about that, too. Every thread emits a signal. For what purpose I don't know and can't imagine. If you live long enough maybe you'll be the ones to find out."

"Boost trace can't be run," Whispr countered. "The signal is way too weak, and omnidirectional."

"It's not omnidirectional." Morgan reached into a carved wooden box resting on an end table. Withdrawing paper and an actual old-fashioned writing stylus (a "pen," Ingrid realized) he scribbled furiously but briefly before passing her the result.

"Here's a bit of key information that can't be traced back to me electronically. Show it to Nokhot and ask her to follow the directions. Don't tell her where you got it, and make sure when you're finished with it to destroy it completely."

She perused the succession of hastily jotted words and figures. "What is this?"

"Coordinates and instructions for how to boost the signal so you can run a proper trace. Without them she'll get nowhere no matter how hard she tries. Maybe the results will give you pause." He started for the front door. "Now you must leave. I have to pack what little I'm taking with me."

Ingrid inquired without thinking. "Where are you going?" It was a question Whispr, who knew better, would never have dared ask.

They were at the door. "Elsewhere," Morgan told her. "It doesn't matter. Anywhere beats where you're going."

A resigned Whispr nodded knowingly. "That's for sure, since we're going to Nowhere."

Their host shook his head. "Close but not quite accurate. You're going to Hell."

IT WAS NOT SURPRISING to find Orangemund's smaller shops located on two levels below the central marketplace. Subterranean climate control was simpler and cheaper. So was the real estate. Vendors sold fruits and vegetables but no meat or fish. The latter were banned by mutual agreement since the smell in an enclosed space would have imposed more than just a minor inconvenience on sellers and shoppers alike. Similar markets could be found anywhere in the world.

Relegated to shop space below the surface were hardworking vendors of secondhand goods, electronic trinkets, cheap children's toys, superficial manips, dubious meld repairs, temporary cosmetics, designer knockoff clothing, practitioners of traditional medicine, exploiters of local endangered species, and the inevitable Chinese-run general store. Within the rock-walled surroundings the raucous chatter of customers and salesfolk ranged from muted to deafening depending on the nature of the transactions that happened to be taking place at one time. The more respectable enterprises such as those that sold validated entertainment, packaged foods whose use-by dates had not yet expired, on-site custom-fashioned clothing, front-line furniture, pornography, and drugs, occupied the main market aboveground. Ringing the marketplace were service facilities that dealt with delivery vehicles and large goods which could not be accommodated underground.

Nokhot's place was tucked back in a corner between an old woman who sold local weavings and an armored shop that dealt in jewelry both new and used. The location was darker than most because the peeling luminate on the walls and ceiling was long overdue for reapplication. Ingrid's initial reaction on seeing the sole occupant of the shop was to inquire as to the owner's whereabouts. Having dealt with similar establishments on another continent Whispr knew better than the doctor that the owner was already present.

"Got a small job for you," he said by way of introduction.

"No job too small for Nokhot" was the giggly response.

Ingrid had the feeling the shop's teenage proprietor giggled a lot. She was very pretty, almost delicate, with sapphire-stained hair styled in counterwoven braids that hung below her shoulders, a wide mouth, and bright black eyes. They made her oversized ears look even more out of place. At five times the size of normal human ears they constituted an extensive meld. The inward-curving rims would serve to amplify sound waves even more. Additionally there were two extra arms that gave the girl four in total. The little finger of each hand had been doubled in length. Each fingertip terminated in a different tool fashioned of reinforced bone. Ingrid decided Nokhot looked like Little Miss Muffit *and* the spider all rolled into one.

In response to a meaningful glance from Whispr, Ingrid drew forth the protective capsule and handed it to the Meld. Giggling pensively, Nokhot turned it over and over in her many fingers as she contemplated the thread within.

"What do you want me to do with this? Run a compositional analysis? See what's on it?"

Whispr shook his head. "It's putting out a really weak signal."

He glanced over at Ingrid. "We'd like to know where it's being sent. Where it's being received."

Nokhot nodded, eyed Ingrid. "I'll have to take it out of its container."

"Go ahead. Just don't drop it into a crack or anything. Or snap it."

The girl crossed her top two arms indignantly as the slightly lower pair went to work on the capsule. "I'll have you know, missy, that I treat my customers' goods like my own."

The thread slid into a receiving slot in the middle of a complex of coupled electronics that comprised the most jury-rigged mass of gear Ingrid had ever seen. Cold lights flared to life from floor to ceiling. With two hands the quadridexterous Nokhot swung her box projection around and forward so that it hovered between her and her customers. The other set of fingers were busily at work deep within the jumbled mass of equipment.

"We were told this would be of help." Ingrid handed over the sheet of paper Morgan had filled with instructions and symbols. Nokhot studied it closely.

"Never seen anything like this." She chuckled. "It calls for a power boost that while brief is strong enough to get me arrested."

"So you can't run the trace the way the paper suggests?" Ingrid was downcast.

The girl giggled loudly. "Didn't say couldn't do it. Said could get me arrested. No biggie. I been arrested before." Her hands went back to work.

Looking on, Ingrid was not particularly shocked by the shop owner's meld-supplemented dexterity. For example, there were any number of meld surgeons who flaunted similar manips. She personally knew two who had six arms. Others might have opted for even more except that tests, trial, and unfortunate error had shown that Hindu mythology notwithstanding, half a dozen upper limbs seemed the limit the human torso could comfortably accommodate.

Ingrid was prepared to wait as many hours as necessary for the trace to be run. Five minutes later the girl's workseat rolled back, a long finger stretched out to depress a single control, and she said, "Here goes . . ."

For a brief instant every light and telltale in the shop put forth the maximum radiance of which they were capable. Then they went dark almost as quickly. As did the lights in every shop within view. Within a couple of seconds the lowest level of the underground market had become dark as a cave. Not as silent, though, as shopkeepers and customers fumbled for emergency lights while shouting vivid imprecations in more than a dozen languages.

Ingrid counted off seconds. Thirty-one, thirty-two—light sources began to flicker back to life. Complaints were overwritten by questions, then resignation, then laughter, and soon it was business as usual again.

Nokhot grunted as she studied several readouts. "Couldn't have held a boot that strong for a full minute. As it is, despite the shunts I programmed into it I'll be lucky if they don't trace it to my little hole in the ground and raid me." She looked back at Ingrid. "This will cost you."

The doctor sighed. "Everything does. Never mind that. Was the trace successful?" Next to her eagerness radiated from Whispr's face. Or maybe it was just sweat.

The girl shifted her seat to where she could better study her instrumentation. Within the hovering box projection there was a distressing lack of imagery; only numbers.

More time passed in light than had in darkness, but without illumination. An impatient Ingrid finally prompted the tech. "Well? Where's the signal going? What's the destination?"

Nokhot absently brushed aside a falling braid as she looked back at her anxious customer. For a change she was not giggling.

"I don't know the destination. I don't know that there is a destination. But the direction is up."

Whispr nodded sagely. "Refracted signal. Can you identify the satellite?"

"There is no satellite anywhere near the line of transmission. It's all empty space." Four hands turned palm upward. "Your little thread is broadcasting to emptiness."

Ingrid struggled to make some sense of what the tech was telling her. "Moon?" she ventured uncertainly. "Mars, maybe?"

"The signal is going out at an angle that would not take it near any solar bodies. Not even the asteroid belt is in line. It's just broadcasting out into nothingness. Unless it's aiming at an unlisted military satellite or a relay not listed in catalog." Nokhot indicated the slot that held the thread. "Pretty fancy-nancy piece of tech just for nothing. If that little smidge of a signal is given a proper boot like we just did, according to the parameters on that paper you brought me, it seems to repropagate itself. There's an algorithmic unfolding takes place like I never seen before." Her gaze narrowed as she examined her oddly matched customers more closely. "Where did you get your little thread?"

Whispr stepped forward and extended an open palm. "It was the prize in a box of Cracker Jack. Hand it back, please."

She stared at him a long moment, then burst out giggling. "Okay, okay! Big secret man. Spends all kinds of time and money to communicate with nothing nowhere." One hand reached back to open the slot and remove the thread. After carefully replacing it in its transparent capsule she started to pass it to the waiting Whispr.

Ingrid interceded. Her companion voiced no objection and took no visible offense as the doctor accepted the capsule and slipped it back into the tiny concealed compartment inside her shirt.

"Thank you for your efforts, Nokhot. What do I owe you?"

The girl named a price. For a change, it was reasonable. As Ingrid conducted the transfer Nokhot erupted in a fresh burst of girlish laughter.

"Hey, I know! I got it all figured out for you now!"

"Really?" Ingrid nearly forgot to log out of her extensively manipulated account. "What? Where?"

The girl's dark eyes met hers. "Aliens! Your thread is talking to aliens!" She might have been trying to say more, but any additional words were overwhelmed by a flowering of giggles.

"Yeah, that's it," Whispr commented dryly. "You got it. Thanks for your efforts." Rising, he turned and exited the shop. Ingrid followed. Insofar as she could tell, no one bothered to track their progress as they headed for the lift that would take them back to the surface.

Aliens. Thanks to Morgan Ouspel they knew what was on the thread, and while puzzling and more than a little sinister, it had nothing to do with aliens.

The rest of the day was spent in making preparations for departure. Whenever a curious shopowner would inquire as to their need for certain supplies they replied simply that they were going camping and bird-watching—which was half truthful. This explanation invariably prompted a caution from every salesperson.

"Watch where you go...don't stray too far from town or the river...keep an eye out for lions and especially for leopards...

the cheetahs won't bother you...no bandits to worry about in the Namib, they don't like the heat any better than we do...take plenty of water...take plenty of food...be sure to let someone know your general itinerary and when you plan to return."

They paid dutiful attention to every recommendation—except the last two, having no intention of informing anyone of even their direction of travel. As soon as they were more than a day or two's walk out of Orangemund they would be completely on their own.

"It's insane, of course."

Sitting at the outdoor café watching the sun set over the western desert and the Atlantic beyond, Ingrid waited for her cappuccino to finish brewing.

"What is?" Whispr was carefully masticating the last of his dinner. It was astonishing how much energy he could muster on so little caloric intake, she mused.

"The signal from the thread. That it could be directed at something alien."

He took a half swallow of water and very carefully put down the glass. "She was joking. The Meld was joking." He paused a moment, added bemusedly, "You're not joking."

Irritated, Ingrid looked away. "I don't know what I'm doing. None of this makes any sense, Whispr. It hasn't from the beginning. The thread is made of a metal that shouldn't be possible. Yet somehow it retains its structure and composition. According to that Morgan person it contains not information but nanoscale implants of a kind I've maybe seen twice, and they shouldn't be possible either. Now some amateur African technician insists that the minimalist signal it's broadcasting, energized by a minuscule power source we don't understand, is being beamed out into empty space. That *is* possible, but it makes even less sense than everything else."

"Okay, doc—slow down. Suppose for the sake of wacky after-dinner conversation we assume everything you just said is true and supported by evidence. Which is more likely that it points to? The existence of little green men from outer space? Or to some good old down-home manufacturing and technical expertise by a consortium like the SAEC? Which is certainly big enough, resource-rich enough, and powerful enough to accomplish everything you just said?"

"I don't know, Whispr. I don't know." Picking up a sugar stick she stirred her coffee. "But 'wacky' as it may be it certainly would go a long way toward explaining how something exists that it shouldn't be possible to manufacture on Earth. What I can't figure, even if you go way out on the end of the farthest limb, is what it has to do with nanoscale devices implanted in the cerebrums of teenagers who are suffering from the aftereffects of botched cosmetic melds."

Whispr couldn't repress a snigger. "Maybe the tech's aliens are planning to open a world-dominating chain of manip beauty shops."

She glared at him over her cappuccino. "It's not funny, Whispr. The thread is real, the implants are real, and the transmission that goes nowhere is real."

"Well, we're going to Nowhere, so maybe we'll find the answers there. And I bet they don't involve aliens. Unless you're trying to say that aliens are running SICK, Inc."

"No," she muttered. "No, of course not. SICK, Inc. has been around forever and their board of directors and administrators are well-known businesspeople whose individual lineages can easily be traced. I just can't keep from thinking back to some of the things Morgan told us. About what he said he saw that made him break his work contract and leave illegally, at some danger to himself. He never did tell us."

Whispr shrugged. "None of our business."

"It is now," she argued. "But it's too late to press him for details. I'm sure he's already on his way out of here."

"Yeah, he was in a hurry, all right." Her companion shook his head and grinned. "Teenagers. Maybe SICK is trying to control what kind of cosmetics and manips they buy."

She didn't laugh. "Maybe SICK is just trying to control them, period."

Whispr blinked. "To what end? And why single them out? Plenty of adults suffer from bad cosmetic meld work. Why not implant them as well? Why not politicians and engineers and teachers? Why only teenagers who've had bad luck with their manips?"

Leaning forward, Ingrid rested her elbows on the table as she held her head with both hands. "I don't know. I just don't know."

"Well I *do* know. It doesn't involve aliens, and it is about money."

Raising her gaze, she stared at him through cappuccino steam. "How do you know that?"

"Because—Ingrid—I've lived long enough and hard enough to learn one thing, and that's that it's *always* about money." He slugged down the rest of his water. "Of course, I could be completely wrong and you could be completely right and there really are aliens at the research facility and they're running SICK, Inc. and doing something horrible to unsuspecting adolescents." He smiled thinly. "The explanation is obvious. We're being invaded." He pushed back from the table. Around them other diners chatted amusedly, romantically, inconsequentially. "At least it would explain today's teen music."

They exited the café together. Insofar as Whispr could tell, no one followed them.

"Do you find everything worthy of sarcasm?" she challenged him.

"Everything." He confessed without hesitation. "It keeps me sane."

"Good. You're going to need your sarcasm and everything else to keep you sane when we're trekking across the desert." Tilting back her head she eyed the bowl of night. The atmosphere of the southern Namib was utterly devoid of pollution and the sky was rife with stars like flecks of molten silver.

Stars and nothing else, she told herself firmly as they walked back to their hotel.

EPILOGUE

Napun Molé hated the desert—but not as much as he hated failure.

ABOUT THE AUTHOR

ALAN DEAN FOSTER has written in a variety of genres, including hard science fiction, fantasy, horror, detective, Western, historical, and contemporary fiction. He is the author of the *New York Times* bestseller *Star Wars: The Approaching Storm* and the popular Pip & Flinx novels, as well as novelizations of several films including *Transformers*, *Star Wars*, the first three *Alien* films, and *Alien Nation*. His novel *Cyber Way* won the Southwest Book Award for Fiction in 1990, the first science fiction work ever to do so. Foster and his wife, JoAnn Oxley, live in Prescott, Arizona, in a house built of brick that was salvaged from an early-twentieth-century miners' brothel. He is currently at work on several new novels and media projects.

www.alandeanfoster.com